sf

# SKY
# KNIFE

# SKY KNIFE

## MARELLA SANDS

A Tom Doherty Associates Book
New York

SKY KNIFE

Copyright © 1997 by Marella Sands

This book is printed on acid-free paper.

A Forge Book
Published by Tom Doherty Associates, Inc.
175 Fifth Avenue
New York, NY 10010

Forge® is a registered trademark of Tom Doherty Associates, Inc.

Library of Congress Cataloging-in-Publication Data

Sands, Marella.
    Sky Knife / Marella Sands.—1st ed.
       p.   cm.
    "A Tom Doherty Associates book."
    ISBN 0-312-86126-5 (acid-free paper)
    I. Title.
    PS3569.A51966S58    1997
    813'.54—dc21                        97-14292
                                          CIP

First Edition: September 1997

Printed in the United States of America

0 9 8 7 6 5 4 3 2 1

*for*
Brian

# Acknowledgments

Thanks, of course, to those Alternate Historians, past, present, and honorary, who have helped me more than I can say in this small a space, including Laurell K. Hamilton, Deborah Millitello, Thomas Drennan, Janni Lee Simner, N. L. Drew, Rett MacPherson, Robert Sheaff, and Richard Knaak. Thanks, too, to Sue Bradford Edwards, who made me promise not to mention we'd been best friends for twenty years. Don't worry, Sue. It's not twenty years. Not . . . quite. Last, but far from least, I would like especially to thank Mark Sumner, who not only "discovered" me in his editorial slush pile and sponsored me into the Alternate Historians, but who also introduced me to his agent and (as if that weren't enough) also wrote a really cool computer program that allows me to convert Mayan Long Count dates to Calendar Round and Gregorian calendar dates. You didn't think I did it all in my head, did you? A million thanks, Mark!

# I

›››››››››

# WEST

## Where Day Dies When It Is Old

9.0.0.0.0
8 Ahau 13 Ceh

# 1

>>>>>

R ed Jaguar of the East! Jaguar of Life, Jaguar of Morning!
Protector of the innocent, prince of the powerful, terror to
our enemies—hear our prayer!"

Sky Knife shuddered as Stone Jaguar's words rang throughout the Great Plaza. Stone Jaguar's face was hidden behind a
mask of feathers and shells and the voice that spoke from behind the mask boomed eerily into the night. Kneeling as he
was just to the left of Stone Jaguar, Sky Knife could see the
sweat drip down the man's neck. Sky Knife was glad he didn't
have to wear a mask, too.

Though the night was hot, Sky Knife felt a cold tendril
creep up his back. Sorcery. Tonight, Stone Jaguar would make
sacrifice, for the old *katun* had ended and a new one would
begin. Stone Jaguar would petition the gods for luck, enough
luck to carry the city of Tikal through the next twenty years
until this *katun*'s end.

"Black Jaguar of the West! Jaguar of Death, Jaguar of
Night! Prince of merchants and all those who travel. Punisher
of the evil, terror in the dark—hear our prayer!"

Stone Jaguar threw his arms out wide, and his jaguar skin

cloak blew back slightly in the sorcerous breeze. The bone and jade bead fringe of the cloak swung dangerously near Sky Knife. He drew back to avoid being touched by it; it would be bad luck indeed for the sacred cloak to touch a mere temple assistant during the ceremony.

Sky Knife himself was dressed in a simple cotton loincloth that had been dyed blue. Blue was the color of water, of luck, and honor. Solid blue garments could be worn only by those who participated in sacred ceremonies, to remind the gods of the luck they brought to Tikal.

"White Jaguar of the North! Jaguar of Rain, Jaguar of Evening! He Who Walks Among the Fields! Prince of the corn, protector of the farmer, terror to the unjust—hear our prayer!"

Sky Knife brushed sweaty palms against his bare thighs as a glow bathed the temple. The light was a sickly orange that flickered and changed in intensity so quickly it nauseated him. Sky Knife tried to ignore the musty, unwholesome smell that always accompanied the temple glow. It was as if it had crept up from a tomb full of rotting corpses.

Stone Jaguar stepped back and Death Smoke, also covered from head to toe with fine ornaments of shell and jade, stepped to the smaller north altar and placed a cigar upon it. Death Smoke spread his hands wide, closed his eyes, and clapped his hands together. The end of the cigar burst into flames. It sputtered for a moment, and a trickle of black smoke wafted up. Then the cigar glowed brightly red. Sky Knife relaxed as the cigar continued burning. Not only was tobacco sacred, but the death gods could not bear its smell. They would be driven away from the ceremony and their bad luck with them.

"Yellow Jaguar of the South! Jaguar of Heat, Jaguar of Day! Prince of the wise, vengeance of the strong, bringer of drought, terror to the unlucky—hear our prayer!"

Stone Jaguar finished the fourth and final invocation with a shout. A cold, dank gust of wind hit Sky Knife, and he shivered. That had never happened before. Sky Knife glanced up toward

Stone Jaguar, but the priest merely waved his left hand and the strange wind died down to a ticklish breeze.

"Let the sacrifice come forth!" boomed the voice of Stone Jaguar.

A musician at the base of the pyramidal temple struck a tortoise shell with a stick in a slow, measured rhythm. The hollow *tok-tok* sounds echoed around the Great Plaza. The crowd gathered in the plaza was absolutely silent as a second musician, this one shaking a gourd filled with small pebbles, joined the first. No one besides the musicians dared make noise—for any quarrelling or other uproar would bring bad luck on the ceremony and drive all the good luck away.

As one, the crowd raised open hands to their chests, palms out, and hummed a single, low note. Heart pounding in excitement, Sky Knife did the same. It was the call for the sacrifice. The people of the city—old and young, men and women—sang for the sacrifice to stand forth.

Across the plaza, a flash of blue. Sky Knife's heart jumped in anticipation, staring at the spot where the sacrifice would first appear. Moments later, he did.

The young man was swathed in lengths of blue cotton. Blue paint stained his face, hands, and feet, as befitted his status as an unmarried youth. Head held high, the young man stepped forward into the plaza. He was preceded by young girls who flung flowers in his path.

The young man walked slowly, in time to the rhythm of the turtle shell drums. When he reached the base of the great pyramid, he paused and bowed to the priests and attendants on the temple platform above. The sacrifice mounted the red-painted first step of the temple—past which only the priests, attendants, and sacrifices could go without bringing disaster to the city.

Sky Knife shivered in excitement. The smell that had nauseated him before changed the moment the sacrifice touched the pyramid. Now the subtle smell of sweet, ripe fruits and the spicy scent of flowers wafted about him, blown by the sorcerous breeze. The sickly orange light stopped its flickering and shone steady and white.

Sky Knife's spirits raised in joy. All the signs were good. Sky Knife prayed that they would remain so. He had no idea how the gods would plague Tikal if the sacrifice were found wanting—and he didn't want to know. Everything had to go perfectly. It *had* to.

As the sacrifice mounted the stairs, he shed the lengths of blue cotton behind him as a moth sheds its cocoon. Finally, naked, he stood on the thirty-sixth and last step. He bowed again to Stone Jaguar. Shells on the jaguar-skin cloak chinked together as Stone Jaguar spread his hands wide.

Sky Knife and the three other temple attendants stood. Sky Knife's feet tingled as he straightened up; he didn't usually kneel on the stone temple platform as long as he had had to tonight.

The tingling passed quickly. Sky Knife and the other three attendants took their places around the circular altar on the platform. The sacrifice lay down on the altar. Sky Knife, acting tonight as the Attendant in the West, grasped the young man's left shoulder and pinned it to the stone below. The other attendants, each one at a cardinal point, held the young man down by shoulder and knees.

Claw Skull and Death Smoke threw *copal* onto the burning coals in the stone bowls on the back corners of the temple platform. The heavy, musky smell choked Sky Knife even as it seemed to make him see and hear more clearly. He took a deep breath of the strange, heady odor caused by the *copal*, tobacco, and the sorcerous temple smell.

Sky Knife suppressed a sense of unease: the fourth priest, Blood House, was not in evidence, and the ceremony could not wait. Normally, four priests, four attendants, and the sacrifice formed a complete set of nine. With Blood House missing, there were only eight people on the temple. Although on occasion the ceremony was performed with fewer than nine, it seemed inappropriate to Sky Knife that this special ceremony should be short. Too much was at stake for anything to go wrong.

"All gods above the earth! All gods beneath the earth! Itzamna—Lord of All! Accept this life—that which was freely bestowed by you is now freely returned!" Stone Jaguar raised his right hand. In it, he held an obsidian blade some eight inches long, hafted onto a handle made from the wood of the sacred *ceiba* tree. The blade glowed a bright, bright blue. Sky Knife looked away.

The sacrifice shifted slightly. Sky Knife pressed down on the shoulder and glanced at the young man. Sweat marred the young man's face, leaving streaks behind in the blue paint.

It always happened. No matter that the sacrifice came of his own will, chosen among the dozens who had applied for the honor. It still always came down to this. Fear. Upon seeing the knife, they were always afraid. Afraid of the glowing blade. Afraid of the pain. Afraid of failure.

If the gods did not find this young man's sacrifice worthy, if even one thing went wrong, Tikal would suffer twenty years of bad luck. The young man had reason to fear. With so much at stake, how could he not doubt, just a little, his own worthiness?

Sky Knife wished there was something he could do to make it easier for the sacrifice—he always did. But there was nothing he could do. What the sacrifice did, he had to do alone.

Sky Knife glanced up toward the sky. The Jade Necklace, a brilliant constellation of seven stars, touched the high point in the sky. The new *katun* would begin at any moment.

With a final shout Stone Jaguar plunged the blade down into the sacrifice's stomach. Sky Knife bore down hard on the sacrifice's shoulder as the young man jerked and screamed.

Blood spurted out of the gaping wound onto Sky Knife, the other attendants, and the platform. But a glowing blue haze surrounded Stone Jaguar now, and the blood did not touch him.

Stone Jaguar withdrew the knife, transferred it to his left

hand, then plunged his right into the wound and thrust his hand up under the sacrifice's ribs. The young man screamed again as Stone Jaguar grabbed his heart. Sky Knife broke out in a cold sweat—no matter how many times he attended a sacrifice, he never got used to this moment, when the sacrifice felt Stone Jaguar's fingers enter his chest and squeeze his heart. The high, ear-splitting shriek was like no other sound Sky Knife had ever heard. The young man's final scream pierced Sky Knife right down to his gut.

But that was the last. The sacrifice's sufferings were—as always—over quickly. Stone Jaguar withdrew his hand from the sacrifice's chest. In his clenched fist, he held the young man's heart. It quivered and convulsed rhythmically.

Not a drop of blood defiled Stone Jaguar. He lifted the heart toward the heavens. The heart continued to beat, powered now by Stone Jaguar's sorcery.

"Accept now this sacrifice!" shouted Stone Jaguar over the shrieking of the gale that suddenly descended upon the temple. Sky Knife hunkered down against the cold wind that battered him from all directions. His shoulder-length black hair slapped his face, got into his mouth and eyes.

Tendrils of light—all colors of the rainbow—rained out of the sky and twisted around themselves, around the sacrifice's body, up to Stone Jaguar. The swarming colors climbed his arms and poured into the spasming heart.

Streaks of blue leaped from the sacrifice into the sky. Orange and red swirls danced around the temple. Where they touched Sky Knife, they tickled.

The wind gained in intensity. Sky Knife leaned on the sacrifice, refusing to be swayed. Then the colors, the noise, all descended upon the heart and entered into it. The glow around Stone Jaguar brightened until it hurt to look at him. Sky Knife blinked, but would not look away. The fate of his city hung in the balance. Would the sacrifice be accepted? He couldn't *not* look.

With a loud crack of thunder, the heart in Stone Jaguar's hands exploded into a thousand colored shards. They rained upon the temple, upon the crowd waiting below. The shards sparkled like stars and the entire plaza was lit as if it were noon rather than midnight.

Sky Knife hugged blood-soaked arms to his chest, laughing with joy. The gods approved. The sacrifice had been accepted.

Sky Knife said a silent prayer of gratitude to the soul of the sacrifice. Not that it needed his help or his gratitude; acceptance would mean the soul would reside forever in the blissful paradise of the seventh, and highest, heaven—the heaven reserved only for true heroes.

The young man was just such a hero. Without him, this night would have ended in disaster. Sky Knife was grateful for the young man's bravery. His courage had conquered the bad luck that lurked everywhere, waiting to victimize the city and its people. The sacrifice's bravery was worthy of song, and of paradise.

Sky Knife relaxed as the light in the plaza died and the glowing shards of heart faded into wisps of colored vapor that dissipated into the darkness of the night.

Stone Jaguar's sorcery had snuffed all the fires in the plaza. Tonight, a fire would be kindled in the gaping, bloody hole in the sacrifice's chest, and all the new ceremonial fires would be taken from it.

Sky Knife reached out to the body of the sacrifice and smoothed the young man's hair. The body was still warm. Sky Knife touched the body a last time in farewell and turned away.

A sneeze caught his attention. Sky Knife looked back toward the altar and his heart stopped cold in his chest. There, just behind the altar, stood a terrible figure. Its fleshless face and chest exposed bleached, white bone, while what skin it had was covered in black and yellow blotches. The figure convulsed with a second sneeze. Slowly, it raised its fleshless hand and pointed at Sky Knife. Dread and terror lanced through Sky Knife. He knew what this was—this was Cizin, the god of death. *Cizin.*

Before Sky Knife could react, the figure leapt off the top of the pyramid and was gone, only the sound of another sneeze remaining behind to give witness to its presence.

Sky Knife dropped to his knees in horror. If Cizin were strong enough to appear here—especially *now*, with the sacrifice still warm on the altar—something was wrong. Terribly, horribly wrong.

Sky Knife glanced toward the others on the temple, but the others laughed and smiled, apparently unaware of the evil thing that had just visited them. That Sky Knife was the only one that had been granted the eyes to see Cizin terrified him. Who was he to see the god of death if the priests could not?

He wasn't sure what the omen meant, except he knew it to be bad. And bad omens left bad luck behind in their footsteps.

# 2

›››››

Sky Knife," said Death Smoke. He was a skinny, white-haired man. Sky Knife stood on shaky legs. Death Smoke's breath stank, and the rotting black stumps of his teeth disgusted Sky Knife, but Sky Knife swallowed his feelings and stepped toward the old man.

"Yes, *Ah kin?*" he asked. Technically, Sky Knife should be allowed to address Death Smoke by his name rather than his title now that the ceremony was over, but Death Smoke was touchy about such things.

"Blood House—where is he? He should be the one to kindle the new fire." Death Smoke's breath hissed out of his throat when he finished speaking. It brushed against Sky Knife's face, sickeningly foul.

"I don't know," said Sky Knife. "I'll look for him if you wish."

Death Smoke dismissed Sky Knife with a wave. "Go," he barked.

Sky Knife dashed down the steep thirty-six temple steps—four terraces of nine steps each—as fast as he dared. At the bottom of the steps, he walked into the joyous crowd. The men and women of Tikal drank *pulque* and ate delicacies the merchants had prepared for this special occasion: turtle soup, roasted river snails, and, most prized of all, wild pig baked with sweet potatoes.

Sky Knife pushed his way through the crowd and tried to ignore the gurgling in his stomach. In preparation for the ceremony, all priests and attendants had not eaten for a day. The overpowering, heavy smell of the *pulque* and the food only made him feel more hungry. Sky Knife waved away a *pulque* vendor, and hurried south toward the acropolis.

Even more than his hunger, Sky Knife was tortured by his awful vision. His heart was in his throat. He knew bad luck was coming—he needed to tell someone, so that the priests could prepare for the bad luck to follow. Blood House was a man of great wisdom. In the six years since Sky Knife had lived with the priests, Blood House had always been kind and patient with him. Blood House would know what to do.

To the south of the Great Plaza, on a small hillock, stood the southern acropolis, home of the priests and attendants to the temple. No red-painted step marked the acropolis' boundary, for no disaster would rain upon the city if anyone besides the priests entered, but still, the people of the city gave it a wide berth. As soon as Sky Knife climbed the first step, he left the crowd behind.

Sky Knife pushed aside the blue cotton drapery that hung over the main entrance and stepped inside. A fire burned inside the main room, which was shallow, but wide. Stone benches lined the walls. The meager light from the fire lit the center of the room, but the corners and vaulted ceiling were left in the shadow of midnight. Sky Knife turned away from the fire and walked toward the dark entrance of Blood House's personal quarters; as a priest, Blood House's quarters were close to the airy, open front room. Attendants were crammed into smaller, smoky rooms deeper in the stone structure.

Blood House's quarters were dark. The feeling of unease

that had plagued Sky Knife all night blossomed into a terrible dread. He retreated to the fire and pulled out a flaming brand. He walked back to Blood House's quarters.

Blood House lay on the stone bench that served as his bed. His hands were clamped down on a tobacco leaf that had been pressed against his bare abdomen. His tattoos, which normally stood out in stark contrast with his lighter skin, now seemed blurred, as if Blood House were bruised over his entire body. Blood stained Blood House's face around his mouth and nose. In contrast to the blood that stained Sky Knife's arms, which was dark and sticky now, almost dry, the blood on Blood House's face was bright and wet.

Sky Knife, trembling, stepped closer. He touched Blood House, but the priest's skin was clammy and cold. He did not seem to be breathing. In the flickering light from the small tongue of flame Sky Knife carried, it was difficult to tell anything at all for sure, but inside he knew. Blood House was dead. No wonder Cizin had appeared. The god of death gloated over the bodies of priests as he gloated over no other—for they knew the secrets of the gods, and kept the rituals pure and holy. How sweet it must have been for Cizin to breach the wall of good luck around the temple and appear on its very summit. How terrible for the city of Tikal.

Grief tugged at Sky Knife's heart. Blood House had been a good teacher, a mentor to Sky Knife. The priest had had a gentle soul and a kind way that had helped Sky Knife in his first frightening days at the temple, when his grief over his parents' deaths had been new and raw. Stone Jaguar was a hard but fair man, a man Sky Knife could respect, but Blood House alone had been someone Sky Knife could not only respect but admire.

Sky Knife brushed away the tears that rained on his cheeks and pushed his grief away. He put the flickering light as close to the body as he dared, looked at the tobacco leaf, and tried to think around the hard knot of sorrow in his heart and mind.

From around the edges of the tobacco leaf dribbled a dark,

sticky liquid. A tobacco leaf over tobacco juice—Blood House had treated himself for some sort of bite or sting. Gently, Sky Knife lifted the edge of the leaf. Two small puncture wounds marred the priest's skin.

A bite. Bleeding, bruising. A relatively quick death. Sky Knife knew what had happened here. The snake called Yellow Chin had bitten Blood House. Yellow Chin lived in fields as well as jungle, but rarely entered the city itself, and never entered the dwellings of man if it could help it. Sky Knife shook his head. He knew Blood House had not left the acropolis all day—none of them had, until the time for the ceremony. So Yellow Chin had had to come here.

Yellow Chin might still be here. Alarmed at the thought, Sky Knife swung his meager light about, looking for a small, brown and black serpent with the diamond pattern on its back. The room was cluttered with the copious garments Blood House had planned to wear to the sacrifice. Yellow Chin could be hiding in a fold in any one of them. Or behind the water jug, or any of a dozen other places in the dark corners of the room. Sky Knife backed out of the room slowly, unwilling to touch anything.

Sky Knife turned and ran into someone. He yelped and dropped his makeshift torch.

"What took you so long, boy?" asked the tremulous voice of Death Smoke. "Did you find Blood House?"

"Yes," whispered Sky Knife. He stepped away from the older man. "Dead. He's dead." Sky Knife's voice cracked with emotion.

"What?" shouted Death Smoke. "That can't be—the ceremony went perfectly. There's no room here for bad luck." He shoved Sky Knife aside and mumbled the fire-calling incantation. Flames spouted into existence above Death Smoke's head, filling the vaulted ceiling, and illuminating the entire room and Blood House's quarters with a brilliant blue light.

The blue drapery to the outdoors was swept aside and Stone

Jaguar strode in, his jaguar skin cloak still in place. "What's going on?" demanded Stone Jaguar. His searching gaze swept past Sky Knife, dismissing him. "Death Smoke? Claw Skull went ahead and kindled the new fire. It would have been unlucky to wait any longer. Where's Blood House?"

"In here," called Death Smoke. "It would seem that the ceremony didn't go as well as we thought. Yellow Chin has been here."

Stone Jaguar's face wrinkled in a terrible frown and his face purpled in rage. Sky Knife backed up, unwilling to call attention to himself while Stone Jaguar was so angry.

"Yellow Chin?" said Stone Jaguar. "The *Bolon ti ku* take the Yellow One and cast him into the lowest hell," he hissed. "Itzamna!"

Sky Knife's gut twisted painfully as part of the import of Stone Jaguar's words hit him. *Yellow*—the color of death, the color of evil. Of course it had been Yellow Chin who had come to do the bidding of Cizin, the Yellow One. Cizin wasn't content to merely gloat over this death; he revelled in it. And had shoved the noses of the priests in it for good measure.

Angry as Stone Jaguar was, he needed to know what Sky Knife had seen. "The Yellow One," Sky Knife said softly. "He was here."

"Of course he was," snapped Stone Jaguar. "He has taken Blood House."

Sky Knife fought the urge to run out into the night, away from the priest's anger, away from the bad luck that undoubtedly clung to this entire building.

"No," said Sky Knife. He straightened his shoulders and spoke firmly. "He was on the temple. After the sacrifice. I saw him. Actually, I heard him first. He sneezed."

"Can't stand the smell of tobacco," cackled Death Smoke from the other room. "Thought I heard sneezing, too, but I didn't see anything."

"He was *on the temple?*" roared Stone Jaguar. "Has our luck deserted us completely? Cizin *here*, and only an attendant with a bad luck name saw him?"

Sky Knife lowered his gaze and dropped to his knees before Stone Jaguar. He knew his name was bad luck, even if his mother said she'd received instructions in a vision to name her child after the Knife of Stars that swung in a slow circle overhead during the year. Still, Sky Knife thought his work in the temple, his efforts to please the gods, merited him luck. To hear Stone Jaguar as much as blame him for Cizin's presence rocked him.

But then, Stone Jaguar had never been happy that the previous *Ah men*, Vine Torch, had sponsored Sky Knife to the gods' service. Vine Torch had claimed Sky Knife was a good omen, that the iguanas who had ringed the house while his mother was in labor had been the servants of Itzamna come to pay tribute.

So Vine Torch had promised Sky Knife to Itzamna. Although Vine Torch had died in the same sweeping sickness that had killed Sky Knife's parents and one of his brothers, Stone Jaguar could not undo what had been done. He'd had to accept Sky Knife into the temple's service.

"Our luck may yet be salvaged," said Death Smoke. "And bad luck name or not, I believe the young man will play a part in it. He was born to his name for a reason. His parents saw it. Vine Torch saw it."

"Have you seen this in the *copal* smoke, or are you just babbling?" asked Stone Jaguar. "Our luck has turned to evil, and you think an attendant can save us?"

"I think the gods can save us," said Death Smoke. "But perhaps not tomorrow or the next day. The gods, too, are slaves to time. They must wait for the time to be right."

"But how will we know when that is?" asked Sky Knife. Stone Jaguar glared at him, but said nothing.

"We don't know," said Death Smoke. He came out of the other room and extended a thin, wrinkled hand toward Sky

Knife, just as Cizin had. Sky Knife's heart dropped in his chest and he fought the urge to bolt from the room. "But Itzamna, the Lord of All, knows. He will tell the gods, and all the *chacs*, high and low. He will tell the spirit of the *copal*, and the *copal* will tell me. He will not desert mankind, or Tikal."

"And what happens when news of our bad luck travels to other cities?" asked Stone Jaguar. "How long do you think it will take Uaxactun to start a war with us? Their sun-rotted king has been itching for the chance to attack."

"It is in the hands of the gods," said Death Smoke.

"In the hands of the gods or not, we must tell the king," said Stone Jaguar. "He must be prepared for whatever happens now that the *katun* has begun so terribly." Stone Jaguar arranged the jaguar-skin cloak, then looked at Sky Knife. "You will come with me. Get a cloth and clean yourself."

"Me?" asked Sky Knife, his voice barely more than a squeak. Still, he moved to obey. He grabbed a cotton towel and rubbed his arms vigorously. The dried blood flaked off easily. "Why me?"

"You saw Cizin," said Stone Jaguar with a frown. "An omen that strange can't be unimportant."

Sky Knife's knees trembled. The king! Storm Cloud, King of Tikal, was a figure larger than life. Born in the north of a princess of Tikal who had been wed to a foreigner to cement an alliance, Storm Cloud had grown up the youngest of many brothers, each royal, each ambitious. Fifteen years before, when Sky Knife was still an infant, Storm Cloud had come to his mother's people and had demanded the kingship. Though his army was small, and his claim tenuous, he had not been opposed.

Sky Knife had never been in the king's presence before—he didn't have the status to even consider it. He was merely the son of a farmer, born in a simple house in the middle of his father's *milpa*. Fear rose in Sky Knife's throat and choked him. He couldn't move.

Stone Jaguar grabbed Sky Knife by the shoulder and pro-pelled him out the door. Sky Knife stumbled into the blackness of the night, the weight of his fear as heavy and as oppressive as the humid tropical air.

# 3

>>>>>

The crowd of revelers hadn't thinned a bit, and the plaza was brighter for the many new fires that had been started. Stone Jaguar strode on ahead and pushed past a group of tattooed men, potters, to judge by the damp clay smell that clung to them, and walked eastward toward the house of the king. Sky Knife hurried along in his wake.

Just before the steps of the king's house stood a tall, rectangular slab of stone, a stela, elaborately carved with the date of the king's accession to the throne and an image of the king in his ceremonial regalia. In the torchlight, Sky Knife could make out few details, though the date, 8.19.4.7.13 4 Ben 1 Xul, was easy enough to read in the dim light.

Stone Jaguar bowed briefly before the stela, then walked straight up the stairs. Sky Knife knelt at the stela and touched his forehead to the ground before it, then stood and jogged after Stone Jaguar. Warriors with their slings and spears in hand stood on each step and watched, but did not interfere. Still, the skin on Sky Knife's neck crawled, as if the gazes of the warriors could pierce his very soul.

Stone Jaguar needed no introductions, and no one seemed

concerned that a temple attendant followed him. Warriors merely stared impassively, their bare chests glistening with sweat in the torchlight. Sweat streaked Sky Knife's body as well, but it was a cold sweat. The king. He was going to meet the king in the king's own house.

The house was similar, but larger, than the acropolis where the priests and the attendants lived. Long, narrow rooms with steeply vaulted ceilings were lined with benches. Colorful cotton blankets covered the benches and the walls had been painted in brilliant reds and blues. In the flickering torchlight, the images of gods and the king's ancestors walked on the walls, their stern stares ever watchful, ever forbidding.

Stone Jaguar stopped. Sky Knife stood behind him, waiting.

"Tell the king I am here on important business," said Stone Jaguar. A warrior nodded, turned, and brushed past a heavy cotton drape. The warrior on Sky Knife's left shifted his weight slightly. Sky Knife didn't dare stare at the warrior, but flicked his gaze toward the tall man several times, awed to be in the warrior's presence.

Sky Knife was taller than many men in Tikal, but the warrior was a head taller than Sky Knife. His earlobes, stretched carefully over time, were wrapped about red-painted spools of wood encrusted with nacre from seashells. Grease coated his hair and plastered it flat to his skull, showing off its fashionable elongated shape. A long, aquiline nose jutted forth from his face, making his skull appear even longer and his eyes slightly crossed.

Sky Knife suppressed a surge of envy; the warrior had a face women would sigh over, lust after, dream of. Sky Knife's small nose was the plainest part of his plain face. His forehead did not have that perfect slope, and his eyes, no matter how hard he tried, absolutely refused to cross. None of the young women remarked on him, or watched him in the marketplace, or let him know by shy glances that they found him attractive.

The warrior wore a skirt of brilliant blue-and-yellow-striped cotton that was wrapped around his waist several times and bunched together in a knot in front. Rope sandals, newer and far finer than Sky Knife's, for these were decorated with cowrie shells, were strapped to the warrior's feet.

The warrior shifted his weight again and fixed his gaze on Sky Knife, who ducked his head and stared at his feet, heart pounding. His thick, straight hair fell forward in his face, obscuring his view. He didn't brush it back, but let it hang as it was.

The sound of the drape being pushed aside caused Sky Knife's knees to tremble. This was it. He would be in the presence of the king.

Stone Jaguar stepped forward into the next room. Sky Knife took a deep breath, pulled his shoulders back, and walked as confidently as he could, though he kept his gaze fixed on the middle of Stone Jaguar's back.

This room was slightly wider than the others, but was still a comfortable, familiar, shape. The paintings on the walls were intriguing, but Sky Knife got no more than a glimpse of a sacrificial scene before having to stop behind Stone Jaguar again. Stone Jaguar knelt. Sky Knife scrambled to his knees and lowered his forehead to the floor.

"My king," said Stone Jaguar in his deep, melodious voice. In this room, his voice seemed to carry in a way it did nowhere else—at least nowhere else that Sky Knife had heard it.

"Stone Jaguar," replied an even deeper, heavily accented voice. The accent jarred Sky Knife; he had not forgotten that the king had been born far to the north, but he had somehow not quite expected the King of Tikal to sound like a foreigner. Storm Cloud was king, father, and protector to the city. It only seemed right that he should speak as a native.

"I have grave news," said Stone Jaguar. "Cizin has been seen." He recounted the events of the evening. Sky Knife kept his head to the floor and listened intently. To either side of him, he heard the rustling of clothing and the bright, clattery sound of jade beads clapping against each other as the king's attendants moved about.

"And this is the one who saw Cizin?" asked the king when Stone Jaguar finished.

"Yes, my king," said Stone Jaguar. A small draft hit Sky Knife in the face, and he realized Stone Jaguar had moved aside.

"And who is he?" asked the king. "What is so special about him?"

Stone Jaguar hesitated.

"Well?" demanded the king.

"My predecessor, Vine Torch," said Stone Jaguar, "said that, though this boy was born to a farmer, he was destined to be more than a farmer. Vine Torch said there were omens at his birth: shooting stars, parades of iguanas outside the house, *yax-um* feathers falling from the sky at his feet. He is the fourth son of a fourth son. And the *Ah kin* says the *copal* told him the boy was born to do work no one else could do."

Storm Cloud absorbed this for several moments. "So, boy," he said at last, "omens tend to follow you, eh?" The king chuckled. Sky Knife tried not to tremble visibly.

"You may look upon me, boy," said the king.

Sky Knife gathered his courage and straightened up, but stared at the chipped stone tiles of the floor in front of him.

"I said, you may look upon me." The deep voice held a hint of laughter. Sky Knife blinked and raised his gaze to the king's.

Except for the image of the owl painted on the wall behind him, the king and his court were wholly Tikal. The king sat cross-legged on a knee-high stone dais, which was covered with layer upon layer of blankets.

Storm Cloud, King of Tikal, was dressed in a red cotton skirt covered in a pattern of green and yellow flowers. His chest, tattooed with the figure of his spirit animal, the crocodile, was covered by strings of beads and shells that hung from his neck. Jade ear spools swung gently from Storm Cloud's ears. On his head, the king wore an elaborate crown of shells, jade beads, and short, brightly colored feathers. Long, iridescent blue-green feathers of the *yax-um*, the sacred bird that dwelt in the far mountains, were fastened to the crown. Some of them stuck up into the air, and some trailed down Storm Cloud's shoulders.

He was an imposing sight and he stared at Sky Knife as one might consider an insect. Sky Knife stared back, trapped in the king's gaze, unable to look away. Sky Knife longed to put his head down on the floor again, to abase himself before this mighty figure.

"Hm," said Storm Cloud. He turned his attention back to Stone Jaguar, no trace of amusement in his manner now.

Sky Knife, released, breathed a silent prayer of relief.

Storm Cloud addressed Stone Jaguar. "Thank you for coming so promptly. This is indeed important news, though unwelcome."

Stone Jaguar bowed slightly. "It is certainly strange, Lord, that such a successful sacrifice would be followed by such terrible luck."

"Perhaps the sacrifice was not successful, then," said Storm Cloud. He glanced over at one of his attendants, a man whose eyes seemed half-closed in weariness. "Well?"

The attendant clutched at the jade beads around his neck and shook his head. "The sacrifice went perfectly, from what could be seen from the plaza," he said. His voice was high and thin, like the voice of a reed flute. He ran his fingers through his graying hair. "All the signs were good."

"Perhaps another sacrifice would reverse our luck," said Stone Jaguar. "We could sacrifice in the morning for the new sun."

Storm Cloud rubbed his smooth chin with one hand. "No," he said. "The people should know of the sacrifice before it is done, so that they may prepare. Besides, how would you find a sacrifice so quickly? Most of the young men will be sleeping off too much *pulque.* "

"In times of trouble, sometimes the sacrifice of a young man is not enough," said Stone Jaguar. "I am sure a sacrifice could be found."

Storm Cloud shook his head. "No."

"I am *Ah men*, High Priest, and *Ah nacom*, He Who Sacrifices," said Stone Jaguar. "I know if a sacrifice is needed."

"And I say we will not have one," said Storm Cloud in a clipped, angry voice. "Do you question me, priest?"

Stone Jaguar bowed, anger in his face. "Of course not. It will be as you wish, Lord."

Storm Cloud looked away from Stone Jaguar, glanced instead at Sky Knife. "Cizin pointed at you. What do you think it means?"

"I'm sorry, Lord, I don't know," said Sky Knife. His voice sounded stronger than he had hoped it would.

Storm Cloud brushed a *yax-um* feather away from his shoulder. "Still, the vision was yours. All this bad luck," he said. "How could it happen when the sacrifice went so well? Why is Cizin here—tonight? What do you think the omen means?"

"It must be the work of sorcery," said Sky Knife, surprising himself at his boldness. The words poured out of his mouth, and he couldn't seem to stop them. "This much bad luck must be the work of a man, or men, in league with the powers of evil. The gods do not send such bad luck after accepting a sacrifice."

Sky Knife closed his mouth before he could blurt out any more and dropped his gaze. It was not his place to say what the gods would or would not do—he was only a temple attendant! Stone Jaguar would be angry with him for presuming too much.

No one spoke. Sky Knife, convinced he had insulted both the priest and the king, leaned forward to abase himself once more.

"No," commanded Storm Cloud. Sky Knife froze midgesture. "I feel you are right. The stink of evil men is behind such bad luck. You will find them for me."

"My Lord, he is only a boy," said Stone Jaguar. "The other priests and I know what to do. We will petition the gods and they will reveal the evildoers to us. We will offer sacrifices of our blood. A hunter can be sent to trap a jaguar, so that we may send its spirit to intercede for us."

"You may petition the gods all you want," said the king. "And cut out as many animal hearts as you wish. But I have walked many miles, and have visited many cities. I have learned that it takes a man to ferret out another man, not a god."

"My Lord," protested Stone Jaguar.

"Silence," barked the high-voiced attendant. "The king has spoken."

"Oh, sit up, boy," said Storm Cloud. "Perhaps this is the work the *Ah kin* foretold for you. Let's see if Itzamna continues to hold you high in his esteem. May he grant you the wisdom and the skill to discover and defeat the enemies of Tikal."

Sky Knife straightened slowly. This time, he could not keep his hands from trembling.

"My staff," said the king. One of the attendants, an old, white-haired man in a black and red skirt, bowed and brought out a black cloth. He unwrapped it and drew out a short, cylindrical stone object. The old man carried the object to the king. Tiny jade beads dangled from each end of it. They made a crackling sound as they clinked against each other.

Storm Cloud took the staff, held it briefly to his forehead, then held it out horizontally in front of him. "What is your name, boy?" he asked.

Stone Jaguar leaned forward as if to say something but a sharp glance from the king stopped him. Stone Jaguar bit back whatever he was about to say and sat still as the stones he was named for.

Storm Cloud looked back to Sky Knife for an answer.

"Sky Knife," he said. It came out as a whisper.

Storm Cloud jingled the jade beads slightly four times before speaking. "I am Storm Cloud, King of Tikal," he said in a loud, commanding voice. "This is my command. Sky Knife, attendant to Stone Jaguar in the Temple of Itzamna, shall go forth from my presence to seek out those who would bring bad luck to our city. The rules of status no longer apply to him. He may go anywhere and speak to anyone. No one may take this task from him, nor interfere with him. And when he has finished his task, he shall report to me alone. So I have said."

"So you have said," echoed the attendants. The old man picked up a gourd out of a box and shook it four times. The eerie rattle of the gourd echoed into the corners of the room and crawled up Sky Knife's spine.

"So that all may see that my authority travels with Sky Knife, a warrior from my personal guard shall assist him and shall be responsible for his protection. So I have said."

"So you have said," whispered the attendants. The old man shook the gourd four more times, then placed the gourd back in the box.

Storm Cloud returned the staff to the old man, who rewrapped it in its black cloth. Storm Cloud raised his left hand, palm out, to Sky Knife and Stone Jaguar, then looked away from them.

"You are dismissed," hissed one of the attendants, a short, bald man with a jade ring in his nose.

Sky Knife lowered his forehead to the floor again briefly, then stood and waited to see what Stone Jaguar would do. Fear nearly strangled him and he felt as if he couldn't breathe.

The priest bowed, then turned and left. Sky Knife followed him back outside to the stela, relieved to be out of the royal presence, bewildered and terrified of his new responsibility.

Stone Jaguar stopped before the stela. He turned and placed his hand on Sky Knife's shoulder. "Sky Knife," he said in a voice more kind than he had ever used with Sky Knife before. "You know I never agreed with Vine Torch about you—I admit that freely. But now the king has chosen you as well and, who knows, perhaps I have been wrong about you. Perhaps Vine Torch was right."

Sky Knife blinked in surprise but Stone Jaguar wasn't finished.

"The king is entrusting you with an important task," said Stone Jaguar. "Whatever it takes, however much courage is required, you will have to do it. Even if you feel you aren't capable, that your task is beyond your abilities to perform, you will still have to do it. Do you understand?" Though Sky Knife could not see Stone Jaguar's face in the dark, he heard the concern and anxiety in the older man's voice.

"Yes, Stone Jaguar," he said. "I understand."

Stone Jaguar sighed. "I will be honest with you; I think it would be wiser for one of the older attendants or one of the priests to be given the task. But the king has spoken. We can do nothing but obey."

"You are Sky Knife?" barked a growly voice. Sky Knife's heart jumped in his chest in surprise. He stepped back and looked back at the king's house. The warrior of the beautiful face and the yellow and blue skirt stood there.

"This is the attendant in my temple whose name is Sky Knife," said Stone Jaguar smoothly. "Do you require something of him?"

The warrior ignored Stone Jaguar and nodded to Sky Knife. "I am Bone Splinter," he said. "The chief of the household has told me I am to assist you in carrying out the king's command."

"Very well," said Stone Jaguar. "You may come to the south acropolis at dawn. Tonight, Sky Knife must accompany me back to the temple, so that we may purify ourselves and begin the burial of our brother Blood House."

Bone Splinter continued to ignore Stone Jaguar. "I am commanded to go with you," he said to Sky Knife.

Stone Jaguar made a rude sound, loud enough for Sky Knife to hear. He was sure the warrior heard, too. Sky Knife flushed with embarrassment. He was used to thinking of Stone Jaguar as a great man; to get angry with the warrior for carrying out his duty was childish.

"Come along, boy," snapped Stone Jaguar. He turned and walked quickly back toward the acropolis, bypassing the ball courts and the remaining revellers.

Sky Knife glanced over his shoulder. The warrior followed along behind him. The sour taste of regret sat on the back of his tongue. Why couldn't he just have said he didn't have an answer to the king's question?

Too late now. Sky Knife, caught between Stone Jaguar and Bone Splinter, began to regret a lot of things.

# 4

## ⟩⟩⟩⟩⟩

The crowd had thinned, but a gaggle of purple-clad nuns from the temple of Ix Chel stood in front of the acropolis on the tile patio and barred their way. The High Priestess, a heavyset woman named Turtle Nest, stood in front of the others. While the others wore their hair braided, the High Priestess' hair had been pulled over her head and interwoven with purple beads made from abalone shells. The nuns who stood behind her did not look happy. Nor did she. Sky Knife hung back and let Stone Jaguar confront Turtle Nest alone.

"Stone Jaguar," said Turtle Nest in her strident voice. She glided down the steps and stood before the priest. "Ix Tabai has visited Tikal. Why this night of all nights?"

Sky Knife's knees almost gave way, but he stood his ground. *Ix Tabai!* Wife of Cizin—one glance at her would drive a man mad.

"Ix Tabai is here as well?" barked Stone Jaguar. "How do you know?"

"What do you mean, *as well?*" asked the High Priestess. "And why does that warrior follow you?"

"Never mind that," snapped Stone Jaguar. "How do you know she was here?"

"Look!" Turtle Nest stepped aside, as did her nuns, and Sky Knife saw what the women had shielded with their bodies. A man. A young man. He sat quietly, and rocked back and forth. Drool ran down his chin and dripped onto his arms. His eyes stared, wide open and vacant.

The young man's rocking slowed when he saw Sky Knife. "The stars!" he cried. "The Knife of Stars!"

Stone Jaguar whirled on Sky Knife, rage in his face. Sky Knife backed up and bumped into Bone Splinter, fear clenching his gut. "What have you done?" asked Stone Jaguar, his voice low and menacing. The sound of it crawled up Sky Knife's spine on spider feet.

"Look," said Bone Splinter before Sky Knife could frame a reply. The warrior pointed toward the night sky. Toward the Knife of Stars.

Sky Knife looked up. Flaming white streaks sailed across the sky. They seemed to come from the Knife of Stars itself. Sky Knife had seen them on occasion before, but never so many all at once.

"The *chacs* throw away their cigars," said Bone Splinter.

Sky Knife continued to watch the celestial display. Surely hundreds of cigars had been thrown by the *chacs* just since he started watching. Why would the *chacs* discard their cigars like this?

"It is a warning!" called out the creaky voice of Death Smoke from the acropolis. "A challenge to the death gods. The smoke from their cigars will drive Cizin back to his house, and Ix Tabai with him."

Sky Knife pulled his attention away from the sky. Death Smoke stood framed in the doorway of the acropolis, silhouetted by the fire behind him, his white hair fanning out around his face. Death Smoke pointed toward Stone Jaguar.

"And it is a sign. The Knife of Stars will be our guide."

Death Smoke dropped his hand back to his side. Stone Jaguar glanced back at Sky Knife, but this time, his look was thoughtful.

"Come," growled Stone Jaguar. "There is still Blood House to consider."

"His soul wanders in the twilight of Xibalba," said Death Smoke. "Consider him not. Other problems await our attention."

"And Ix Tabai?" asked the High Priestess. Sky Knife jumped. He had forgotten about her.

"The *chacs* and the Knife of Stars," said Stone Jaguar angrily, "have apparently taken care of the matter." He walked past her and past the slobbering man on the patio. Sky Knife followed after him, bowing slightly to the High Priestess as he passed.

"We will be back to demand answers to our questions!" shouted Turtle Nest. Death Smoke stood aside while Stone Jaguar and Sky Knife entered the acropolis. Death Smoke let the drapery drop behind Sky Knife. Bone Splinter did not enter.

"At least the warrior shows some respect," said Stone Jaguar. "His father should have taught him better manners."

"He is another sign," said Death Smoke.

"Signs, signs," barked Stone Jaguar. "Is that all you can see? Why don't you look out of that *copal* fog you're in and tell us who has done all this to our city."

Claw Skull stepped up to the fire. "All the other attendants besides *him*," he said, pointing toward Sky Knife, "are gone. Some of them will be back, I'm sure, but several said they would no longer stay in a temple the gods have abandoned. We won't be able to give Blood House a proper burial."

"Death Smoke says we needn't worry about Blood House," said Stone Jaguar bitterly. Stone Jaguar removed his jaguar skin cloak carefully and placed it on a bench in the corner. He took off his blue cotton shirt and threw it into the fire. The flames roared up and devoured it quickly. Stone Jaguar watched the flames a moment, then turned his back on them. Strapped to his back was a gourd filled with a mixture of tobacco and lime, a symbol of his office. Every priest wore one, and it was his alone. Blood House's would be burned at his funeral.

"He was my friend, too," said Claw Skull. "We have to have a funeral for him."

"We don't have the time," said Stone Jaguar. The words seemed forced out of him. "The king is concerned—rightly—that this bad luck is the work of men who wish us evil. He has ordered Sky Knife to seek out these men before they do us more harm. We must help him in any way that we can."

"Blood House's body can be buried tonight in the north acropolis," said Death Smoke. "After this is over, we will have the rites."

"This? What is *this?*" asked Claw Skull. "Why did you go see the king? Why was the High Priestess of Ix Chel here with that madman?"

Death Smoke cackled. The sound was dry and brittle as kindling. "Sky Knife saw Cizin on the temple. And Ix Tabai has taken a stroll through the market. Even the *chacs* are active tonight. Before we know it, Itzamna himself will come to the temple and level it to the ground."

"Blasphemy," hissed Claw Skull. He hitched up his blue and purple skirt. "Itzamna would never destroy Tikal."

Sky Knife, forgotten where he stood by the door, contemplated sneaking outside. But he couldn't move. He'd never seen the priests bicker among themselves. To the attendants, the priests were teachers, mentors, dispensers of knowledge and discipline in equal measure. They were not fractious, confused men. They couldn't be. They were the priests of Itzamna.

Sky Knife bit his lip and fought to keep his trembling knees from buckling under him. If even the priests didn't know what to do, other than argue amongst themselves, who was he to find the source of the bad luck? The king had made a mistake, but Sky Knife could not say so aloud. The king had spoken.

Claw Skull sighed and sat down on a bench. "What will we

do?" he asked. "There are only three of us. How can we defeat the bad luck?"

"We do not have to defeat it," said Death Smoke. "In the end, the bad luck will defeat itself."

"Very comforting," said Stone Jaguar. He turned and spat into the fire. "I'm sure the people of Tikal will appreciate the sentiment."

"No matter what happens, we must be strong," said Death Smoke. "There is an added danger."

Stone Jaguar nodded. "Yes. Storm Cloud has been looking for any excuse to bring worship of the Feathered Serpent to Tikal. He has continually pushed me to have at least one festival in the Feathered Serpent's honor each year. So far, I have managed to persuade him out of such folly."

Sky Knife trembled. Surely the king would not let Teotihuacano gods rival Itzamna in Tikal! Such blasphemy was unthinkable. But Storm Cloud *had* been born in a foreign land. Sky Knife gritted his teeth, and prayed the king would not do such a terrible thing.

"But if the bad luck continues," said Death Smoke, "he will not be so compliant next time."

"Yes," mumbled Stone Jaguar. "The king—and all the people—must see that we are not helpless. We have the ear of the gods. The people depend on us to petition our gods for good luck. We do not need a foreign god to aid us. We know the *p'a chi* well. We need no northern rituals."

"Another sacrifice?" asked Claw Skull. "It will take some time to arrange. It will be difficult to find a volunteer so soon after the last sacrifice, especially with bad luck in the city."

"A jaguar," said Stone Jaguar. "We can send the hunters out into the forest to trap one for us. The jaguar is fierce and strong; he will make an excellent representative. The jaguar can intercede for us."

"It's seldom done," protested Claw Skull. "Dogs, crocodiles, turkeys. But a jaguar—think of the danger. It's too risky."

"Risky or not, we need to do something, and I believe a jaguar is our best hope," said Stone Jaguar. "Come. After we carry Blood House to the northern acropolis, we can send for the hunters."

Claw Skull nodded. He stood up wearily and walked into Blood House's quarters.

"We will not need you to lay our brother to rest," said Stone Jaguar to Sky Knife. He raised a hand in dismissal. "Go with the warrior and begin your search."

Sky Knife bowed to Stone Jaguar, then retreated past the drapery to the cooler, danker air outside. Bone Splinter stood just to the right of the door. He had probably heard everything. Sky Knife was embarrassed for the priests—to have their argument witnessed not only by a simple attendant, but by one of the king's household guard as well! Bad luck just seemed to pile upon bad luck.

Sky Knife paused by the warrior, but didn't know what to say. He settled for saying nothing. Sky Knife strode across the patio and down the steps to the Great Plaza. A few celebrants were still out, but most had gone. The merchants had departed back to their camps as well.

Sky Knife walked to the base of the pyramid and sat on the red step. Bone Splinter stood patiently several feet away.

"What do I do?" asked Sky Knife. He wasn't sure if he were asking Bone Splinter, the king, or the gods.

"First of all, don't listen to them," said Bone Splinter. Sky Knife glanced at him, surprised.

"What?" he asked.

"The priests," said Bone Splinter. "They don't know what's going on any more than you do. Don't let them tell you differently."

"They can speak to the gods," protested Sky Knife. "They are great men. The gods listen to them, and do what they ask."

"I'd rather trust my spear and my brother warriors," said

Bone Splinter, "than the chance that the gods will listen to those men. You should trust yourself."

Sky Knife stood, anger growing in his heart. "They are great men!" he insisted.

Bone Splinter shrugged. "Where will you go first?"

Sky Knife was not blind to the warrior's blatant attempt to change the subject, but he was glad to go along with it. He would have to put up with Bone Splinter as a companion until he had finished his task. There was no point in arguing with the man.

"I don't know," said Sky Knife. "Do you have any ideas?"

Bone Splinter scanned the plaza. "You can talk to the merchants tomorrow and ask them if they know of anything unusual that has happened recently. Merchants often know more than you think. But for now, I think the temple of Ix Chel is the place to go."

"Why?" asked Sky Knife. He was not eager to enter the realm of Ix Chel. Wife of Itzamna, she was the mistress of the healing arts. But she also brought disease. On the nights when she left her glowing sky palace, the moon, it was so lonely for her it refused to shine. In the darkness, Ix Chel walked in the forest, and pestilence came with her. Her nuns could heal in her name, or bring a plague upon those unlucky enough to anger them.

"Ix Tabai has been seen, and the nuns of Ix Chel seem to know about that. Perhaps they know something else, as well. Besides, it is not so bad," said Bone Splinter with a smirk that Sky Knife did not understand. The nuns of Ix Chel were sworn never to lie with a man, just as the king's personal guard were sworn never to lie with a woman. As far as Sky Knife knew, there was no contact between the nuns and the king's warriors. Why, then, should Bone Splinter know about the temple of Ix Chel? Sky Knife itched to know, but he didn't dare ask.

"All right," said Sky Knife. He walked to the temple, the

westernmost in the city. The sprawling structure, painted in bright red, orange, and purple designs, was at once garish and compelling.

As they approached the door, Bone Splinter laid a hand on Sky Knife's shoulder. "Wait," he said. Sky Knife halted obediently.

Bone Splinter went up to the purple drapery. "Sky Knife, representative of the King of Tikal, to see the High Priestess," he bellowed.

Someone scurried up to the drapery and pushed it aside a few inches. "You do not belong here, warrior," said a high female voice. "And neither does he."

"The king has declared that Sky Knife may go anywhere and speak to anyone," said Bone Splinter. "He has pronounced it upon his staff."

"What the king does with his staff," said the voice sharply, "is his wife's concern, not ours."

"That is foolish talk," said Bone Splinter. "Now, let us enter."

The drapery was pulled aside and Bone Splinter entered. Sky Knife followed him slowly. Bone Splinter stepped aside as soon as Sky Knife entered.

The woman who faced him was probably his age. She barely came up to Sky Knife's collarbone. Long black hair hung loose down her shoulders and back, held back only by a beaded thread tied around her forehead. A sleeveless dress of darkest purple fell to her ankles. The neckline plunged toward her navel. From his vantage point, Sky Knife could see rather more of the nun than he wished. He swallowed and focused his attention on the jade pendant at her throat.

She smiled. "A man who can resist temptation," she said. "That says more about you than the king's decree." The woman's perfume hung in the air between them, thick and sweet. Sky Knife concentrated on the pendant.

"Go fetch the High Priestess, girl," said Bone Splinter. "You've tested him enough."

The woman nodded to Bone Splinter. "Of course, warrior," she said. She spun around so that her skirt twirled about her ankles. The hem touched Sky Knife's knee. He stepped back. The laughter of the woman hung in the room along with her perfume long after she left.

Sky Knife breathed deeply, relieved she was gone, embarrassed by the tight bulge pressing against his loincloth.

"Why?" he asked. "They can't . . ."

Bone Splinter grunted, though he was grinning. "They play the part for those like you who haven't been here before, who are here to see Turtle Nest. It's an act, designed to rattle you."

Sky Knife whispered, "It worked."

A tinkling of beads announced the arrival of Turtle Nest before she even entered the room. Sky Knife took a deep breath and waited.

Turtle Nest swept into the room, four attendants in her wake. The attendants spread out to the corners of the room. Each of them was dressed as the nun earlier had been, but without the jade pendants. The High Priestess herself was covered from neck to wrists to toes in layer upon layer of purple cloth. Shells dangled from her ears and wrists. Multiple strands of jade beads hung around her neck and rested between her pendulous breasts.

"Yes?" she asked, her voice cold and harsh. "Why have you come here?"

"The king . . . the king . . ." stammered Sky Knife. The women in the corners stood silent, but their postures were inviting, enticing. Sky Knife's gaze kept being drawn to them.

"What, are you an idiot?" asked Turtle Nest. "Speak up, man, or leave."

Red anger swept though Sky Knife and took away his fear. "I am here on the king's business," he said as he took a step forward. "You have no right to treat me this way. I will not be bullied by you."

"You speak nonsense," said Turtle Nest. She turned to go. "You are wasting my time."

"I am not," spat Sky Knife. "I am tired of your games." Inwardly, he was appalled by the disrespectful tone in his voice, but he kept on. "Send your nuns away so that we might talk."

The High Priestess paused, then waved toward her attendants. They departed silently. The High Priestess turned back to Sky Knife. She smiled slowly, but her smile was as friendly as the crocodile's.

"All right," she said. "What is your business?"

"The king wants to know the source of the bad luck that has come to our city tonight," said Sky Knife. "Since Ix Tabai was seen earlier, I hoped you might have an idea."

The woman stroked the beads around her neck. "Tell me," she said. "What did Stone Jaguar mean earlier when he said Ix Tabai has been seen *as well?*"

Sky Knife hesitated. He had no reason to answer her question, and every reason not to—no doubt Stone Jaguar did not want her to know, or he would have told her earlier. But Stone Jaguar was not here to tell him what to do. What was it Bone Splinter had said, that he must trust himself? How simple that sounded.

"Answer my question first," he said. "What is the source of the bad luck?"

Turtle Nest spread her hands wide. "I don't know," she said. "For Ix Tabai to feel safe here on the night of a sacrifice—it is unheard of. I would think an object or a person must be doing this. It must be sabotage." Her eyes narrowed. "Perhaps the king of Uaxactun is planning an attack, and wants to send us bad luck first."

"And where was Ix Tabai seen?" asked Sky Knife.

"Here," hissed Turtle Nest. "Just outside, on our patio. Ix Chel protect us!"

"The man—what did you do with him?"

Turtle Nest shrugged. "He is here for now. But tomorrow—I don't know. We don't take care of the insane here." She frowned at Sky Knife. "He seemed to know *you*, though."

Sky Knife said nothing.

"Now answer my question," said the High Priestess. "What did Stone Jaguar mean?"

Sky Knife hesitated. But she had answered his questions. "Cizin was seen," he said at last, hoping he made the right choice. "Or rather, *I* saw Cizin. On the temple, just after the sacrifice."

Turtle Nest reacted as if Sky Knife had struck her. She stepped back and her hands flew to her face. "No," she whispered. "Oh, Ix Chel, no."

"And now Blood House is dead," continued Sky Knife. "And the *chacs* burn tobacco in the heavens."

Turtle Nest lowered her hands and clapped them once, loudly. Her attendants rushed back in and knelt behind her.

"Prepare the inner sanctum," said the High Priestess. The nuns rose and hurried out.

The High Priestess stepped toward Sky Knife. "I do not have an answer for you, but if you need the assistance of the temple of Ix Chel, you have only to ask. We shall fast and meditate. Perhaps Ix Chel will have pity on us and send us an answer."

The High Priestess turned and left the room. Bone Splinter grunted. "So they will fast and pray. And the priests will fast and pray. Do you see, Sky Knife, why you must be the one to find the answer to the question?"

Sky Knife almost protested, but inside, he felt the truth of Bone Splinter's words. He stepped back outside, his mind already planning where he would go next.

In the east, the glow of dawn brightened the sky over the Great Pyramid. It was the end of an unlucky night, and the dawn of what would likely be an unlucky day. Sky Knife's stom-

ach growled in hunger, and his eyelids felt heavy. But this was
no time to sleep.

Sky Knife was determined that, before the day was out, he
would have part of his answer. For the gods. For the king.

For himself.

# 5

**〉〉〉〉〉**

Sky Knife walked quickly to his quarters in the southern acropolis. Both Stone Jaguar and Turtle Nest had mentioned Uaxactun as a possible source of the bad luck. There ought to be merchants in the city who had recently been to Uaxactun. They might know something.

They might even be responsible.

Still, Sky Knife didn't want to look disheveled when he went among the merchants. He left Bone Splinter in the street and ducked into a small side entrance to the acropolis and walked down the narrow hallway to his tiny room.

The room was rectangular and not much longer than Sky Knife was tall. A single stone bench covered in a plain cotton blanket jutted out of the wall. Sky Knife reached under the bench and brought out a jar filled with water. He poured some of the water over his head and rubbed it through his hair. Then he dried his hair with the cotton blanket and brushed it back over his ears with his fingers.

Sky Knife returned the bowl to its place under the bench and pulled out a small, flat bowl that was covered with a lid. The bowl had been painted in bold blue designs, and the handle of the lid was shaped like a frog.

Sky Knife removed the lid and dipped his fingers into the blue paint inside the bowl. Since he was unmarried, he didn't merit tattoos; he had to satisfy himself with paint. Sky Knife drew two blue lines across each forearm and thigh. Then he painted a line down each cheek.

Sky Knife blotted the remaining paint from his fingers on the cotton blanket and replaced the lid on the bowl.

Bone Splinter stood outside the acropolis, facing the street. He stood with his feet slightly apart, his arms crossed. Sky Knife bit his lip, conscious that his spindly limbs and reed-thin body could not compare to the wide shoulders and rippling muscles of the warrior.

Sky Knife took a deep breath and walked out into the street.

"No," said Bone Splinter.

Sky Knife turned to look at the warrior. A frown creased Bone Splinter's features.

"What?"

"No," repeated Bone Splinter. "You have the king's grace." He grabbed Sky Knife by the upper arm and pushed him back into the acropolis.

"Where are we going?" asked Sky Knife.

Bone Splinter didn't answer. He shoved Sky Knife down the corridor until they came to a large room where a temple attendant, Peccary Spine, ate a breakfast of corn gruel and fruit.

"Fetch some paint," commanded Bone Splinter. "And food."

Peccary Spine shrugged. "Only the priests can order me, warrior," he said. "Get it yourself."

Sky Knife tried to back out of the room—Peccary Spine was the son of a priest, and a bully. He had always teased Sky Knife about his bad luck name and his humble beginnings. Sky Knife tried to avoid being near him if he could help it.

To Sky Knife's surprise, Bone Splinter smiled. "I am here on the orders of the King of Tikal," he said. "My orders are his orders. Get the paint and the food. Get them now."

Peccary Spine frowned and opened his mouth.

"Before I get angry," Bone Splinter added.

Peccary Spine apparently thought better of what he was going to say. He put down his breakfast and left the room hurriedly.

Sky Knife sat down on a bench and waited. Bone Splinter stood immobile by the door. When the attendant returned, Bone Splinter took the bowl of paint and knelt in front of Sky Knife. The attendant put the food down on another bench, grabbed his own breakfast, and left.

Bone Splinter dipped his fingers in the paint and drew two additional lines on each of Sky Knife's forearms and thighs. He added another line to each of Sky Knife's cheeks, then painted a line down his forehead to the tip of his nose and finished with a dot on Sky Knife's chin.

"I can't go out like this," whispered Sky Knife. Only the royal family merited this much paint, and four—*four*—stripes on each arm and leg.

"Of course you can," said Bone Splinter. His tone was firm, but patronizing, as if he spoke to a child. "You are the king's own representative in this matter. You can go anywhere, be with anyone, ask any question, and your questions must be answered."

For the first time, Sky Knife met Bone Splinter's eyes. The warrior's gaze was impassive, but there was a spark in his eyes. Humor, perhaps. Or pride. Perhaps both.

"You will succeed," said Bone Splinter. "If you only listen to your own heart."

Sky Knife opened his mouth, but nothing came out. No one had ever spoken to him like this! Not even his father, who had believed in the omens that plagued Sky Knife's young life, believed them enough to dedicate his fourth son to the service of Itzamna. Depend on himself? He was only a man, a man with questions. A man who would age and die. The gods were eternal. Only they knew the entire mystery of life. Only they were forever. Only they had the answers.

Sky Knife ate breakfast quickly and in silence, his heart in turmoil. Bone Splinter ate also. His actions were precise and meticulous. All over again, Sky Knife fought back envy. Why had the king sent Bone Splinter to him—Bone Splinter was so perfect, so beautiful. Next to him, Sky Knife was nothing.

When he finished, Sky Knife left the acropolis quickly, before any of the priests could spot him wearing the extra paint. They would be angry at the pretention.

At the door of the acropolis, Sky Knife paused. The sun had climbed higher in the sky and shone down through the canopy of the *ceiba* trees that stood at the south end of the acropolis. People passed by on the street without giving Sky Knife a second glance and he relaxed slightly. Perhaps Bone Splinter was right. Perhaps Sky Knife should forget his station and go out as if he truly were a member of the royal family.

Sky Knife gathered his courage and strode into the plaza. Merchants had set up their wares in a haphazard manner and the people of Tikal swirled by the merchants in a colorful, dazzling mass of humanity.

Sky Knife stood in the plaza for a moment and watched the men and women bustle about. Several children ran through the throng, their small white-and-brown-spotted dogs barking at their heels. The children stopped when they saw him. Or perhaps they were staring at Bone Splinter.

"Go on," urged Bone Splinter. "Back to your mothers."

The children darted off, their dogs following them.

Sky Knife took a deep breath and plunged into the crowd. It was a good bet that someone in the plaza knew about Tikal's bad luck, knew about where it came from. Knew, perhaps, how to stop it.

"Come, sir," urged a large woman in a bright red dress. She sat under a small tent, which was merely a blanket hooked over a couple of sturdy sticks. "You are just a young maize plant today, but soon you will flower. I have rabbits here. Take a look."

Sky Knife blushed. He'd often been a target for the vendors who bartered love gifts—every man was before he had his first tattoo. Rabbits were most prized of all, for they had to be imported over a great distance. They were rare and beautiful; the perfect gift to use to woo the affections of a girl.

Sky Knife reached down into the basket that sat beside the woman and stroked one of the rabbits. Its fur was the softest thing he'd ever touched. The rabbit, which was brown with a white streak down its nose, wiggled its nose vigorously.

"He likes you, see," said the woman. "There must be a special girl in your life. This rabbit is for her, yes?"

Sky Knife shook his head. "No," he said. He didn't bother to hide the disappointment in his voice. "There's no girl."

The woman frowned. "A strong lad like you?" she asked. "You should be thinking of marriage, and children. It's the beginning of a new *katun*. What luckier time could you choose?"

Sky Knife stood quickly and walked away. "Come back later," called the woman after him. "I'll save this one for you, yes?"

Sky Knife ignored her and walked around a salt vendor and a man selling charms to keep snakes away from houses and fields. Toward the center of the plaza, he saw a flash of white and green.

"What's that?" he asked Bone Splinter.

A dull throbbing filled the air and a strong, deep voice sang in a language Sky Knife didn't know. He walked forward slowly, toward the sound.

A merchant in a white-and-green-striped skirt sat in sunlight that poured into the plaza. The merchant sat in the open without even a blanket over his head. His hair fell over his shoulders, down to his waist. A lock at each temple had been braided with leather thongs. Shells dripped off the ends of the braids. The merchant's assistant beat a small wooden drum with a hide-covered stick while the merchant sang.

Sky Knife stood, mesmerized, until the song was over. He had never heard a voice so smooth, so powerful.

The crowd applauded when the merchant finished.

"I am Red Spider," announced the merchant in fluent, lightly accented Mayan. "I have fine drums here, and rattles. Perfect for any ceremony or occasion. I also have several fine pieces of jewelry, made by an ancient technique known only to a selected few who reside in Teotihuacan, the Great City of the North, the Jewel of the Civilized World!"

The merchant stood and spread his hands wide, accepting the praise of the crowd. He was taller than any man Sky Knife had seen before, taller even than Bone Splinter. He was thin and his nose was small. But his eyes—they were deep-set, hooded. Like an eagle's. This man was no spider; he was a bird of prey.

The merchant sat back down and beckoned the crowd to come inspect his wares. For a moment, his eyes met Sky Knife's. Sky Knife shivered in his skin, trapped in the other man's gaze. Time slowed, and only the piercing brown eyes of the tall man seemed important. Then the merchant looked away and Sky Knife could breathe again.

"I don't like him," said Bone Splinter. "The merchants from Teotihuacan often know magic, and all of them are trained in combat. See how he moves?"

Sky Knife nodded. He could see what Bone Splinter meant. Red Spider moved with the silky grace of a warrior, displaying a confidence in his abilities most people didn't have.

Sky Knife had heard of the warrior-merchants of Teotihuacan, but he had never before seen one. It was said that their merchants were only the first line of invasion, that armies followed in their wake. The merchants were not exactly welcome in the lowland bazaars, but no one dared kill them, lest they arouse the ire of the Teotihuacano king.

Sky Knife strode forward and knelt by the merchant's wares. He fingered a necklace made of obsidian beads the same sparkling dark green as the *ceiba* tree's leaves.

"It is beautiful, is it not?" asked Red Spider. Sky Knife started as he realized that the exotic accent of Red Spider was the same that colored Storm Cloud's speech. Except Storm Cloud's accent, even after fifteen years in Tikal, was thicker.

"Yes," said Sky Knife. He hesitated, unsure how to ask the questions he wanted to ask. He looked up into the eyes of the merchant. Red Spider's gaze was level and open.

"But you are not here to buy," said Red Spider. He waved a fly away. His fingers were long and slender, more like a musician's than a warrior's.

"No," said Sky Knife.

Red Spider turned to his assistant and barked out a few words in a foreign tongue. The assistant nodded. Red Spider flicked a long braid across his shoulders. The shells clinked against each other.

Red Spider stood. "Come," he said. He wandered away from his wares. "Tell me why you have such a long face on such a lucky day."

Sky Knife walked beside Red Spider, framing his questions. "Why are you here?" he asked at last. "I've never seen a merchant from Teotihuacan here before."

"I'm here to trade my wares," said Red Spider. "Not to cause trouble, as your question seems to imply."

"You speak our language well," said Sky Knife.

"Thank you," said Red Spider. "I've worked at it for many years. One should know the language of the people if one wishes to trade with them."

Red Spider's path led them to the base of the Great Pyramid. Sky Knife stepped up on the red step in order to be able to look Red Spider in the face.

"Have you been to Uaxactun lately?" asked Sky Knife.

Red Spider shrugged. "I spent the rainy season there. Since the rains left, I have been in several cities." Red Spider smiled. "I saw you at the sacrifice last night," he said. "You didn't have *him* with you then."

Sky Knife's gaze caught Bone Splinter standing several yards away. The warrior watched Red Spider intently.

"No, I didn't," said Sky Knife. "Tell me, have you been able to trade many of your wares today?"

Red Spider paused and glanced toward Bone Splinter. His eyes narrowed. "Is this a threat? Are you asking me to leave?"

"No," said Sky Knife quickly. He cursed the sudden squeak in his voice. "It's only a question."

Red Spider looked back at Sky Knife and smiled slowly. It was a warm smile, yet it froze Sky Knife's blood. "The answer is no, I haven't. And that's strange—today should be a lucky day, a day to barter, a good day for trade. So why should I be hearing stories of bad luck from the people of Tikal?"

"What kind of stories?" asked Sky Knife.

"Stories. Just stories."

Sky Knife felt like slapping the smug look off the merchant's face, but he didn't dare. Instead, he stared at the man. Red Spider frowned, but Sky Knife didn't drop his gaze.

Red Spider shrugged. "They say the priests have sent hunters into the jungle to trap a jaguar for sacrifice. They say the king has seen the god of death and will die before the rains come. They say the king of Uaxactun will march here with his troops and make Tikal pay tribute to him."

Bone Splinter spat. "Stories to scare ignorant peasants."

"It speaks!" exclaimed Red Spider. He laughed. "And it is probably right. They are just stories, as I told you."

"The jaguar part is true enough," said Sky Knife, angry at the rudeness of the merchant. Red Spider jerked, as if surprised. Bone Splinter frowned. "But the rest is not true. The king did not see the god of death—I did."

Red Spider's eyes grew wide and he stepped back. Sky Knife jumped down from the step and stood in front of Red Spider. "And neither Uaxactun nor Teotihuacan will take advantage of our bad luck if I can help it," he said. "Remember that."

Red Spider smiled. "As I said, I want no trouble with anyone. I just want to trade. I am a merchant."

"And a warrior," said Sky Knife.

Red Spider shrugged. "I don't deny it," he said. His gaze darted over Sky Knife's shoulder, and he smiled even wider.

Sky Knife turned. The nun from the temple of Ix Chel walked into the plaza. Today she was dressed from neck to toe in a flowing white dress. A red flower was tucked behind an ear, and she had a small brown monkey on a leash. The jade pendant at her throat flashed in the sun. Sky Knife let his breath out slowly.

"A dazzling vision," said Red Spider. "A goddess on earth. A fruit just ripe for the picking, don't you think?"

Anger rose in Sky Knife's throat. That this man—a foreigner, by Itzamna—should lust after a nun of Tikal! It was a disgrace, a slap on the woman's honor, on Ix Chel's honor.

"I should get back to my wares," said Red Spider. "Unfortunately, there's no such thing as an honest assistant. Excuse me."

Red Spider walked toward the nun and spoke to her. The woman laughed, and Red Spider moved off in the crowd. Sky Knife clenched his fists.

"How dare he!" he said. "She's a nun!"

Bone Splinter laid a hand on his shoulder. "No, she isn't."

Sky Knife turned to the warrior. "But she was in the temple!"

Bone Splinter grimaced. "Only because the king has nowhere else to send her. That's Jade Flute, his wife's niece. You don't think nuns have pet monkeys, do you? Or can speak of the king the way she did?"

Hope and despair clashed in Sky Knife's heart. Jade Flute was not only his age, she was the most beautiful woman he had ever seen. And unmarried. And *not* a sworn virgin.

And she was beyond his station. Sky Knife could never aspire to woo the niece of the king's wife.

"Go on," urged Bone Splinter. "Talk to her—why not?"

Why not, indeed. He had the king's own permission to speak to anyone. Sky Knife stepped toward Jade Flute, determined to introduce himself properly this time.

Behind him, someone screamed.

# 6

>>>>>

Sky Knife whirled around to see what was wrong. Bone Splinter, too, had turned toward the sound of the scream.

Several men ran into the plaza shouting about the *Bolon ti ku*, the Lords of Night. Sky Knife broke out into a cold sweat. Surely the Lords of Night weren't going to appear, too! The *Bolon ti ku* weren't malevolent like Cizin, but neither were they particularly well-disposed toward mankind. They reigned over the nine underworlds, the fifth and lowest of which was Xibalba, the land of the dead. Sky Knife had no desire to meet any of the *Bolon ti ku* one hour earlier than he had to.

Sky Knife ran up the steps of the Great Pyramid. From the summit, he scanned the plaza below. The crowd milled about in apparent confusion. The men who had run through shouting about the Lords of Night were gone.

Another scream. Sky Knife strained to see the danger. Suddenly, the mass of people in the plaza began pushing against each other, trampling merchants' tents and wares underfoot. More screams rent the air.

A horrible growl rose over the screams, and echoed between

the stone buildings that surrounded the plaza. Sky Knife trembled. A jaguar! A jaguar was loose in the plaza of Tikal.

Something large and black leapt at a child. The child fell underneath the weight of the beast. A black jaguar. The child's last scream gurgled into silence, and her blood splattered on the pavement, on the men and women running by. Sky Knife's heart went cold in his chest at the sight of the dead child. She could be his sister—she was surely someone's sister. Now she lay broken on the tiles of the plaza.

The jaguar stepped over the body of the child and looked around as if searching for something. Sky Knife held his breath. No wonder the men had shouted about the *Bolon ti ku*—the black jaguar was their messenger. Only the black jaguar could make the journey between earth and the underworlds and return in safety. Only the black jaguar could speak for the Lords of Night.

The cat sat down, panting. It sniffed the child's body briefly, then resumed scanning the plaza. Two other bodies littered the ground of the plaza, blood from their wounds dark and wet on the pavement stones.

The cat stood and stretched slowly. It yawned, blinked, and shook its head. Its gaze traveled to the only human left in the plaza: Bone Splinter. It took a step toward him.

"No!" shouted Sky Knife. He darted down the steps as fast as he could and tried to step in front of Bone Splinter. A fierce determination rose in his gut. No one else would die before his eyes today! No one!

A thick arm blocked his way. "Stay behind me," said Bone Splinter softly. Sky Knife halted, but remained tensed, ready to move, to spring, to do *something*.

The cat's gaze traveled slowly from Bone Splinter to Sky Knife. Its ears perked up when it saw him.

"It's you," said Bone Splinter. "It wants you."

"Me?" gulped Sky Knife. "But . . ."

The great cat roared. Its glistening fangs looked yellow in the late morning light.

"Stand still!" called a voice. It took Sky Knife a long moment to place it. Stone Jaguar.

Sky Knife looked away from the cat reluctantly. To his left, Stone Jaguar, Death Smoke, and Claw Skull spread out on the south end of the plaza. Claw Skull beckoned to someone. Sky Knife looked to his right. Several hunters, spears and nets in hand, fanned out on the north end of the plaza.

"It seems the priests' plans for a jaguar sacrifice have gone astray," said Bone Splinter. He sounded amused. Sky Knife couldn't imagine how anyone could find the situation funny.

The hunters approached the cat, which only acknowledged them with a flick of an ear. The cat tensed, still staring at Sky Knife.

"Don't move!" shouted Claw Skull.

Sky Knife wanted to shout that he wasn't moving—not an inch!—but he didn't dare speak. Suddenly, Bone Splinter screamed and jumped toward the cat.

The cat backed up, toward the hunters. One of the hunters jabbed at it with his spear, but the cat swerved and swiped the hunter with a paw. The man went down in a spray of blood and didn't move.

Another hunter lunged at the cat with his net and dropped the net over the cat's head. A cheer of triumph rose up from the other hunter. Sky Knife's voice joined his.

The cat jumped backward and snapped the net, then darted forward and locked its teeth onto the net-holder's throat. The man's eyes widened in fear. Then he slumped over and the cat let him go.

"Itzamna, help us!" shouted Claw Skull. He ran toward the cat and picked up the first hunter's spear. The cat ignored him and the remaining hunter and loped toward Sky Knife. Bone Splinter pushed Sky Knife out of the way and got in front of the cat. Sky Knife stumbled, then picked himself up quickly and turned back to the plaza. The great cat was only a dozen yards away, poised to spring at Sky Knife. Bone Splinter surged forward and caught the cat around the neck.

Claw Skull plunged his spear into the cat. The cat howled in pain and twisted away from the spear and from Bone Splinter. It pounced on Claw Skull, dug its claws into his chest and its teeth into his face and shook him like a dog shakes a bone. Sky Knife couldn't look away.

With a sickening crack Claw Skull went limp.

Sky Knife, unthinking, rushed forward and leaped onto the back of the jaguar. He wrapped an arm around its throat and squeezed. The coarse fur of the jaguar smelled musty in his nose.

The cat snarled and flung Sky Knife away with a twist of its back. Pain exploded in Sky Knife's shoulder and head as they connected with the pavement. He bit back a scream.

The third hunter and Bone Splinter jabbed the great cat with spears. Bone Splinter impaled the cat right through the neck.

The cat twisted in agony, its roars turned into pitiful mewlings. Then it was still.

Bone Splinter pulled out his spear and tossed it down. He jogged over to Sky Knife. "Are you injured?" he asked.

Sky Knife shook his head. "A little," he said, embarrassed by the way his voice shook.

Bone Splinter laid a hand on Sky Knife's uninjured shoulder. "That was stupid," he said. "To go against a jaguar without a weapon."

Sky Knife hung his head, ashamed that Bone Splinter would think so little of him.

"It was also very brave," said Bone Splinter. He squeezed Sky Knife's shoulder. "But next time, pick up a weapon first. All right?"

Sky Knife looked up into Bone Splinter's blood-spattered

face. The warrior wasn't angry—he was smiling! Sky Knife smiled back. "All right," he said.

Bone Splinter nodded and stood up. He extended a hand to Sky Knife. Sky Knife took it and let Bone Splinter pull him up.

"Our luck truly has flown," mourned Stone Jaguar. He knelt by the broken body of Claw Skull.

"Two priests in less than a day," said Death Smoke. He bent over to look at the dead cat. "It will be difficult to replace one, but two!" He shook his head sadly.

"The cat didn't want *him*," said Bone Splinter. "Or these other people. It wanted Sky Knife. It came for him."

Stone Jaguar stood and faced the warrior. "The cat came because the hunters trapped it, but it got away from them somehow. Why would a jaguar want Sky Knife? He's just a boy."

Bone Splinter said nothing, but turned back to Sky Knife. "Come," he said. "Our wounds can be tended to in the House of the Warriors."

"Sky Knife should go to the acropolis, where he belongs," said Stone Jaguar.

"Sky Knife belongs anywhere he chooses to go," said Bone Splinter over his shoulder. "The king has said so."

Stone Jaguar glowered. Sky Knife almost ran back to the acropolis, back to his small room, but he didn't. Curiosity overcame his fear of Stone Jaguar's wrath. Like any other boy, he'd always wondered about the House of the Warriors, for only the king's personal guard could enter. If Bone Splinter were willing to allow him to enter the House of the Warriors, Sky Knife had to go.

"*Bolon ti ku!*" shouted Death Smoke.

Sky Knife spun around, visions of the jaguar suddenly returning to life and ripping out Death Smoke's throat dancing in his mind.

Death Smoke stood, unharmed, by the body of the cat. Sky Knife breathed a small tired sigh of relief, but his breath caught in his throat. The body of the jaguar writhed in mock death throes on the pavement. Its limbs quivered and its abdomen distended as if something inside were trying to escape.

"What's happening?" demanded Stone Jaguar.

Sky Knife stared, mouth agape, as butterflies—blue butterflies—climbed out of the jaguar's wounds and took to the air. In mere moments, hundreds of butterflies, each the size of Sky Knife's hand, fluttered about Death Smoke. The cloud of butterflies spread outwards toward Sky Knife and the others.

The remaining hunter dropped his weapons and ran, shouting incantations against evil as he went. Sky Knife fought the urge to follow him. Butterflies were an evil omen. Butterflies meant decay; they spoke of death. They stole the souls of children who were left unattended. They swarmed the newly dead on their trip to the underworld to make them lose their way.

Bone Splinter batted at the butterflies. He hissed and drew his hands back.

"What's wrong?" asked Sky Knife.

"They bite," said Bone Splinter.

Sky Knife stared at the butterflies warily. The butterflies hovered in the air, reflecting the bright light of the sun like a thousand blue jewels.

"Get back," said Bone Splinter.

"What?" asked Sky Knife.

"Get back," Bone Splinter repeated. "The jaguar came for you—perhaps the butterflies are meant for you as well."

Sky Knife walked backwards a few steps, but the butterflies didn't follow him. Instead, they floated higher and higher into the sky until they were above the Great Pyramid. Then the cloud dispersed. Butterflies flew everywhere, in every direction.

A few flew down toward Sky Knife and flapped up into his face. He batted at them. Where he touched them, his hands stung as if he'd angered a bee. Bone Splinter grabbed the butterflies attacking Sky Knife and crushed them in his hands, only a grimace betraying the pain they caused him.

"Itzamna," hissed Stone Jaguar. "They'll spread throughout the city. No one will be safe! Death Smoke—come!"

Stone Jaguar jogged back to the southern acropolis, Death Smoke at his heels. A sprinkling of butterflies trailed them, but no more remained to bother Sky Knife or Bone Splinter. Sky Knife felt a surge of relief. The priests would be able to handle the threat. Their power was great. Sky Knife took a deep breath. His shoulder throbbed and his head ached. He wanted to sit down, drink some water, and try to forget his pain.

"Come," said Bone Splinter. He walked east past the Great Pyramid, toward the House of the Warriors. Sky Knife walked close behind him.

# 7

›››››

Two warriors stood straight and tall on the patio in front of the House of the Warriors. They nodded to Bone Splinter, but looked askance at Sky Knife.

"He has the king's grace," said Bone Splinter. The warriors' faces cleared and they bowed to Sky Knife. Sky Knife fidgeted, embarrassed.

Bone Splinter entered the building and walked down several narrow, windowless corridors. Sky Knife struggled to keep up with the warrior. His eyes felt gritty and tired, and he ached all over.

Bone Splinter walked into a garden enclosed within the building. Sky Knife gasped, his pain momentarily forgotten. He'd never suspected the House of the Warriors contained such a place.

Vines dripped down the walls and flowers bobbed in the faint breeze. Small shrubs of a type Sky Knife had never seen before lined the garden. Several warriors sat in the center of the garden, the leaves of a *ceiba* tree shading them from the early afternoon sun.

Bone Splinter approached the warriors. Sky Knife gritted

his teeth and stumbled after him. The warriors cheered, and Sky Knife heard the sound of dry bones cracking against each other. The warriors were apparently throwing bones in a game of chance.

"Brothers," said Bone Splinter. The others looked over to him. One of them stood.

"You must be Sky Knife," said the standing warrior. He was not as tall as Bone Splinter, but his arms and chest were as big as two men's. Sky Knife had never seen such a massive person before. "I am Kan Flower. You are welcome here."

Sky Knife nodded and stood still, fighting to stay on his feet.

"Come, sit," said Bone Splinter. He latched onto one of Sky Knife's elbows and guided him to a low bench. Sky Knife sank onto it, knees trembling, grief over the death of Claw Skull and the remains of his fear clutching at him.

"He is tired and injured," said Bone Splinter. "There was a black jaguar in the plaza. Sky Knife leapt onto its back to try to save another's life."

"Bone Splinter killed it," Sky Knife said. "And he killed the butterflies, too."

"Butterflies?" asked Kan Flower. He knelt in front of Sky Knife.

"You've been killing butterflies?" laughed one of the others. "Did you chase them down in the fields and bite them in two like a dog?"

Bone Splinter held out his hands. Sky Knife gasped. Bone Splinter's palms were crisscrossed with small, round bites that oozed blood.

Kan Flower grabbed Sky Knife's hands and turned them palms up. Sky Knife's palms were marred by several bites, but the pain from them was drowned out by the throbbing in his shoulder and head.

"Looks like you killed a few of them yourself," said Kan Flower softly. "Itzamna!"

The other warriors crowded around. "Some butterflies," said the one who had laughed earlier.

"You've come to the right place," Kan Flower said. "We'll take care of these for you. Are you hurt anywhere else?"

Sky Knife nodded. The warrior probed his face and head gently. Sky Knife winced as pain shot through his skull.

"That's quite a knot on your head," said the warrior. He felt Sky Knife's shoulder. Sky Knife jerked as a sharp pain sliced through his shoulder and down his side.

"Here," said Bone Splinter.

Sky Knife looked up. Bone Splinter held out a wooden bowl full of water. Sky Knife took it and gulped it down gratefully.

"Come on, now," urged Kan Flower. "Lie down here."

The warriors moved the bones they had been throwing, while Kan Flower helped Sky Knife lie down on a cotton throw. Sky Knife tried to relax as Kan Flower probed his injuries again. He concentrated on the gentle waving of the *ceiba* leaves overhead. They appeared fuzzy, out of focus. Sky Knife squinted, but the pain in his head grew worse and he stopped.

"Bone Splinter, you too," said Kan Flower.

"I am not badly injured," protested Bone Splinter.

"You're supposed to protect Sky Knife. To do that, you need two good hands. Now lie down." Kan Flower sounded angry, but it seemed far away to Sky Knife.

Sky Knife couldn't keep his eyes open any longer. The weariness in his bones leeched into his mind. He sighed and relaxed. Even the throbbing of his injuries seemed to lessen in importance. He felt Bone Splinter lie down beside him.

The sharp cracking sound surprised him. Sky Knife jerked, heart pounding, then relaxed as he realized one of the warriors had merely pounded a stick onto the head of a small wooden drum. The sour taste of fear sat on the back of his tongue.

"Easy," urged Kan Flower. "We are going to sing the healing chant."

Sky Knife blinked, surprised again. A healing chant? He'd never known warriors could do such things.

The drum sounded again and Kan Flower laid his hands on Sky Knife's chest. He began chanting in a low, slow tone. Sky Knife shivered, though curiosity began to get the better of his fear. He felt as if thousands of insects were crawling over and under his skin. He closed his eyes and gritted his teeth. The feeling wasn't painful, but it made him want to brush the insects off, to get up and get away from the crawly feeling of his skin. He could feel their feet, all their tiny, tiny feet. . . .

Sky Knife held his breath while the urge to run or scream overwhelmed him. He balled up his fists and screwed his eyes shut. He would not scream. He would not!

Kan Flower shrieked an impossibly high note and lifted his hands off of Sky Knife. Sky Knife let out his breath in a rush, suddenly free of the terrible crawling sensation.

Sky Knife opened his eyes. The *ceiba* tree leaves nodded back and forth in the slight breeze just as they had before, but this time, he could see them clearly. His vision was no longer cloudy, and his shoulder and head didn't pain him. Cautiously, he sat up.

The warriors sat in a circle around him and Bone Splinter. Bone Splinter grabbed Sky Knife's hand and examined the palm. The butterfly stings had healed without scars.

"Good," he said.

"What about you?" asked Sky Knife.

Bone Splinter displayed his own palms, which had also healed.

"I never knew warriors could do healing magic," said Sky Knife. He flexed his shoulders, but not even a twinge of pain remained.

"No one outside the House of the Warriors knows," said Kan Flower. "And no one ever will. This is our secret, as secret as the existence of this garden."

"You have the king's grace," said the laughing warrior. "So we must trust you with our secrets."

"I will tell no one," said Sky Knife, suddenly uneasy. He would never want any of these men angry with him. He could imagine that no one who told the secret lived long.

"Now, tell us about this jaguar," said Kan Flower.

"And the butterflies," added another warrior.

"Food first," said Bone Splinter. "He is our guest."

"Yes, of course," said Kan Flower. He and another warrior got up and left. The others retrieved their throwing bones.

The bones had been carved with glyphs depicting the twenty day names. Sky Knife leaned closer for a better look.

The warrior holding the bones threw them down in front of Sky Knife.

"Today is Ahau," he said. "See—here it is, next to Cauac."

"But how do you play?" asked Sky Knife.

The warrior laughed.

"To train you in the game would take as long as it would take to train you with a sword or a sling," said the warrior. "Everything depends on the pattern of the bones when they fall, and which days touch, overlap, or cross the others."

"You see, Sky Knife," said Bone Splinter, "this is what mighty warriors do with their lives."

The other warrior appeared insulted. "That's not all we do," he said to Sky Knife. "We guard the king, and fight his wars, too."

"And have poetry contests," offered another. "Bone Splinter is one of our best poets."

"Poetry?" asked Sky Knife. Could it be true? Did the king's personal guard actually compose poetry on long, sleepy afternoons? Sky Knife had always assumed the warriors discussed, well, fighting, and wars. Battles won and battles lost. Hearts taken, blood spilled. Sky Knife couldn't help but smile.

"Poetry is the heart of a warrior," said Bone Splinter. "Or it should be." He leveled a disdainful gaze on the laughing warrior.

"Poetry is merely a bunch of pretty words," said the other. "A sword is what is important. A spear, a shield, a knife. Feeling an enemy's blood run across your fingers. Hearing his screams. Seeing the life bleed out of his eyes."

"There is more to life than violence," said Bone Splinter. "A warrior is more than one who kills."

Sky Knife sat quietly and listened. Bone Splinter and the other warrior spoke without passion, as if they had had this discussion a hundred times before. Perhaps they had.

Kan Flower returned with bowls of fruit, breadnuts, and cornbread. The warrior behind him carried an entire baked turkey.

"*Pulque* is coming," said Kan Flower. He set the bowls down in the center of the group. Sky Knife's stomach growled and his mouth watered at the sight of the food. The warriors sat down, but didn't reach for the food.

Bone Splinter gestured toward the bowls. "Sky Knife, you must eat first. You are our guest."

Sky Knife blushed, embarrassed that the king's personal guard would defer to *him*. He reached for a chunk of cornbread and ripped a leg off the turkey. The warriors smiled approvingly and reached for their own helpings.

"Now," said Kan Flower, "tell us about the jaguar."

"And the butterflies," piped in a warrior with a high, squeaky voice.

Bone Splinter told the tale, but it didn't seem to agree with what Sky Knife remembered. For one thing, Bone Splinter ascribed more courage to Sky Knife than he could recall displaying. For another, Bone Splinter did not see Stone Jaguar and Death Smoke's flight as a heroic attempt to save the city, but a cowardly retreat that left the body of their friend and companion Claw Skull behind on the plaza tiles.

Sky Knife fidgeted—he, too, had left Claw Skull's body behind without a thought. Suddenly, the food did not seem as appetizing. Sky Knife put down the remainder of the turkey leg and the bread.

"It's got to be the work of that sun-rotted king of Uaxactun," said Kan Flower. "Mark my words—he'll be here with an army before the rains."

"I don't think so," said the warrior of the squeaky voice. "I think it's the work of that Teotihuacano—what's his name?"

"Red Spider," answered Bone Splinter.

"Oh, *him*," said Kan Flower. He tapped his fingers on his thigh. "Could be. Storm Cloud's the youngest of his brothers and the only one besides the eldest to be a king. The others might want to come here and take his place. Red Spider could be here as an advance scout. He could have brought charms and spells with him to give us bad luck."

The others nodded. Sky Knife frowned. There was something wrong with the idea that Red Spider was behind the bad luck. Sky Knife had not liked Red Spider, but still, something wasn't right.

"Red Spider is from Teotihuacan, like Storm Cloud," he said. "Why bring a Teotihuacano king bad luck on behalf of some minor noble who wants to be king?"

"He's a merchant. Wealth is important to him," said Kan Flower. "He could be paid to do it."

"He's a warrior, too," said Sky Knife. "Would *you* accept wealth as a substitute for honor?"

Kan Flower tensed. The cords in his neck stood out. "Not I!" he said. The others echoed him.

"Merchants have no honor," hissed the laughing warrior. "Warrior or no, Red Spider is a filthy, stinking merchant."

"Uaxactun still seems a better bet," said Sky Knife. "It's only one day's walk—anyone could have come from there and be in Tikal now, and we'd never know."

"True enough," said Kan Flower.

"Then perhaps we should start looking for such people," said Bone Splinter. "And find out if they're here or not."

Kan Flower and the other warriors nodded. "We'll start today," he said. "With all the trouble, no one will think twice about a few extra warriors patrolling the city. We'll report anything we find to the king, and to you."

"Good," said Sky Knife. Whether it was the food, the healing, or the support of the warriors, he didn't know, but he felt sure now that the answer would be easily found. Whoever the king of Uaxactun had sent to curse Tikal would be found out, and the bad luck would be dealt with. Sky Knife felt more hopeful than he had since seeing Cizin on the temple.

"This calls for a poem," said the warrior of the squeaky voice. "Bone Splinter?"

Bone Splinter smiled a tight smile. He closed his eyes a moment. Finally, he took a deep breath.

> "Cizin
> On the temple
> Sneezes bad luck
> Out his nose."

Sky Knife joined the warriors in laughter. It felt good to ridicule the death god rather than to fear him. Bone Splinter didn't laugh, but he did nod approvingly at the response to his poem.

Sky Knife and Bone Splinter took their leave of the warriors. As they walked out of the garden, Kan Flower spoke.

> "Sky Knife goes
> Bone Splinter follows—
> Bad luck, beware!"

Sky Knife felt heartened and honored by their confidence in him, their willingness to share their secrets with a mere temple attendant. The House of the Warriors was nothing like he had expected it to be—strength could be found within, but so too could beauty.

Outside in the street stood a temple attendant, one of those who had been with Sky Knife on the pyramid the night before.

The attendant ignored Bone Splinter and gestured to Sky Knife.

"Hurry," he said. "Death Smoke says you and I must come to the northern acropolis."

"Why?" asked Sky Knife.

The attendant shook his head. He seemed agitated. "I don't know," he said. "Hurry!"

The attendant dashed off in the direction of the northern acropolis. Sky Knife ran after him, Bone Splinter in his wake.

# 8

>>>>>

Sky Knife hesitated in the plaza just short of the patio of the northern acropolis. The low stone building had been built so long ago that no one except the priests knew what gods had been worshipped there. The trees of the jungle crowded the structure; vines covered part of it. The building was supposed to be haunted by the spirits of dead and forgotten gods. No one but priests could enter and expect to exit safely.

Death Smoke had undoubtedly extended whatever protection was required to Sky Knife, but Sky Knife doubted Death Smoke would consent to protect Bone Splinter. He turned to the warrior.

"Perhaps you should stay here," he said.

Bone Splinter frowned.

"I'll be safe enough with the priests," said Sky Knife. "They'll know how to deal with the ghosts that walk here."

The warrior nodded and glanced around at the people that occupied the plaza. "I'll look for anything unusual out here," he said. "Not that anything in the plaza will look *usual* today."

Sky Knife scanned the plaza and saw what Bone Splinter

meant. Although the bodies of Claw Skull, the hunters, and the black jaguar were gone, few merchants had returned to the plaza. And very, very few people had come back to look at their merchandise. The plaza more closely resembled Uayeb—the Five Unlucky Days—than the first day of a new *katun*.

Sky Knife looked, but didn't see Red Spider among the merchants in the plaza this afternoon.

"See if you can find Red Spider," Sky Knife said. "I'm interested in knowing how he's reacting to the bad luck."

Bone Splinter nodded. Sky Knife turned back to the acropolis and walked across the cracked patio toward the largest of three doors. The patio was uneven; roots had pushed their way up and around the tiles. Sky Knife stepped carefully, heart pounding. The roots resembled dried and shrunken fingers. It was easy to imagine angry spirits of the jungle stretching out their fingers over the centuries, reclaiming this area for the trees, grabbing the ankles of anyone unlucky enough to come across them.

The entrance was dark. Sky Knife took a deep breath, clenched his fists, then plunged inside. The moment he stepped inside, he was in darkness, as if no light from the outside could pass the entrance.

"Death Smoke?" he shouted. "Stone Jaguar?"

"Come on, boy," croaked the thin voice of Death Smoke. "A few steps in the dark won't hurt you."

Sky Knife stepped forward carefully. The floor here was smooth and even. On the fourth step, Sky Knife suddenly found himself in a room lit brightly with a blue sorcerous glow. Even the far reaches of the high, vaulted ceiling were filled with light.

The room was long and narrow, stretching out to his left and right. On the walls, scenes of sacrifice painted in bright oranges and blues vied for space with lists of dates. Sky Knife caught one very imposing date: 8.2.5.14.2 7 Ik 20 Tzec—almost four hundred years before! Proof, if Sky Knife had needed any, of how ancient this structure was. It *had* to be haunted. Sky Knife resisted the urge to look over his shoulder. He could almost imagine skeletal fingers reaching for his throat.

Death Smoke, Stone Jaguar, and the other attendant sat in the center of the room around a large clay bowl filled with water.

"Come, come," said Death Smoke. "Sit." He gestured to a place in between himself and Stone Jaguar.

Sky Knife sat.

"We are four. The circle is complete," said Death Smoke. His fetid breath hung around Sky Knife. Sky Knife shivered and tried not to breathe deeply.

Sky Knife looked across the circle to the other attendant. The man's eyes were wide and sweat rolled off his face. Sky Knife made an effort to sit up straighter. *He* would not give in to such fear.

Stone Jaguar drew a cigar out of a pouch in his lap. He held it over the water.

"Itzamna, Lord of All," said Death Smoke. "Give us light."

One end of the cigar began to smoulder. Stone Jaguar waved the cigar over the water four times, then put the cigar to his mouth and inhaled deeply. He blew out the smoke slowly.

Stone Jaguar passed the cigar to the other attendant, who also put it to his lips once. He blew out the smoke in a quick, jerky breath.

Death Smoke took the cigar and puffed. A smile spread across his face as he handed the cigar to Sky Knife.

Sky Knife's eyes watered as he inhaled the essence of the tobacco. The cigar tasted spicier, and danker, than any tobacco he could remember smoking before. The hot smoke filled his lungs. Sky Knife blew out the smoke, and it joined the rest of the sweet-smelling fumes that hung about the heads of the four men. He gave the cigar back to Stone Jaguar, who dropped it into the water.

Death Smoke laughed, startling Sky Knife. "The tobacco gods are pleased," said Death Smoke. Sky Knife looked in the water. The cigar had sunk to the bottom, yet continued to burn and smoke. The surface of the water churned as the smoke moved within it.

"We have lost two of our brethren in the past day," said Stone Jaguar. "And the law of Itzamna is that four priests must always be in the temple."

"The voice of the *copal*, and the voice of the waters, is clear," said Death Smoke. "We shall lose another priest before this month is out."

"What?" asked Sky Knife. "Who?"

"Such bad luck is unprecedented," said Stone Jaguar. "Death Smoke has seen his own death in the *copal* embers. We must act quickly to replace our fallen brothers before yet another is lost to us. The two of you will serve for now, Itzamna willing."

"But, what of the others?" asked Sky Knife. There were always junior priests and senior attendants in the temple. Surely young men, without rank or tattoos, could not be considered as potential priests.

"You will serve, Sky Knife, because the gods seem to have their hands on your fate," said Stone Jaguar. "If there is any luck in that, we must have it for the temple, too."

"The others are fled," said Death Smoke. "When the test came, they proved themselves unworthy. Bad luck has come, and they hide their faces."

"Several have remained true," corrected Stone Jaguar. "And if Death Smoke has seen truth in the smoke, then I shall be choosing another from among you before long."

"Reach your hand into the water," commanded Death Smoke. "And take out whatever your hand closes upon."

Sky Knife stretched out his hand and held it briefly over the violently churning water. Then he reached into the water. It was cold, colder than anything Sky Knife had touched before, colder than rain, colder than water drawn from the depths of a *cenote*. Sky Knife shuddered, but didn't hesitate. He reached to the bottom of the bowl and grasped something solid. It was larger than the cigar. He closed his hand around it and pulled his hand out of the water.

Sky Knife turned his hand over and opened his fist. He stared in awe at the object in his hand. It was a temple knife, a sacrificial knife. The blade had been chipped of blackest obsidian, the handle carved from the branch of the *ceiba* tree.

"Behold the Hand of God," said Death Smoke. "It is yours from this day, until Itzamna or his High Priest requires it of you."

Stone Jaguar handed Sky Knife a deerskin pouch. "The pouch is blessed by Itzamna," he said. "The blade will rest within it quietly."

Sky Knife took the pouch and placed the knife inside. Then he tied the pouch around his waist.

"Now, you," barked Death Smoke.

The other attendant stretched his hand toward the water. His hand shook so much, Sky Knife doubted he'd be able to grasp anything, but he said nothing. The man plunged his hand into the water.

The man froze for a moment. Then he jerked his hand back to his chest and screamed. It was a scream of pure terror laced with pain. Sky Knife leaped up and rushed to the man's side.

"Idiot!" hissed Death Smoke. "You have broken the circle."

Sky Knife ignored the older man. He put an arm around the attendant's shoulders and held him while the man whimpered. Sky Knife reached for the hand the man kept close to his chest.

"What is wrong?" he asked. "Let me see."

The man relinquished his hand to Sky Knife. Sky Knife pried open the man's fist. On the man's palm were two small puncture wounds.

"Bah," said Stone Jaguar. "The gods have rejected this one. Now we are only three."

"When I die, there will be just you and Sky Knife," said Death Smoke. "Two more must be found. Quickly."

As Sky Knife watched, the puncture wounds smoked as if a fire burned inside the man's hand. The man screamed again, then slumped against Sky Knife.

Sky Knife felt for the man's heartbeat, but couldn't find it. "He's dead," he whispered.

"Of course he's dead," said Stone Jaguar. "No one may see this ritual and live without becoming a priest of at least the lowest rank. That is not the problem. The problem is that we must find two more men to train as priests. Tikal has enough bad luck already—who knows how bad it could become if there are not enough priests for the temple."

"Worse and worse," said Death Smoke. "I . . ." Death Smoke's voice trailed off.

"What is it?" asked Stone Jaguar. "Ah, gods. Navel of the World—now what?"

Sky Knife lowered the body of the attendant to the floor and looked to see what had alarmed Stone Jaguar and Death Smoke.

The water in the bowl had stopped churning. Floating belly-up in the water was a rainbow-colored snake. The snake stuck out its tongue once and bravely tried to right itself, but the effort was too much for it. It went limp.

Sky Knife's gut twisted in dread. This snake was not the one responsible for the attendant's death, for this was a *chic-chac*, a rainbow serpent. *Chic-chacs* did not have fangs or poison. Their duty was to bring rain and life to the people of the earth. They were good and generous protectors of mankind. Sky Knife had never thought he would be blessed enough to see one. Now he had seen one, and it was dead. Sky Knife was grieved by the thought of the little snake's death and horrified to consider what it might mean.

Would the rains even come this year if the *chic-chacs* died? Would Tikal become a barren and dry land?

Troubling, too, was the question: who would be cruel enough, evil enough, to kill a rainbow serpent, a being of protection and goodwill?

Sky Knife reacted. He grabbed the little snake, which was barely as long as Sky Knife's arm from wrist to elbow, and clutched it to his chest, stroking its cold scales.

"Let it go," said Stone Jaguar. "It is just another omen of our bad luck."

"No," whispered Sky Knife. He couldn't bear the thought of the *chic-chac* dead. He rubbed the dull scales vigorously and prayed silently to Itzamna. *Let the snake live*, he begged. *It is so small and helpless.* Tears rolled down his face and dripped onto the damp body of the snake.

The snake quivered. Sky Knife stopped stroking it, afraid he was imagining things. But the snake trembled again. Its tongue flicked out once. Then a second time.

"Itzamna," hissed Death Smoke. "It's alive!"

"The gods be praised," said Stone Jaguar. His voice was low and harsh. Sky Knife glanced up at the priest. A single tear rolled down Stone Jaguar's face. It seemed he was as affected by the snake's survival as Sky Knife.

The snake raised its head. Eyes the deep purple of the edge of the rainbow stared into Sky Knife's face. Sky Knife hardly dared breathe. The snake flicked its tongue out toward Sky Knife several times in quick succession. Slowly, it slithered up his arm and around his neck. Sky Knife stroked it, amazed that it did not crawl away and return to its home, to *chun caan*, the land at the bottom of the sky. The snake's head rested on his collarbone, and the tip of its tail made a small curve at the hollow of his throat.

"Well, well," said Stone Jaguar. "Finally. A piece of good luck."

"But for whom?" asked Death Smoke.

"What do you mean?" asked Sky Knife. "The *chic-chac* . . ."

"Is a message from the gods," said Death Smoke. "You have denied the message. It is good luck for the *chic-chac*, but not necessarily for you. Or for Tikal."

"Bah," said Stone Jaguar. "The *chic-chac* lives. That has to be a good thing. No harm can come from a rainbow serpent. And it might prove useful."

"How so?" asked Death Smoke.

"Evil cannot look upon it," said Stone Jaguar. "Perhaps Sky Knife can find the man the king seeks by discovering who cannot see the rainbow serpent."

"Few are bound to be wise enough to see a *chic-chac*, no matter how pure they are," said Death Smoke. "That's a foolish idea."

Stone Jaguar turned to Sky Knife. "Perhaps so," he said. "But keep it in mind, just in case it's not."

"No matter," said Death Smoke. He waved his hands over the dark and still water. "The ceremony is over. Sky Knife has been elevated to a priest of the lowest rank. We welcome him to our brotherhood."

Stone Jaguar stared at Sky Knife a moment, his expression dour. "It seems he has already elevated himself to the royal caste," said Stone Jaguar. Sky Knife, remembering the extra paint Bone Splinter had put on him, flushed with embarrassment. "No matter," continued Stone Jaguar. "We will begin your training soon. Guard the knife you carry."

Sky Knife nodded.

"Death Smoke and I will take care of the body," said Stone Jaguar. "Later we must consider which two other attendants to offer into the service of Itzamna."

"We have other things to consider," said Death Smoke. "The boy is a priest but unmarried."

"There'll be time enough after Sky Knife finishes his task for the king to find a wife for him," said Stone Jaguar. A look of pain crossed his face, and then, just as quickly, was gone. Sky Knife glanced away. Stone Jaguar's wife had died several years before, and he had yet to take another.

"It is unseemly," said Death Smoke.

"Unseemly or not, Sky Knife will live a bit longer without

a wife," said Stone Jaguar. "And that's all I will say on the matter."

Death Smoke frowned but nodded. He waved his hands over the water again. "Evening falls," he said. "The second day of the new *katun* will soon begin. Itzamna grant it be a luckier day than this one."

Death Smoke waved Sky Knife away. Sky Knife bowed slightly to each priest, then stood and walked out of the room. This time, he did not step into darkness. The little snake at his throat shone brightly enough to light his path. The warmth from its scales burrowed into Sky Knife's soul and touched his heart with love.

# 9

››››› 

Bone Splinter sat on the steps of the northern acropolis, facing the plaza. Sky Knife walked up behind him.

"Did you find Red Spider?" he asked.

Bone Splinter shook his head. "No," he said. "But Kan Flower sent someone to tell me that he has detained several merchants that have been to Uaxactun recently. If you wish, I will . . ." Bone Splinter stood as he talked and turned to face Sky Knife. His eyes widened as he saw the snake. His voice jumped. "I will . . . take you to where Kan Flower has them. That is a rainbow serpent you wear around your neck."

Sky Knife nodded. He couldn't tell Bone Splinter what had happened in the acropolis; none but the priests could know that. Sky Knife was awed by the thought that now *he* was considered a priest. The thought seemed very strange.

"I don't think I'll go see them now," he said.

"Why not?" Bone Splinter frowned. The light from the setting sun glinted off the mother of pearl inlay in his ear spools.

"Let them squirm tonight," said Sky Knife. "They don't know why they've been detained, do they?"

A slow smile spread across Bone Splinter's perfect features. "I don't believe so," he said.

"Besides, with Kan Flower watching them, they won't be able to work any more bad luck magic against us," said Sky Knife. He yawned. Now that the light of day was dimming, and the excitement of the ceremony wore off, he remembered he hadn't slept at all last night. His eyes were dry and gritty. He rubbed them wearily.

"You there, boy!"

Sky Knife looked around for the source of the shout. A purple-clad nun strode across the plaza, ignoring the curses of the merchants as her long skirt disrupted their wares. Salt cakes and obsidian blades fell to the plaza in her wake. The blades smashed against the tiles with bright, sharp sounds.

"Who's going to pay for these?" shouted the obsidian merchant.

The nun ignored him. The merchant half-rose, then apparently thought better of confronting a nun who could curse him with the power of Ix Chel, and sat back down, muttering.

"Yes, priestess?" said Sky Knife as the woman approached.

"Come to the temple," she barked. "The High Priestess wishes to see you."

"Then perhaps she should find a messenger with manners," said Sky Knife. He resisted the urge to turn his back and ignore this rude woman.

The nun stopped in front of him. She frowned. "Come along, boy," she said. "Who are you to say no to the High Priestess of Ix Chel in any matter?"

Bone Splinter stepped forward, but Sky Knife waved him back. "I am Sky Knife," he said. "A representative of the King of Tikal, and a priest now, in the Temple of Itzamna."

Bone Splinter's eyes widened at that. The nun seemed unimpressed. "You are a temple attendant," she said. "Who apparently has ambitions beyond his years or his station."

Sky Knife considered walking past the nun and ignoring her. But if the High Priestess knew anything that could help him, he should go to her and see what she had to say.

On the other hand, he didn't necessarily have to go with this particular nun.

"I am very busy," he said. "And you have offended me. If the High Priestess wishes to see me, she can send another messenger."

"I don't think so," said the nun. "Come with me or . . ."

"Be very careful about what you say next," said Bone Splinter softly. "He is under my protection."

"I've had quite enough of this," said Sky Knife. He fought to suppress a yawn. His anger helped chase away some of his weariness. "I will go see the High Priestess."

The nun smirked.

"But I shall report your unseemly behavior to her," said Sky Knife.

The nun tossed her head, sending braids flying around her shoulders. "My mistress will put you in your place, boy."

"We'll see," said Sky Knife. He stepped down from the patio and strode toward the Temple of Ix Chel. Bone Splinter walked just behind him, but the nun had to struggle to keep up. She was panting by the time they reached the temple.

Bone Splinter stepped ahead and drew aside the purple curtain. Sky Knife walked in without announcement.

"No, wait," called the nun. She jogged the last few steps into the temple. "You can't just come in here like this."

"I can go anywhere I wish," said Sky Knife, though he didn't move from the room. He might have the king's permission, but he certainly didn't have Ix Chel's leave to wander the inner recesses of the temple.

Turtle Nest strode into the room. "Thank you for . . ." she began. Then her eyes widened and she stepped back, hands at her throat. "Oh, Ix Chel!" she whispered. "Is it true? Is it really a rainbow serpent?"

"It is," said Sky Knife. "It . . . it seems to like me."

"A rainbow serpent?" asked the rude nun. She looked around the room, at Bone Splinter and Sky Knife. "Where?"

"What luck," said Turtle Nest. She walked forward slowly, eyes never leaving the *chic-chac*. "You have brought luck to my temple. Thank you."

Sky Knife didn't know if she spoke to the snake or to him, so he kept silent.

"This man was most rude to me," said the nun. "I had to ask him several times to come. He claims to be a priest instead of an attendant, too."

Turtle Nest blinked and stepped back, her gaze thoughtful. "Foolish girl," she said. "What do you think is in that bag at his waist? If he bears the Hand of God, he must be a priest." She looked into Sky Knife's eyes. "Stone Jaguar, I assume, plans to use whatever luck you can bring for his own temple, and so has elevated you. Congratulations."

"You mean he *is* a priest?" asked the nun. "He doesn't seem like one to me."

Turtle Nest frowned and turned to her nun slowly. "Look at this man and tell me what you see around his neck."

"Nothing but an old braided cord," huffed the nun.

The High Priestess walked toward her nun, the grace of the jaguar in her movements. "Oh, it is not a cord," she said, her voice silky and low. The sound of it sent a shudder up Sky Knife's spine.

The nun stepped back, surprised. "What?" She glanced from Sky Knife to Turtle Nest. "What's going on?"

"You slut!" barked Turtle Nest. The nun's jaw dropped open in shock and horror. Turtle Nest slapped the nun. The nun shook her head and tried to speak, but her High Priestess slapped her again. The nun fell down into a sobbing heap. "Get up!" screamed the High Priestess. She kicked the nun, whose wails grew ever louder.

Several other nuns ran into the room. They stopped in surprise when they saw their High Priestess kicking the nun on the floor. "Who is he?" shouted Turtle Nest. "Who is he? Who made you forget your vows to Ix Chel?"

Sky Knife bit his lip, suddenly understanding. The nun had lain with a man—she was no longer consecrated to Ix Chel. She was defiled. No wonder she couldn't see the snake—she lived in a terrible state of dishonor, without repentance, without remorse.

The gods, even Ix Chel, might forgive. But only if a person repented, and offered penance.

"Ix Chel curse you," said the High Priestess. "You have no honor. You have no name. You are nothing. At the moment the sun dies on the horizon tonight, you shall join him in the underworld, where the beasts shall burn your dead flesh with their cigars and roast your heart for their supper." Turtle Nest turned her back on the nameless woman. "Take her away," said the High Priestess. The other nuns rushed forward and dragged their former sister out of the room. The screams of the defiled nun echoed down the narrow corridor.

Turtle Nest turned to Sky Knife. "Xibalba shall be her next home," she said. "For any insult this nameless woman gave, I offer my apology."

Sky Knife nodded.

Turtle Nest cocked her head. "You find something amusing, warrior?" she asked.

Sky Knife turned to Bone Splinter. The taller man looked as though he were swallowing a laugh.

"I was thinking that, in the House of the Warriors, if a brother were found to be defiled, we should take his life's blood then and there, without bothering to curse him or make a speech. But I think the curse is appropriate. She will carry it into Xibalba with her like a tattoo."

Turtle Nest nodded. "Even so. She has failed the temple, Ix Chel, me, her sisters, her parents—everyone."

Sky Knife cleared his throat. "There was a reason you sent for me?" he asked.

Turtle Nest sighed. "Yes, although now my heart is weighed so heavily with sorrow, I almost forgot. I was going to tell you that I burned *copal* today and petitioned Ix Chel to send me a sign in the smoke. I asked her to tell me who brought evil to Tikal. And she answered."

"Yes?" asked Sky Knife. His body quivered in excitement. "Who is it?"

"The goddess does not give names, young priest," said Turtle Nest. She smiled. "But she does help those who are faithful. In the smoke, I saw a tall man with a dark heart. An ambitious heart. I could not see his face. At first, I thought I wouldn't tell you—a dark heart is scarcely something one can just go out and look for. But perhaps you will find a way. You bear luck with you at your throat, luck enough perhaps to outweigh your name."

Sky Knife lowered his gaze. "My mother said she was told by Itzamna himself to name me after the Knife of Stars," he said. He glanced back up at Turtle Nest.

The priestess nodded. "I thought it might be something like that. A woman just doesn't go looking for bad luck for her child without reason. Perhaps for you, the name is good luck—it should be, if it's Itzamna's choice. If Itzamna wants you named after the Knife of Stars, then you and your name may be good luck, not only for yourself, but for Tikal as well. And now you have an ally in the *chic-chac*. Do not underestimate that."

"Providing the snake stays with me," said Sky Knife, hoping what Turtle Nest said about his name and Itzamna was true. Turtle Nest's duty was to Ix Chel, not Itzamna, but she was more familiar with the ways of the gods than Sky Knife. She might be right.

"One cannot rule the desires of a serpent's heart," said Turtle Nest. "You can only hope it will stay for a few days before returning to *chun caan.*"

Sky Knife nodded. Turtle Nest bowed slightly to him. "Go in peace, priest of Itzamna. My temple shall continue to serve in whatever way we can."

"Thank you," said Sky Knife. He turned and walked out of the temple. The sun was low on the horizon. Sky Knife didn't watch it go down, didn't want to be reminded of the nameless woman who had shed her duty, her honor, and now, her life.

Sky Knife stumbled back to his quarters and dropped onto his bed, the wails of the nameless woman still ringing in his ears. But the warmth of the *chic-chac* burned away the screams until only pleasant thoughts, and untroubled dreams, remained.

# II

>>>>>>>>>

# EAST

## WHERE KNOWLEDGE BEGINS

9.0.0.0.1
9 IMIX 14 CEH

# 10

›››››

Sky Knife woke slowly. The first thing he did was put his hands to his neck. The *chic-chac* was still there. Its feather-soft tongue touched his hand. It tickled. Sky Knife felt relieved, and honored, by the snake's favor.

The cotton blanket had slipped to the floor, and the paint on his arms and legs had flaked off. Sky Knife poured some water over his head and ran his fingers through his hair. He took a towel and scrubbed off the bits of paint that remained on his skin, then scooped out some fresh paint with his fingers. He hesitated, but went ahead and painted himself with four stripes on each arm and leg.

Bone Splinter lay on a bench in the corridor outside. As soon as he saw Sky Knife, he sat up. The warrior ran his hands through his hair and patted it down close to his scalp. His ear-lobes, bare of the ear spools, dangled in loose hoops around his chin. Bone Splinter retrieved the ear spools from a fold in the cotton blanket on the bench, and fitted them back onto his ears.

"Let's get something to eat," said Sky Knife. "And then visit the merchants Kan Flower has detained. Unless you've heard of more bad luck in the city?"

Bone Splinter stood and stretched. "No," he said. "No bad luck seems to have occurred since Kan Flower rounded up the merchants."

"And Red Spider is not among them?"

"No."

Sky Knife nodded and wandered toward the back of the acropolis, where the cooks would have prepared the morning meal. He stepped outside into the cooking yard and took a deep breath. The scent of the jungle mixed freely with the smoke of the cooking fires and the dry, sweet smell of ground corn.

The women in the yard used their round *manos* to grind the corn on heavy granite *metates*. The granite had to be imported from the highlands for the local stone was too soft to grind corn with. *Metate* merchants always made a good living.

Sky Knife walked into the yard, but Peccary Spine barred his way.

"Sky Knife," said Peccary Spine with a small bow. "I will get you something to eat." The man's eyes never left the snake around Sky Knife's throat.

"That will not be necessary," said Bone Splinter before Sky Knife could say anything. "I'm sure this priest of Itzamna has better things to do this morning than look at your face."

Sky Knife bit his lip, embarrassed, but at the same time, a malicious glee crept into his heart. Peccary Spine had tormented him for years. Now, suddenly, with Sky Knife's fortunes improved, the man couldn't torment him any longer.

"Sky Knife!" called a deep voice. Sky Knife turned around. Death Smoke stood in the door of the acropolis.

"Yes, Death Smoke?"

"Move your things to Blood House's room," said Death Smoke. "You're not to sleep back here with the attendants any longer."

"Of course, Death Smoke," said Sky Knife. A slight tremor

ran up his spine. The bad luck that had come to Blood House could still be lingering in the room. Sky Knife didn't want to move there. He didn't want to be reminded of finding Blood House's body. He didn't want to think about Yellow Chin entering the room.

The *chic-chac* squeezed his neck slightly, then relaxed. Sky Knife breathed deeply. The snake seemed to be telling him he didn't need to fear. It was probably right. The good luck of a rainbow serpent had to be more than enough to outweigh the bad luck of Blood House's untimely death.

A woman brought Sky Knife and Bone Splinter some cornbread and water. Sky Knife accepted the food and ate it quickly, as did Bone Splinter. The woman took the empty bowls when they had finished the water.

Sky Knife went back to collect his things. Bone Splinter took the paint jar and water bowl while Sky Knife carried the cotton throws.

Blood House's quarters were empty. Not even a blanket remained to remind anyone of his presence here. Sky Knife tried not to think about Blood House's body on the bench as he threw his blankets down on it.

Bone Splinter deposited the bowl and jar in a corner.

"All right," said Sky Knife. "Let's go."

Bone Splinter nodded. He led Sky Knife out of the acropolis, eastward toward the House of the Warriors. Just to the south of that building sat a small, rectangular outbuilding.

Bone Splinter stepped aside and let Sky Knife enter first. The room inside was a few feet deep, but stretched out to his left for eight or ten yards. Between him and the end of the room stood Kan Flower, his burly arms crossed over his chest. A smile raced across his face as he saw Sky Knife. The smile faltered as he caught sight of the serpent, but he said nothing.

"Ah, Sky Knife," he said. "We've a few men here for you to speak with."

"You're fish waste," called a high, stringy voice from behind Kan Flower. "You can't keep us here. We've done nothing!"

Kan Flower's expression looked pained. "There are seven merchants here. But *that* one is vocal enough for all," he said.

Kan Flower stood aside and Sky Knife stepped past him. Six men sat on the floor and stared at Sky Knife dully. The seventh stood rigidly, arms folded across a chest bare of tattoos. He was bald and a jade hoop hung from his nose. He was almost Sky Knife's height, but his pudginess made him look shorter.

"I am Nine Dog," said the merchant. "Of the great city of Monte Alban. Who are you, monkey dung?"

Sky Knife leaned against the wall. "I am the king's representative," he said. "In this matter, at least."

Nine Dog waved plump arms at Sky Knife. "What matter? The bad luck? About time, I say. This backwater village could use some shaking up."

"You've been to Uaxactun recently?"

The merchant nodded. "Last week," he said. "They're a good market for shells from the western sea. And salt, of course."

"What about wood?" asked Sky Knife. Wood from the *ceiba* tree could be used for many magical purposes. Charms and spells could perhaps be stored in it, to be released at a later time. "Or bones?"

The merchant ran a hand over his bare scalp. Sweat dripped down his face. "It's too hot in this country," he said. "And no, I don't deal in wood or bones. I can't imagine why I should choose to market such common stuff."

"What about the rest of you? I'm sure Kan Flower has already determined what it is you sell, and where you are from, so there's no reason to lie to me now."

The others shook their heads. "I'm leaving," said one. He had a strong highlands accent. "Next time I leave Copan, I'll think twice about coming here."

"And you?" Sky Knife asked the merchant from Copan. "What do you sell?"

"*Yax-um* feathers," said the man. "And *metates*. Three of these men are my assistants."

Nine Dog laughed. "I bet they get to carry the *metates*," he said.

"You won't be leaving," said Sky Knife. "No bad luck has happened to Tikal since you were brought here. Do you understand what that means?"

Nine Dog stepped forward and spat at Sky Knife. "It means you think one of us is bringing the bad luck on purpose."

"You would, too, wouldn't you?" said the merchant from Copan in a weary voice.

"But not while I was still *here*," protested Nine Dog. "I don't want bad luck around me—what if it follows me onto the trail home?"

"If you were going back to Uaxactun," said Sky Knife, "and the bad luck followed you, you could ask a priest to drive it away."

Nine Dog's eyes narrowed. "Perhaps," he said. "But maybe I wouldn't want to see a Mayan priest at all. You don't worship the gods the way we do. Only a Zapotec priest could help me."

Nine Dog turned his back on Sky Knife. The men on the floor returned to looking at their feet. Sky Knife went back to the entrance.

"Kan Flower," he said. The warrior stepped close to Sky Knife.

"Yes?"

"Will it be a problem to keep them here a while longer?"

The warrior shook his head. "No. I can keep them here a day or two at least. But then the king will want something done with them."

"Something?" asked Sky Knife.

Kan Flower grinned. "We can always just go ahead and kill

them. If the bad luck stays away, the rest of the merchants won't mind."

"No," said Sky Knife. "Not yet, anyway. Let's just keep them here and see what happens."

Kan Flower nodded, but rolled his eyes. "If you don't tell me to let them go soon, I will be sorely tempted to kill the bald one, at least."

Sky Knife grasped Kan Flower's arm and smiled, partially appalled at his actions. A few days ago, he'd never dared get close to a warrior, let alone touch one. How long ago that time seemed. "I'm sure he is in good hands."

Kan Flower nodded and walked back to his post. Sky Knife stepped outside. "Nine Dog certainly hates Tikal enough to bring us bad luck," he said as he joined Bone Splinter. "Why would he come here at all, anyway?"

"Men will follow the path of wealth wherever it leads," said Bone Splinter. "Even to death."

Sky Knife walked back toward the plaza. "He didn't see the *chic-chac*. But he wasn't very tall."

"Taller than Turtle Nest. And I don't think any of them saw the snake. I doubt you'll find many merchants who will be able to."

Disappointment hovered over Sky Knife, but he refused to give in. The person or persons causing Tikal's bad luck would be found. Between himself, the warriors, and Turtle Nest, they had to be found.

The sun topped the trees behind him and warmed Sky Knife's back. His shadow preceded him into the plaza.

The plaza was busy today; the merchants who stayed away yesterday afternoon after the incident with the jaguar had returned. The hubbub of a thousand voices washed over Sky Knife. He strode through the plaza, looking for Red Spider.

No one stared at Sky Knife as he passed; apparently, Death Smoke was right when he said most people would not be able to see the *chic-chac*. The vendor of love gifts winked at him and pointed in her basket at the brown rabbit, but Sky Knife shook his head. The vendor didn't react as if she'd seen something unusual.

"There," said Bone Splinter. He pointed to his right. Sky Knife looked, but, from his height, couldn't see what Bone Splinter was pointing at.

"What?" he asked.

"Red Spider," said Bone Splinter. "He is talking with a customer."

"Show me."

Bone Splinter walked through the crowd confidently. The people in the plaza made way for him. Sky Knife followed in the taller man's wake.

Sky Knife didn't see Red Spider until Bone Splinter stepped aside. The Teotihuacano merchant talked to a pregnant woman, his hands gesturing about him in almost comical fashion.

The woman leaned over to study the jewelry more closely. Her orange dress was embroidered with shell beads and her hair had been carefully coiled about her head. She was almost as tall as Sky Knife.

Red Spider glanced toward Sky Knife, then glanced away. He did a swift double take and stared at Sky Knife, eyes on the *chic-chac*.

"Excuse me," he said to his customer. "One of my assistants can help you, I'm sure."

Red Spider strode past the woman, who watched him depart, then turned and left the area, ignoring the fawning attendant completely.

Bone Splinter stood close to Sky Knife and slightly out in front, so that his bulk was effectively between Sky Knife and Red Spider. Sky Knife was grateful for the support, for Red Spider's gaze never left Sky Knife's throat.

"Where did you get that?" asked Red Spider. "It is exquisite. What would you take for it?"

Bone Splinter held out an arm in front of Red Spider. "Come no closer to him," he said.

Red Spider ignored the warrior. "What is it made of?" he asked, his voice soft as a whisper. "I have never seen a carving so realistic. I can almost see it breathe."

"It is breathing," said Sky Knife, somewhat perturbed. Red Spider could see the *chic-chac*, but he didn't realize it was a true serpent, and not a piece of jewelry. What did that say about Red Spider's heart?

"It can't be." Red Spider frowned and leaned over Bone Splinter's arm. Sky Knife felt the snake move slightly. Red Spider's eyes grew wide and his mouth dropped open. "Feathered Serpent, it is! I saw its tongue. Only for a moment, but still! It is alive! May I touch it?"

Bone Splinter frowned, but Sky Knife nodded. "I think that is up to the *chic-chac*," he said. "You can try."

Red Spider reached a long finger toward the snake. Slowly, he touched it once briefly. Then he touched it again, and this time, he stroked it slightly. "It's warm," he said. "I can't believe it." Red Spider dropped his hand.

Sky Knife stepped back slightly. "If you don't mind," he said. "I'd like to ask you a few more questions."

"All right," said Red Spider. "I . . ."

A drop of rain struck Red Spider's face, and he flinched. Sky Knife looked into the sky. A strange black cloud swirled about angrily overhead. Another drop came down from the cloud and landed on Sky Knife's arm. He looked at it.

The water was black.

# 11

›››››

Sky Knife brushed the drop off his arm. The water stung his hand as much as the butterfly bites had. More drops fell. The hubbub of voices in the plaza became louder, more shrill. Merchants looked into the sky, then scrambled to get their wares put away and on the backs of their assistants.

Sky Knife turned and ran for the acropolis. Suddenly, lightning cracked and a deep rumble of thunder rang throughout the plaza. The rumbling echoed between the tall stone buildings until Sky Knife felt it more in his gut than heard it with his ears.

A few more drops fell. They were large and dark. The cloud had grown to cover the entire sky. Water poured out of the sky. It stung wherever it touched Sky Knife's skin. He continued toward the acropolis, followed by Bone Splinter. Screams rang through the plaza as people tried to brush off the stinging raindrops.

As soon as he reached the patio, Sky Knife no longer had to contend with the crowd. He dashed across the patio and ducked behind the thick drape, Bone Splinter on his heels.

Sky Knife went to Blood House's—*his*—quarters and brought back two cotton blankets. He handed one to Bone

Splinter and they dried themselves off. The stinging subsided as his skin dried.

Sky Knife went back to the drapery and pulled it aside slightly. The plaza was nearly empty now, only a few stragglers remaining, and they were running away as fast as they could.

"More bad luck," said Sky Knife. "Who ever heard of this kind of rain? I guess this means the merchants Kan Flower has are not responsible—if he saw them working magic strong enough to bring this rain, he'd surely stop them." Sky Knife swallowed his disappointment. He hadn't realized how badly he wanted Nine Dog to be the one—at least then, he would have succeeded in his task quickly. And the man responsible was someone easy to dislike.

"Perhaps," said Bone Splinter. "But they could have accomplices. I'm not sure that Nine Dog has told us all he knows. They might still be responsible, at least in part."

Sky Knife turned back to the small fire in the center of the room and added some wood from a pile in the corner. The fire blazed up, greedily consuming the wood.

A snuffling sound came from the corridor beyond. Sky Knife glanced up, but saw nothing. Bone Splinter walked carefully to the corridor and stepped into the darkness.

"All right, come out of there," said Bone Splinter. He sounded amused.

Bone Splinter came out of the hallway, followed by Jade Flute and her maid. Sky Knife's heart jumped. Jade Flute's white dress was stained by the black rain, and her hair looked wet and bedraggled. Her dress clung to her body and legs, outlining her slender figure in a very immodest way.

"What are you staring at?" Jade Flute asked. She walked straight to the fire and began waving her skirt near it to dry it. The motion also revealed her legs up to her knees. Sky Knife's own knees felt weak.

Sky Knife glanced away. When he looked back, Jade Flute had turned her back to the fire and was waving the back of her skirt close to the flames. A tongue of flame caught the edge of her skirt. Sky Knife stared a brief moment, horrified at the sight of the flame searing Jade Flute's skirt.

Sky Knife leaped over the fire and grabbed Jade Flute's skirt in his hands. He batted at the small flames until only a scorched hole in the skirt remained as witness to their presence.

"What are you doing?" demanded Jade Flute. She whirled around, ripped her skirt out of Sky Knife's hands, and slapped him across the cheek. Sky Knife's face stung with the force of her blow.

Sky Knife stood to face Jade Flute. "Your skirt had caught fire," he said. "Perhaps I should have let the fire burn it away."

"That's disgusting," said Jade Flute. "You wouldn't dare. I am the king's wife's niece!"

"You're a spoiled brat."

"That, too," said Jade Flute. "You might be, too, if your father kept trying to marry you off to every foul-smelling rank-conscious noble within a hundred miles."

Sky Knife was silent for a moment. "Maybe," he said at last. "But that's no excuse to be rude to me."

"I don't need an excuse. You're a nobody, even if you wear all that paint and have a *chic-chac* around your neck."

Sky Knife was stunned. He had assumed Jade Flute could not see the serpent, but see it she did—and she was not impressed. How could she not be?

"He has . . ." began Bone Splinter.

"I know, the king's grace. So you said. I don't care. This man won't find out what's causing the bad luck because the man who did it is already gone."

"What?" shouted Sky Knife. "What do you mean? Who did this?"

Jade Flute flicked her hair back over her shoulders. Her maid stepped forward and arranged the black tresses carefully. "My last suitor, of course. He said he'd call down the wrath of the gods when he left."

"You slapped him," said Bone Splinter.

"He was nothing but a squawking bird. Pretty, but dull," said Jade Flute. "Ouch!" She turned around and slapped her maid. The maid fell to her knees, trembling and sobbing. Jade Flute ignored her and turned back to the fire.

Sky Knife bent down to help the maid, but she flinched from his touch.

"So, what you're saying is that all this is because of you," said Bone Splinter. He sounded amused.

"Of course," said Jade Flute. She turned to the maid. "Oh, get up," she snapped.

The maid stood. She cast a wary glance toward Sky Knife and stepped away.

"Why are you afraid of me?" asked Sky Knife.

The maid dropped her eyes, but said nothing.

"Oh, ignore her," said Jade Flute. "In her city, they sacrifice household servants to the gods—imagine! Sending your servant to talk to the gods. Wretched people. She probably thinks you have designs on her life."

Sky Knife studied the foreign face of the maid, an idea tickling the back of his mind. The maid's hair had been braided and tied back in the style of Mayan servants, but her face was not Mayan. It was too round, her eyes too narrow, her nose small and turned up at the end. Outlandish features, to be sure, but not entirely unpleasant.

"I won't hurt you," he said. The maid shivered, but did not look at him.

"Ignore her," said Jade Flute. "That's what servants are for."

Sky Knife ignored Jade Flute instead, though that was difficult considering the way she kept picking up the hem of her dress to examine it—for what, Sky Knife had no idea. "My name is Sky Knife," he said to the maid. "What's yours?"

The maid glanced at him briefly, doubt in her eyes.

"This is Mouse-in-the-Corn," said Jade Flute. "Why would you want to know something like that?"

Sky Knife didn't press the issue. Mouse-in-the-Corn was obviously frightened of him, and it wouldn't help him to make her more afraid. Not if she could help him in his quest for the source of the bad luck.

Sky Knife walked back around the fire and pulled the drapery aside. Outside, the sun shone brightly and had already dried the patio and the tiles of the Great Plaza. A few merchants had returned, but mostly, the plaza was empty.

"Rain's stopped," he said. "One more curse we've lived through."

Jade Flute pushed past him and stood in the sun. "There will be more," she said. "Until that wretch stops pining over me."

"Somehow, I doubt that," said Sky Knife. "I don't believe the bad luck has to do with your ex-suitor at all."

Jade Flute drew herself up, anger flashing in her eyes. "Don't believe me, then! But you'll see." She stomped away.

As Mouse-in-the-Corn passed him, Sky Knife leaned over and whispered to her. "If you know something, please tell me," he said.

Mouse-in-the-Corn glanced at him warily, but Sky Knife stepped back from her. The maid's gaze lost some of its fear, to be replaced by thoughtfulness. She looked away and ran after her mistress.

"What was that about?" asked Bone Splinter.

Sky Knife watched the lithe figure of Jade Flute cross the plaza and disappear around the north side of the Great Pyramid. "An idea," he said softly. "Because that's what servants are for."

"What?"

"To be ignored," said Sky Knife. He turned to Bone Splinter. The warrior's beautiful features were marred by a frown. "The great ones might keep secrets from each other, but who watches what they say or do in front of their servants? Servants are only visible if they do something wrong."

"So you think the person who has planned this has a servant who would know about it. But how do you intend to find the servant if you don't know the master?"

"Mouse-in-the-Corn," said Sky Knife. He stepped outside into the warm sunshine. "Servants talk to each other. If a servant in the palace knows something, Mouse-in-the-Corn may know it as well."

Bone Splinter joined Sky Knife and stretched. "I don't think this idea of yours will work," he said. "But it's certainly worth trying."

"Anything's worth trying," said Sky Knife. He walked across the patio toward the plaza. "So far, I don't know anything more than I did yesterday."

"You know about Jade Flute's last suitor," said Bone Splinter with a laugh.

Sky Knife smiled. "Did she really slap him?"

Bone Splinter shrugged. "I wasn't there, but it was all over the House of the Warriors. The man offered her a pet parrot that had been trained to speak—but it wouldn't speak to Jade Flute. She returned it and told him what she thought of his gift."

Sky Knife could very well imagine what she'd say. He ran his fingers through his hair. "What kind of love gift do you think she'd appreciate?" he asked.

Bone Splinter slapped him on the shoulder. "I'm sure you'll think of something."

Sky Knife stepped onto the Great Plaza. The love gift vendor would sell him one of her rabbits, of course. But jewelry was another traditional gift. If only Sky Knife could afford it; he had nothing of his own.

Sky Knife smiled at the thought of Jade Flute even though he was too poor to buy her a gift—any gift. But, who knew, perhaps he could find *something*. If he was worthy of the king's wife's niece, he'd have to show her somehow that he was a better choice than any of her other suitors.

One thing was for sure—a talking parrot would not do. Or fruit, unless he wanted her to throw it at him.

Without warning, something hit Sky Knife on the back of the head. Pain shot through his skull and he fell forward onto the hard tiles of the plaza.

# 12

›››››

Sky Knife tried to get his arms under him to push himself up off the tiles, but a strong hand shoved him back down.

"Stay there," said Bone Splinter. "Someone is throwing rocks and it would seem you're the target."

Sky Knife stayed where he was. After a few moments, Bone Splinter removed his hand. "All right," said the warrior. "Get up. I don't see anyone."

Sky Knife pushed himself up into a sitting position. Blood trickled down behind his ear and dripped down his neck. His head hurt, but the stinging of his knees and elbows where they had been scraped by the tiles of the plaza burned brighter than the throbbing in his head.

Pain lanced through his head as Bone Splinter parted Sky Knife's hair and his fingers prodded the wound. Sky Knife gasped. "It's all right," said Bone Splinter. "It'll bleed some— scalp wounds always do. But you're not hurt too badly."

"Badly enough," moaned Sky Knife. He closed his eyes and waited for the pain to recede. In a few moments, it settled down to a more tolerable level.

"Maybe it is Jade Flute's last suitor," said Bone Splinter. He patted Sky Knife on the back. "And he's jealous of your interest in her."

"Very funny," said Sky Knife. He struggled to his feet. Bone Splinter put a hand under Sky Knife's elbow and helped him up.

Sky Knife's vision swam for a moment, but he blinked and the world settled down to look as it always did. Sky Knife scanned the plaza, but saw nothing unusual except for the fact that it was almost deserted.

The love-gift vendor was one of the few that had returned after the rain. She had taken advantage of the thin crowd to take a luckier spot than she had before. She sat right at the steps of the Great Pyramid. Sky Knife got up and walked over to her and sat on the first step.

"You've found a new place," he said.

"Oh, you're bleeding," said the old woman. "I saw you fall—are the gods angry with you?"

"More like a man," said Sky Knife. "A man with a rock to throw."

"Bad enough luck, still," said the old woman. "Here." She handed Sky Knife a small square of cotton cloth. He wiped away the blood from his face and neck, then returned the rag to her.

"Have you come to take my rabbit?" she asked, indicating the basket where the brown rabbit sat patiently chewing something Sky Knife couldn't see.

"No," said Sky Knife. "I was wondering if you knew of anyone who had profited by the bad luck besides yourself."

"It's a good spot, isn't it?" asked the old woman with pride. She patted the tiles next to her, but didn't touch the temple itself. "If I can keep it, I'll do better business."

"As long as people return to the plaza," said Bone Splinter.

"They will," said the old woman with conviction. "They will. The plaza is the center of the city—the heart. Cut it out and you kill the city."

Sky Knife shivered, a cold feeling twisting his gut. Of course the bad luck centered on the plaza—the old woman was right. Kill the heart of the city, and the city would die.

"It seems someone wants the city to die," said Sky Knife. "Who is likely to want that?"

The old woman frowned and stroked a black-and-brown-spotted rabbit she held in her lap. "Not a merchant," she said. "We have to have the plaza alive with people."

"There are always other cities," said Bone Splinter. He knelt on the other side of the woman, but was also careful not to touch the temple itself.

"Ha," said the old woman. "You think all cities are the same? Each one is different—the people of one buy more salt, but ignore the rabbits. In another city, people might buy more rabbits, but little pottery. This is a good city for selling rabbits."

"What about bad luck?" asked Sky Knife. "In what city does that sell well?"

The old woman frowned. "Well, there's always someone around you can buy charms and the like from. Most aren't worth much. But sometimes, you can find the real thing."

"Where?" asked Bone Splinter.

"Sometimes the highlands," said the woman. "And, of course, you can buy anything you can imagine in the Jewel of the North."

Teotihuacan. Red Spider's city. Sky Knife looked around the plaza, but didn't see the tall merchant.

"How about Tikal?" asked Sky Knife as he turned back to the woman. "Where would I go to buy bad luck here?"

The old woman glanced nervously from side to side. "I shouldn't say anything," she said. "Not to a priest and a warrior."

"The king himself has asked for no one to hinder me," said Sky Knife.

"The king—Itzamna bless his name—can't be everywhere," said the old woman. "And I'm old. Who will take care of me if something happens to me or my rabbits?"

Sky Knife opened his mouth to speak, to convince her to help him. But Bone Splinter reached down and untied a string of cowrie shells from his ankle.

"Here," said Bone Splinter. He held out the string of shells. The woman stared at it a moment, then claimed it. The strand disappeared into a fold of her voluminous dress.

"In the west," she said. "Beyond the temple of Ix Chel. In the jungle. There's an old woman—she was old when I was born, or so they say—who knows the secrets the gods whisper in the dark to the mad."

Sky Knife nodded his thanks to the old woman. She smiled and reached into the basket that held the brown rabbit. "Are you sure you won't be taking him now?"

"No," he said. He walked away from her through the near-empty plaza toward the temple of Ix Chel. Bone Splinter followed him. When Sky Knife was sure they were far enough away from the old woman not to be overheard, he turned to the warrior. "Thank you for what you did," he said. "I had nothing to give her."

Bone Splinter smiled. "I know. You are even poorer than I. Still, it was nothing. Anything I can do to aid you serves the king, so I will do it."

Sky Knife felt humbled before the warrior's devotion. But then, if the gods required something of *him*, wouldn't he do it? Even if it meant lying down on the altar to face Stone Jaguar's knife?

Sky Knife shivered at the thought. He'd attended too many sacrifices, pinned down too many shoulders, seen fear on too many faces. Even if the sacrifice were bound for paradise, he had to suffer Stone Jaguar's knife first. The suffering was short, but Sky Knife knew he would be afraid if it were required of him. Very afraid.

"Well, I'm sure you have the king's thanks. I just wanted you to know you had mine, too," said Sky Knife.

Bone Splinter laid a large hand on his shoulder briefly, but said nothing.

The garishly painted temple of Ix Chel loomed to their right. Sky Knife strode past it quickly to the edge of the jungle beyond. The jungle was thick and there was no evidence that anyone lived beyond its boundaries.

"Where should we look?" he asked.

Bone Splinter peered through the branches of the bushes that grew up around the edges of the cleared areas. "I don't know," he said. "Perhaps we should look around in each direction."

"All right," said Sky Knife. He began walking to the south, assuming Bone Splinter would take the north, behind the temple. Sky Knife didn't want to think about the adulterous nun right now, or her fate. Or Jade Flute. The temple reminded him of all those things.

Suddenly, the snake on his neck squeezed slightly. Sky Knife stopped and looked into the jungle. There was a slight break in the shrubbery here.

"Bone Splinter!"

The large man jogged over. "Have you found it?" he asked.

"I think so," said Sky Knife. "At least, the *chic-chac* wanted me to look here."

Sky Knife stepped toward the path, but Bone Splinter grabbed his arm and stopped him. Sky Knife gasped as the pain from his wounds flared again to life at Bone Splinter's touch.

"I'm sorry," said Bone Splinter, "but I should go first."

Sky Knife's arm trembled as Bone Splinter released it, but he kept the pain to himself. Bone Splinter strode on ahead, holding aside branches for Sky Knife.

"Bone Splinter?" asked Sky Knife.

"Yes?"

Sky Knife hesitated. He hadn't had the courage to ask Bone Splinter anything about his life, about why he was in the

House of the Warriors. But Bone Splinter hadn't hesitated to spend wealth in Sky Knife's cause. Perhaps he'd answer a question, too.

"I, uh," began Sky Knife, "was wondering. How did you come to be a warrior?"

Bone Splinter chuckled. "I'm tall and strong," he said. "But then, I could have been a tall and strong farmer, at that. Actually, my grandfather was one of Jaguar Paw's retainers. He promised Jaguar Paw that his son would become a warrior."

Bone Splinter held aside a large vine and Sky Knife ducked under it.

"But my father didn't grow up strong; he had a weak leg and he stuttered. He became a servant in the royal house and promised that *his* son would fulfill my grandfather's vow. And so I did. When I was eight, I went to live with the warriors and I've been there ever since. I have a sister. She's one of Turtle Nest's nuns."

"Only one sister?" asked Sky Knife. He wiped sweat from his face. Above him, iguanas rustled in the branches. Their long tales drooped over vines and leaves, making them look much like vines themselves.

"Yes," said Bone Splinter. "My father died while my sister and I were very young. I told you, he was not strong. My mother died a few years later in the sickness."

"My parents died then, too," said Sky Knife. "And one of my brothers. I have two other brothers, though."

"Older brothers?"

"Yes. Why?"

"You are the fourth son. No wonder you're special."

Sky Knife blushed and was glad Bone Splinter was ahead of him, unaware of Sky Knife's discomfiture. "So was my father," said Sky Knife softly.

Bone Splinter nodded as if that explained everything. Suddenly, he pointed ahead. "There," he said.

A small peasant hut sat only a short way in front of them. The trees grew up around it as if the hut had been built without clearing the trees first.

"Hello?" called Sky Knife.

"Go away," said a thin, hoarse voice from inside the hut.

"I have to ask you a few questions," said Sky Knife. "I come from the king."

There was a slight pause. "I know where you've come from," said the voice, "and where you're going. I know about that bauble around your neck and the stone at your waist. I know many things."

"Please, I need to speak to you," said Sky Knife. There was no answer. Sky Knife stood still just outside the hut, determined to outwait the woman.

The jungle was hot and the air very still. Beetles rustled in the leaves and twigs on the forest floor at Sky Knife's feet. Overhead, birds hopped from limb to limb, but at this time of day, they refrained from singing.

A spindly monkey stared down curiously. It scratched its head as if puzzled by their presence. Then it reached out, grabbed a leaf and plucked it. The monkey shoved the leaf in its mouth and continued to consider Sky Knife and Bone Splinter while it chewed.

"Come in," the old woman said eventually. "Patience should be rewarded in one so young."

Sky Knife stepped up into the house, which, like all peasant huts, had been built on a raised platform of earth. A small fire crackled in the firepit in the center of the hut. Branches, leaves, and fruit hung from the walls and peaked thatch ceiling, making the interior of the hut seem like its own kind of jungle. A musty smell hung in the air. Sky Knife suppressed a sneeze.

Sky Knife sat by the fire slowly, looking around. He saw rags and broken pottery jars scattered in the corners of the hut, but he didn't see the old woman. Bone Splinter sat down beside him.

"Hello?" asked Sky Knife.

One of the rags in the corner moved. It sat up. Sky Knife suppressed a gasp of surprise. Now that the woman was sitting, Sky Knife could make out her skeletal figure. Fine wisps of white hair clung to her mottled scalp, and bare gums showed when she smiled.

"Welcome to my hut, priest of the unlucky name," she said, "and devoted guardian of the king. It has been long and long since any as esteemed as yourselves came into my hut. Not since the great Jaguar Paw's day."

"Jaguar Paw?" asked Sky Knife. "But he died . . . he died in my grandfather's youth."

"Even so, little one," said the old woman. "I have seen kings come and go, but none ever became what Jaguar Paw was. So— what brings you to my home?"

"Ah," said Sky Knife, momentarily forgetting his purpose in his awe. This woman had seen Jaguar Paw! She had to be the oldest person in the world. "Ah, the bad luck," he said finally. "I'm trying to find out who is bringing disaster to Tikal. I believe this man—or men—want to cut out the heart of the city in a terrible kind of sacrifice."

"How so?"

"Well, the bad luck seems to concentrate in the plaza. The plaza, as I have been recently reminded, is the heart of the city. The center. If someone wanted to kill a city, they would only have to keep people out of the plaza."

The old woman laughed. "Only a man would think of such a thing. Youngster, a city is more than a plaza, more than its people."

"Only a man?" asked Bone Splinter. "Do you think a woman does this to Tikal?"

"No," said the old woman. "I know no woman strong

enough to bring such terrible bad luck to our city. No, you must keep searching for a man."

"The priestess said a tall man with a dark heart."

The old woman pointed a bony finger toward Sky Knife. "Most men are taller than a priestess, and all men hide darkness in their hearts."

A dread sort of heaviness hung on Sky Knife's heart. "Then what can I do?" he asked. "Whom do I look for?"

"Your rainbow friend may aid you," said the old woman. "But depend on nothing but your own strength. The eyes of a rainbow serpent see clearly, but not what a man sees."

"How could this bad luck happen?" asked Sky Knife. "Who has the power?"

"Very few," said the old woman. "Not even the king can call the black jaguar. Jaguar Paw could have, but not Storm Cloud."

"Red Spider?" asked Sky Knife.

"Him I know not," said the woman. "For his roots are not here."

Sky Knife nodded to the old woman, convinced his interview with her had been a failure. She had told him nothing that he did not know, and discounted Turtle Nest's words he had thought he could rely upon. Sky Knife stood. "Thank you," he said. "I will not disturb you further."

"Wait," said the old woman. "There is one thing I have seen, but you will not like it."

"And what is that?"

"The darkness of Xibalba lies between you and your goal. Only a perfect sacrifice will free you from it."

Sky Knife hesitated over her strange words, unsure what to say in return. Finally, he settled for nodding to the woman. She smiled slightly and waved him away.

Sky Knife stepped down out of the hut and walked back through the thick, hot jungle to the cleared area next to the temple of Ix Chel. He walked back to the plaza, contemplating the old woman's words.

Bone Splinter interrupted his reverie. "Look," said the warrior. He pointed to the palace. Sky Knife could just see it in the distance. From the roof flew a large white banner.

Bone Splinter grinned. "It is war!"

# 13

## ››››››

"War?" asked Sky Knife. "With whom? Why?"

"I don't know," said Bone Splinter. The warrior speeded his pace and Sky Knife struggled to keep up. "But Kan Flower will."

Sky Knife followed Bone Splinter across the sparsely populated plaza, past the Great Pyramid, to the House of the Warriors. The garden, which, the day before, had been a peaceful place for throwing bones and creating poetry, now swarmed with activity. Warriors painted themselves in red and black and prepared their weapons.

Sky Knife struggled to see Kan Flower amidst the whirl of activity.

"Navel of the World!" exclaimed a warrior near Sky Knife. "A rainbow serpent!"

All the warriors in the garden turned to Sky Knife. Their open-mouthed stares unnerved him. Sky Knife resisted an urge to back away.

Kan Flower stepped out from behind another warrior, a sword in his hands. Two red lines of paint ran down each of his cheeks like bloody tears. He walked to Sky Knife slowly, eyes never leaving the *chic-chac*.

"Is it true?" he asked. "Is it really a rainbow serpent? I saw it earlier, but I didn't dare believe . . ."

Bone Splinter grunted. "As you see."

Kan Flower dropped to his knees. All the warriors in the garden besides Bone Splinter did the same. Kan Flower held out his sword. It had been carved from the wood of the *ceiba* tree. Bits of obsidian stuck out along its edges like tiny black teeth. "Please," said Kan Flower, "touch the sword, Sky Knife. Whatever luck goes with you, share it with me."

Sky Knife reached out and touched the sword, though he felt silly doing so. The *chic-chac*'s luck might be his, or it might not if he believed the strange old woman. Still, it didn't seem to Sky Knife that his touch should prove any benefit.

Kan Flower rose and stepped back. One by one, the other warriors rose and held out their spears, slings, and swords to Sky Knife. He touched each one and tried to behave as dignified as the warriors seemed to expect. He was sure Stone Jaguar would have proceeded in a much more impressive, priest-like manner.

When the last warrior had filed past, Bone Splinter, who had stood to the side all during the strange ritual, stepped forward. "Now, tell us of the war," he said. "Upon whom do we make war, and when?"

"Storm Cloud decided this morning," said Kan Flower.

"Uaxactun," interrupted a man Sky Knife remembered as the laughing warrior from the day before. "We fight Uaxactun. The king has decided our bad luck comes from there."

"How does he know?" asked Sky Knife. He stepped forward, toward the warrior, who stepped back. Sky Knife stopped. "What is going on?" he asked.

Bone Splinter laughed. "You see, Sky Knife? They are all in awe of you because of the serpent."

Red anger rose in Sky Knife's throat. "Wonderful," he said. "But I don't need awe. I need answers." He stepped forward and sat down on the bench he had occupied the day before. "And someone to tell me why Storm Cloud decided to make war."

Kan Flower came and knelt on the ground at Sky Knife's feet. "It was the merchants," he said. "When the king discovered you wanted us to search for merchants who had recently been to Uaxactun, he ordered the war. It shall be tomorrow. A runner has already been sent to Uaxactun to tell them to prepare."

Sky Knife leaned back against the rock wall behind him. "What about Stone Jaguar? Where is he?"

"He is with the king," said Kan Flower, "trying to dissuade him from making war." Kan Flower's voice sounded angry.

"He should be planning a ceremony to aid us, not working against us," said the laughing warrior. He spat. "The priests always try to have things their own way."

Sky Knife stood. "I need to see the king," he said. "Something is wrong. There shouldn't be a war, not when we don't know who is behind this."

"The king's word is good enough for me," said the laughing warrior, "and for any man here. We obey only him."

"And die only for him," added Bone Splinter. "But perhaps even a king can act rashly in this matter. I think Sky Knife should see him."

The other warriors glanced at each other. Only Kan Flower looked right at Sky Knife. "I'm not sure," he said. "But the rainbow serpent is an omen I don't understand. Perhaps the king should see it. It can do no harm."

One by one, the other warriors nodded. Bone Splinter crossed his arms over his wide chest. "All right then," he said. "I shall take Sky Knife to the king."

Sky Knife stood and followed Bone Splinter out of the garden and out of the House of the Warriors. They walked north toward the palace, and past the stela that stood outside. This time, Sky Knife did not abase himself before it. He bowed slightly, but kept on walking. Bone Splinter paid no attention to it.

The warriors who stood at the entrance to the palace stared at Sky Knife. No doubt they saw the *chic-chac*. Sky Knife walked past them quickly into the dark palace.

Sky Knife turned toward the direction of the throne room, but a hand on his shoulder held him back.

"No," said Bone Splinter. "You shouldn't just go in like a servant. I shall announce you first. Wait here."

Bone Splinter moved off down the corridor. Sky Knife wanted to pace back and forth, but if he did, the warriors outside would notice. So he forced himself to stand still and appear calm, though his heart was in turmoil—not only was he going to see the king, but he was going to try to talk him out of a war.

Bone Splinter returned quickly. "The king will see you," he said. "And I think Stone Jaguar is pleased you are here."

Sky Knife headed for the throne room, Bone Splinter just behind him. The corridor was dark, but the glow from the serpent at his throat lit his way. The warrior at the entrance to the throne room pulled the drapery back, but kept his eyes on the floor, refusing to meet Sky Knife's eyes or to stare at the source of the strange light that filled the hall.

The throne room was just as he remembered it, but this time, the fear Sky Knife felt was not fear of the king. He walked confidently down the center of the room to the dais at the far end and knelt before Storm Cloud. Stone Jaguar sat just in front and to the right of the throne.

"You wished to see me, Sky Knife?" asked Storm Cloud, his accent jarring Sky Knife's ears once again.

"Yes," he said with a nod. "Kan Flower told me you plan to make war on Uaxactun tomorrow."

"And I do," said Storm Cloud. He waved toward Stone Jaguar. "Though the *Ah men* of Tikal says it would be foolish."

"If you send the warriors out of the city, there will be a disaster," said Stone Jaguar. "Whoever is causing the bad luck will have a free hand to do as they please."

"I don't see that they're having much difficulty as it is," said Storm Cloud. "Whoever it is was strong enough to call up that darkness-spawned rain this morning. What did you do about that, priest?"

Stone Jaguar was silent. Sky Knife jumped to his superior's defense. "Just so, my king," he said. "Someone was strong enough to call up that rain. That means they were in the city. Uaxactun is miles from here—no one there is causing the bad luck here."

"They may not be there, but I believe they are from there," said the king. "Unless you have found out something since the rain?"

Sky Knife struggled to find an answer for the king. "I talked to someone who felt the answer might lie in Teotihuacan," he said. It wasn't exactly what the old woman had said, but almost. "Perhaps one of your brothers is here to cause you trouble."

Storm Cloud sat back and stroked the jade beads that dangled from around his throat. "The last I heard, my brothers squabbled among themselves about who would rule what. Perhaps one of them decided I would be an easier target. It's possible."

"There is a merchant from Teotihuacan in the city," said Sky Knife. "I was talking to him when the rain came, but he could have an accomplice."

"Red Spider," said Storm Cloud. "Yes, I know him. His family has a great deal of status. He would be a powerful foe."

"You know him?" asked Sky Knife.

The king laughed softly and stepped off the dais to stand in front of Sky Knife. For the first time, Sky Knife realized Storm Cloud resembled Red Spider. Not as tall, and more Mayan-looking than foreign. But they had the same eyes, the same hooded, bird of prey eyes.

Storm Cloud laid a hand on Sky Knife's shoulder. The king was several inches taller than Sky Knife, and much more elaborately dressed. Sky Knife felt like a child before him. Who was he to question Storm Cloud's judgment in anything?

"Oh, yes," said Storm Cloud. "He is family. His mother was my father's cousin, who married one of the warrior-merchants of the city. Red Spider is her eldest son."

"Then he might want to act against you," said Sky Knife.

Storm Cloud, for some reason Sky Knife didn't understand, laughed. He released Sky Knife's shoulder and sat down on the edge of the dais. "I don't think so," he said. "There is something in this city he wants, but she wears a purple dress and throws fruit at her suitors. He would not want to woo a bad luck bride."

"Jade Flute?" asked Sky Knife, his knees suddenly wobbling. He had not thought to wonder what other suitors she might have. But then, what was he thinking? Storm Cloud could never marry Jade Flute to a low-status priest like himself.

"So you've met my wife's niece," said Storm Cloud. "She is another problem. But not the most immediate."

"The war," said Stone Jaguar. "Call off the war, lest ruin overtake us."

Storm Cloud clapped his hands. "Leave me," he said. "And I will consider the matter. And even if I do decide to call off the war, that doesn't mean that the king of Uaxactun will permit me to back away from the promise of a fight. He may insist."

"He may indeed," said Stone Jaguar, "but then let the wrath of the gods be on his head, not yours. You must protect your city."

Anger colored Storm Cloud's features. "You do not tell me what I must or must not do, priest. Remember that."

Stone Jaguar bowed low. "Of course, my king. But give Sky Knife a chance to discover the identity of our enemy. With the protection of your warrior and the *chic-chac*, he cannot fail."

The king frowned. "*Chic-chac?* What is this?"

Cold dread settled into Sky Knife's chest and touched his heart with bony fingers. "My neck," he said. "What do you see around my neck?"

Storm Cloud glanced toward Sky Knife in irritation. "A cord," he said. "Just an old cord. Now get out."

Sky Knife backed away from the king, then turned and walked out of the room. He fought the urge to run from the palace, to run from what he feared.

The king! The king could not be behind the bad luck—what good did it do to rule over ruins? That made no sense.

Still, the king could not see the *chic-chac*. And he was tall. And between two powerful cousins, what kind of bad luck could *not* be wrought?

Sky Knife exited the palace and only then broke into a run. He had no idea where he was going. Just so long as it was away from the palace. And the king.

# 14

›››››

Sky Knife ran until his sides hurt, and his chest heaved in an effort to take in more air. He slowed to a walk and wiped sweat from his forehead.

The Temple of Ix Chel stood just ahead. Sky Knife paused. What should he do now? Should he tell Turtle Nest of his suspicions concerning the king?

No, that would wait. Sky Knife walked back toward the plaza. Ahead, he saw Bone Splinter coming toward him. The warrior waved as he approached.

"Stone Jaguar wants to see you," said Bone Splinter. "The king orders me to the House of the Warriors to await his decision concerning the war."

"And if there is war?" asked Sky Knife.

"I will go with my brothers," said Bone Splinter.

Sky Knife's heart wilted. He had never known someone like Bone Splinter, someone who believed in him, even when he himself found that difficult to do. A jab of loneliness pierced him.

Bone Splinter laid a hand on his shoulder. "I'll see you again," he said. "Unless the gods of war wish to see me first."

Sky Knife nodded, his throat too thick to speak.

Bone Splinter patted him once on the shoulder, then turned and walked back toward the House of the Warriors. Sky Knife watched him go and fought back tears. The *chic-chac* squeezed his neck slightly.

Sky Knife took comfort from the serpent's support and walked to the southern acropolis. The sun was high in the sky and shone down steady and bright. Sweat rolled off Sky Knife's face. The dry season was always a time of oppressive heat, but now it seemed worse than ever before.

The interior of the acropolis was dark and stuffy. Sky Knife walked to Stone Jaguar's quarters. As he approached, he heard Stone Jaguar and Death Smoke arguing.

"He's too young," said Death Smoke.

"The gods have chosen him," said Stone Jaguar, his voice hard and sharp.

"A *chic-chac*'s blessing is not the same as the gods'," said Death Smoke.

"It's all we've got!"

"And when I'm dead, it will just be him and you."

"And if we don't use him, then it will just be me. Talk sense, old man. There's no time to argue. He drew the Hand of God out of the water. He is a priest."

Sky Knife stood still, hardly daring to breathe. Although he agreed more than he liked to admit with Death Smoke, anger rose in his gut. He had not thought he would become a priest, but he had. He intended to do the best job he could as a credit to the gods. And to himself.

"Yes, I know he's a priest," said Death Smoke with a sigh. "It was just done so quickly, with no training. He doesn't know anything!"

"He can learn. We'll start today. Right now, in fact. I've sent for him—he should be here soon."

Sky Knife bit his lip and stepped forward into the room.

Stone Jaguar looked up sharply from his seat on a bench, but said nothing.

Death Smoke frowned. "All right," he said. "Come, boy, you should look like a priest rather than an attendant."

Death Smoke held out a length of blue cotton material. The pattern on the material was of green and white flowers. Sky Knife took the material and wrapped it around his waist, bunching it up in front to match the way the other priests wore their skirts. He tucked the end into the cord of his loincloth.

Stone Jaguar nodded approvingly. "It suits you," he said. "Here."

Stone Jaguar held out a necklace of tiny jade beads. Sky Knife took it, hands trembling. He'd never been given such a precious thing to wear. He dropped the strand over his head. It dangled almost to his belly. The *chic-chac* shifted slightly. Sky Knife felt its tongue touch his chin.

"It would seem your rainbow friend approves," said Stone Jaguar. "Good. I'd like to think that means a little good luck might come our way."

"One more thing," said Death Smoke. "Your ears are not pierced. If you're going to be a priest, you should be able to wear ear spools someday."

"Come over here," said Stone Jaguar. Sky Knife obediently walked over to the priest. Stone Jaguar stood and held out a stingray spine and a cotton towel. He grabbed Sky Knife's left ear and jabbed the lobe with the spine.

Sky Knife flinched slightly at the sudden pain, but made no sound. Stone Jaguar patted the earlobe with the towel, then quickly repeated the procedure with the right ear. This time, Sky Knife managed not to flinch.

Death Smoke handed two wooden spools barely as big around as a dried corn kernel to Stone Jaguar, who thrust them into the newly made holes in Sky Knife's ears. He stood back.

"Good," said Stone Jaguar. "In a few weeks, we'll put something larger in."

Sky Knife's earlobes felt swollen, and his wounds stung. Cautiously, he touched one of the spools. The wood was soaked by his blood.

"Come," said Stone Jaguar. "We must begin your education." Stone Jaguar threw his jaguar-skin cloak over his shoulders and adjusted his necklaces.

Death Smoke and Stone Jaguar walked out of the room. Sky Knife hesitated for a moment, then followed them. The skirt swished against his legs as he walked. It seemed to catch at his knees as if to trip him. No doubt he would get used to it, but for now, it seemed a nuisance.

Stone Jaguar and Death Smoke headed for the northern acropolis. Sky Knife followed slowly, uncomfortable at being outside with his new finery. Fortunately, the plaza was still largely deserted, and those who stared at the priests walking among them stared mostly at Stone Jaguar in his jaguar-skin cloak.

The northern acropolis seemed just as menacing today as it had the day before, but Sky Knife took comfort in the presence of the *chic-chac* at his throat. He followed the other two men into the darkness of the building.

Stone Jaguar clapped his hands as they entered a room. A fire sprang into being in the firepit in the center of the room. Sky Knife glanced around; this was the same room he had been in the afternoon before, the room where he had saved the *chic-chac*, the room where the other attendant had died.

"There should be four of us," complained Death Smoke. "This is highly unusual."

"I already know that," said Stone Jaguar. He sat by the fire. A small cotton pouch was already in place beside him. "But there's nothing we can do. The other candidate was rejected."

Death Smoke and Sky Knife sat down as well. Stone Jaguar took a small pouch, opened it, and threw a pinch of something into the fire. It flashed and a sweet, heavy smell filled the room.

"We offer incense," said Stone Jaguar.

Death Smoke took out his tobacco pouch and threw a pinch into the fire. "We offer tobacco," he said.

The other two looked at Sky Knife. A trickle of blood ran down his cheek and dropped onto his arm. He flung the drop into the fire. "We offer blood," he said.

Stone Jaguar grunted approval. "When the gods first made man, they made him from mud," he said. "But then the rains came and the men washed away."

Death Smoke waved his hands over the fire and closed his eyes. "When the gods made man the second time, they made him from wood. But the wood-men had no emotions, and the gods destroyed them."

Silence fell. Sky Knife glanced at Stone Jaguar, but the older man had closed his eyes as well. Sky Knife took a deep breath and continued the story. "When the gods made man the third time, they made him from maize," he said. "And the men worshipped the gods, and counted the seasons, and offered themselves as sacrifices."

"So the gods were pleased with men," said Stone Jaguar. "And taught him to raise the corn, his brother."

"Man shelters the corn as it grows," said Death Smoke, "and in return, it fills his belly."

Again, there was a silence. But this time, Sky Knife did not know what to say. The others waited for a few moments, then Stone Jaguar continued. "Itzamna taught men how to count, and how to write so that men could keep track of the comings and goings of the stars, and the moon, and the seasons."

"Itzamna is the greatest of the gods," said Death Smoke. "His names and forms are many."

Sky Knife felt lost. The other men spoke as if he should know all the proper responses. He knew Itzamna took on many forms, but he didn't know them all. When Death Smoke paused, Sky Knife jumped in with the first thing he could think of.

"As Itzam Cab Ain, he is the surface of the earth," said Sky Knife quickly.

"He is Itzamna Kauil when he smiles upon man, and Ix Kan Itzam T'ul when he frowns," said Death Smoke.

Stone Jaguar smiled slightly, and Sky Knife's fear eased a bit. Perhaps this was just a test to see what he would say. Sky Knife continued.

"He is the earth iguana, whose home is the treetops. He is the crocodile that floats on the waters of the world."

"He is our lord in heaven and our lord of the earth," said Stone Jaguar. "His anger is terrible to behold, and his mercy is terrible to receive."

"Itzamna, Lord of All," said Death Smoke, "you have called and accepted this man Sky Knife to be your priest. For your signs and omens, we give you thanks. May Sky Knife always remain true to you and serve you well."

"And may your tongue remain as quick," said Stone Jaguar. Sky Knife glanced at the other man. Stone Jaguar smiled and nodded. "Many young priests are too frightened to say anything at this ceremony."

"You have done well," said Death Smoke. "But you would not let fear overtake you, would you? Or you would have let the *chic-chac* drown."

Stone Jaguar sighed and threw another pinch of *copal* into the fire. "Sky Knife, you are a priest in name only today. You have had no formal training. Death Smoke and I will try to instruct you as well as we can before his death. Then it will be up to you and I to recruit two other priests and make our brotherhood complete."

"It will be hard," said Death Smoke. "I do not envy you this task."

Stone Jaguar grunted. "Speaking of tasks, you are still performing a duty for the king. Have you had any luck?"

Sky Knife looked into the fire, fear crowding his thoughts. "No," he said.

"Then why do you fear, boy?" asked Death Smoke.

"He is no boy," said Stone Jaguar. "He is a priest."

Death Smoke hesitated, then nodded. "Tell us," he said. His breath hissed out of his mouth. "What do you fear, Sky Knife?"

Sky Knife felt strangled by his doubt, but he didn't know how to say his suspicions out loud.

"Come, Sky Knife," urged Stone Jaguar. "It has been two days. What have you discovered?"

"Nothing," whispered Sky Knife. "Except . . ."

"Yes?" asked Stone Jaguar.

"Storm Cloud cannot see the *chic-chac*," said Sky Knife, words coming in a rush. "And you said yourself, Stone Jaguar, that the man I'm looking for would not be able to see it. And Storm Cloud is a cousin to Red Spider, who could have brought the bad luck with him for Storm Cloud to use."

The others were silent. The silence pressed down on Sky Knife until he felt he might scream.

At last, Stone Jaguar spoke. "It's true, the king could not see the serpent. But could that really mean the king is behind this? Perhaps it is because he is a foreigner, and unaware of our sacred animals."

Death Smoke shook his head. "Surely the king is innocent of this. Why rule a city of bad luck?"

"If Red Spider brought the bad luck with him, he might have also brought something with him that would dispel it," said Stone Jaguar. "Then, at the proper moment, when we are dead, he can suddenly proclaim that he alone can get rid of the bad luck."

Death Smoke's eyes sparkled. "Yes," he said. "I see. Then the king has no high priests around to bother him. He can bring the worship of the Feathered Serpent here and no one will oppose him."

"But you two are still alive," said Sky Knife. "And Red Spider *could* see the *chic-chac*. If what you say is true, then as a foreigner, he shouldn't be able to see it." Sky Knife frowned. He didn't think the love gift vendor had seen the serpent, either.

"Death Smoke's days are numbered," said Stone Jaguar. "I would not be surprised if mine are as well. Possibly by the king and his cousin Red Spider. In any event, I'm not surprised Red Spider could see the serpent. Teotihuacano merchants are trained in many arcane matters."

"Take care, Sky Knife," whispered Death Smoke. "If you prove too clever, your life may be short, too. Very short indeed."

Sky Knife closed his eyes. This time, not even the warmth of the serpent at his throat could ease his mind. His fear was far stronger, and far, far colder.

# 15

>>>>>

Stone Jaguar reached over and patted Sky Knife on the shoulder. "Come, Sky Knife," he said. "You should have your first lesson."

"You will already know some of it," said Death Smoke, "considering that you knew so much about Itzamna."

Stone Jaguar and Death Smoke stood. Sky Knife climbed to his feet as well. Stone Jaguar led them down a narrow passageway and a flight of steep steps. Sky Knife kept his hands out against the walls to steady himself. The steps had been worn down over time by many feet. Their uneven surfaces were treacherous. Sky Knife slowed and fell behind the other two.

At the bottom of the steps was another narrow passageway, this one low enough that all three men had to duck their heads.

Beyond the sound of the men's sandals on the stone floor and the hiss of his own breath, Sky Knife heard another sound. Water, dripping. He shivered. Caves were holy, of course. But the water of such a cave was truly sacred. It was absolutely pure.

Sky Knife had seen bowls of pure water, but never a pool of it in a cave. Excitement ran up his spine and the hair on the back of his neck stood on end.

More steps. But this time, there were only nine. The ceiling arched overhead. Sky Knife took a deep breath and stood up. Then Death Smoke stood aside and Sky Knife saw what was in the cave. He gasped in awe.

A wide, deep pool of clear water occupied most of the room. Blue balls of light danced around the ceiling, illuminating everything. Sky Knife stepped forward to the edge of the pool. At the very bottom, he saw a gaping black hole—surely an entrance to the underworld. Heart in his throat, Sky Knife stepped back.

"Behold *zuhuy ha*," said Stone Jaguar loudly. His voice echoed back to Sky Knife over and over. "The Virgin Water in the Navel of the World."

*Navel of the World, Navel of the World . . .* The words bounced against Sky Knife's ears painfully.

"We show you this," continued Stone Jaguar much more quietly, "to remind you of your duty to the gods. And because no one besides the priests of the highest status may know of its existence."

Sky Knife glanced toward Stone Jaguar, alarmed. The other man smiled and laid a hand on his shoulder. "I know. You are not yet of the highest status. But, in all likelihood, you will soon be the sole priest of Itzamna of any rank in Tikal. You must know of the pool."

"Come," whispered Death Smoke. He gestured toward a small opening in the eastern wall. Sky Knife followed the old man into a four-sided room with a low ceiling. Death Smoke sat against the south wall. Sky Knife sat at the north. Stone Jaguar took the highest-ranked wall, that of the east.

A ball of blue light followed them into the room and stationed itself against the ceiling.

"You have been taught many things in your years as an attendant," said Stone Jaguar. "You can reckon the days of the Long Count, and the Calendar Round. You know the nine days of the *Bolon ti ku* and the thirteen days of the *Oxlatun ti ku*. You know the names of the Lords of the Nine Underworlds and the Lords of the Thirteen Heavens."

"You have attended *p'a chi*," said Death Smoke. "And held the sacrifices as they were offered to the gods. And today you have made a blood sacrifice of your own."

Sky Knife's hand went unthinking to his earlobe. It still stung, but not as badly as before.

"You know of Ah Mun, the maize god, and Ix Chebel Yax, the wife of the great Itzamna," said Death Smoke. He cackled. "I don't need to tell you about Cizin and Ix Tabai. You have already seen them and their work."

"But there is more to know," said Stone Jaguar. "Knowledge that only the priests may keep."

"More than lore," said Death Smoke, "for there are many who could learn the names of the gods and the ways of the calendar if they wished. But not everyone can take the heart of the sacrifice. Not everyone can call the temple glow, or a ball of flame to light the darkness."

Stone Jaguar put a hand to his mouth. Sky Knife realized the priest was stifling a laugh. "Not that you need help with light just now, Sky Knife," said Stone Jaguar, "what with your glowing friend at your throat."

Death Smoke cast a frown toward Stone Jaguar. "Still, there is no telling how long the *chic-chac* will stay. We must teach him."

Stone Jaguar nodded. "I didn't say we wouldn't, only that, for the moment, calling light in the darkness is not a problem for Sky Knife."

Sky Knife fidgeted, uncomfortable at being in the center of a squabble between the other two men. The serpent moved its head slightly, as if it knew it were being discussed. Sky Knife stroked its warm scales and the serpent settled down around his neck once again.

"Sky Knife," said Stone Jaguar. "Lie down on the floor underneath the ball of light."

Sky Knife scooted to the middle of the floor and lay down, head facing east.

"Good," said Stone Jaguar. "Now, clear your mind. When you feel you have emptied yourself of all thoughts and desires, reach your hand toward the light."

Sky Knife took a deep breath and let all thoughts drift away from him. The world shrank away until it was only him and the light. He reached toward it and touched it with outstretched hands.

The light was warm. And it tickled. Sky Knife shivered and concentrated on the light. Only the light.

"Good," said Stone Jaguar. The sound of the other priest's voice startled Sky Knife and he yelped.

Death Smoke laughed. "He succeeded the first time. Why didn't we make him a priest long ago?"

"Because, you old fool, we had enough candidates without sifting through all the attendants, too."

"Who's the fool, then? You're the one who's supposed to keep an eye open for talent and luck. You were just unhappy that Vine Torch discovered a child of omens before you had a chance to."

Sky Knife closed his eyes and shut out the sounds of the bickering priests. He concentrated on the warm tickle on his palms. It seemed to penetrate right through to his bones. Slowly, it seeped up his arms. The serpent at his throat grew warmer, too. But the heat from the ball and the serpent wasn't like the sun; it didn't burn, it didn't make Sky Knife sweat. It felt good, like happiness. Or health.

Suddenly, it was gone. Sky Knife's eyes snapped open. The room was dark.

"What happened?" he asked.

"Wait," said Stone Jaguar. "I know it's a temptation to lose yourself in the light. We've all tried it at one time or another. Just remember—you must always leave a bit of your soul tied to your body in order to make it back. Take a rope braided from the inner bark of the *ceiba* tree and tie it around your right wrist before you try such a trick again."

"Since you were so successful at touching the light, why don't you try calling it?" said Death Smoke.

"How?" asked Sky Knife.

"Raise your hands," said Stone Jaguar, "and remember the feeling of the light as it touched you. Imagine that feeling back again."

Sky Knife closed his eyes and raised his hands. He concentrated on the memory of the holy light that had touched him. The way it had tickled, and soaked into his bones.

"It's hard the first few times, and you might not succeed today. But don't be discouraged; sorcery takes a while to learn," said Death Smoke.

Light blazed from Sky Knife's hands and illuminated the room with blinding whiteness. He blinked at the brightness.

"Apparently not," said Stone Jaguar. "Don't think on it quite so hard, Sky Knife." Stone Jaguar chuckled.

Sky Knife relaxed and the light died down a bit, though it was still terribly bright. He felt weak, but triumphant.

"An excellent first lesson," said Stone Jaguar. "But I'm sure you're tired now—the strength you use to call the light comes from your own soul. But calling the light will not take so much energy in the future, now that you know how to do it."

"You can call light to see with, as you just did," said Death Smoke. "Or you can concentrate on a small point and think of a great heat, and you can call up a fire as well."

"The way you light the cigars at the sacrifice?" asked Sky Knife.

"Yes, of course," said Stone Jaguar.

"Sit up and return to your place," said Death Smoke. "The weakness will pass, but you will need to eat. I will get you some water."

The older man got up and left the room. Sky Knife raised himself to his elbows, then rolled over and pushed himself to his knees. His elbows and knees trembled. He crawled back to the wall.

Death Smoke returned in a few moments with a wooden bowl filled with water.

"It is from the sacred pool," said Death Smoke. "It will refresh you."

Sky Knife took the bowl and stared into it. The water seemed no different from ordinary water, but he didn't want to touch it. Drinking it would contaminate the water; take the holiness away.

"All of us have tasted the water at some time or other," said Death Smoke. "It is another test of a priest. Drink."

Somehow, knowing this was a test made it easier. Sky Knife gulped down the water. It was cold and wonderful. He drained the bowl.

Death Smoke took the bowl back to his place by the southern wall. "There is just one more thing for today," he said. "Something you must remember always."

"Yes?" asked Sky Knife.

"These things we teach you are secret. Not just from those who are not priests, but from all others. I would sooner tell the secrets of the priesthood to a Tikal peasant in his *milpa* than someone from another city."

"Why? What about their priests? Don't they worship the same gods? What about the priests of Uaxactun or Copan?" asked Sky Knife. "Are they not also Mayan, and sorcerers?"

"But they have their own magic," said Death Smoke. "Every city has its own priests and its own magic. Each is unique."

"Beware any foreign magic," said Stone Jaguar. "Or anything foreign, for that matter. Trust only in the magic and traditions of Tikal. Everything else is heresy."

"Heresy," hissed Death Smoke. The sound sent a shiver up Sky Knife's spine, and he felt cold despite the warmth from the light he had made.

"We must return to the city," said Stone Jaguar. "And let Sky Knife continue with his duty to the king."

Death Smoke nodded. "Another thing to beware," he said. "Step carefully, Sky Knife. Very carefully."

Sky Knife swallowed a lump in his throat and nodded. He got up and left the room, bowed once to the *zuhuy ha*, and made his way up the steps.

The light of the sun outside was a shock after the sorcerous light of the passageways and cave. It seemed to press down on Sky Knife's shoulders and weigh down his eyelids.

"There he is!" shouted a deeply accented voice. Sky Knife shaded his eyes with his hands and searched the plaza for the source of the shout.

Nine Dog, the fat merchant of Monte Alban, stood at the bottom of the steps to the northern acropolis. He pointed to Sky Knife.

"There he is," Nine Dog said again. He drew a flint knife. "And he's mine."

# 16

⟩⟩⟩⟩⟩

What do you want?" asked Sky Knife. He stood on the patio, four steps above the plaza, and waited. Nine Dog made no move to mount the steps.

"Come down here," said Nine Dog. Sweat dripped off his flabby face. "You're the one responsible!"

"Responsible for what?" asked Sky Knife.

"For having me imprisoned for no reason," shouted Nine Dog. "For my being taunted all day by rude guards. For my attendants fleeing me as soon as we were released. Now who will take my goods back home?"

The love-gift vendor walked over. "Bah, your attendants will come back," she said. "Where do they have to go besides home?"

"They were from Uaxactun," muttered Nine Dog. "They'll get home easily enough."

"This is just a boy," said the love-gift vendor. "He couldn't be responsible for everything you say."

"Get out of my sight, old woman," shouted Nine Dog. He shoved the love-gift vendor aside. She fell to the stones of the plaza and lay still.

"No!" shouted Sky Knife. He leaped down the stairs and ran to the old woman's side. He touched her shoulder and she moaned. Blood seeped out of a scrape on her head.

Something struck Sky Knife on the shoulder. For a moment, he thought Nine Dog had slapped him, then pain raced from his shoulder down into his arm and chest. Blood ran down his arm. The *chic-chac* squeezed his neck tightly.

Sky Knife jerked away and retreated a few steps. He turned to face Nine Dog. The merchant stood over the love-gift vendor, flint knife raised above his head. Blood dripped from its dark tip.

"I'm going to kill you, boy," said Nine Dog. He rushed forward toward Sky Knife. Sky Knife ducked under the knife and stumbled up the steps to the northern acropolis. Around him, objects swam in his vision and seemed indistinct. Once on the patio, he dropped to his knees.

The fire in his shoulder wrapped around his chest, constricting his breathing. Sky Knife gasped for air.

"Stop!" ordered a deep voice. Sky Knife looked around for the source, but everything seemed dark and hazy.

Something struck Sky Knife across the face and he fell to the patio. He screamed as his injured shoulder slammed into the pavement stones.

"Get away," shouted Nine Dog. "I am in the right here."

"This is not Monte Alban," said the deep voice. "And nowhere is it seemly for a merchant to attack a priest."

"Priest?" spat Nine Dog. "He's a temple attendant. I asked."

"He is a priest, and he carries the authority of the king," said the deep voice. Sky Knife's confused mind refused to put a name to it. "Leave now or I shall kill you."

"This isn't over," said Nine Dog.

"Yes, it is. If you are not out of the city by sunset, I will kill you anyway for disrupting the king's representative as he went about the king's business."

The sound of footsteps retreating reached Sky Knife's ears. He struggled to sit, but a hand held him down.

"Easy, my friend," said the deep voice. "It's Bone Splinter. Don't worry; I'll take care of you."

"The old woman . . ." whispered Sky Knife.

"She is all right," said Bone Splinter. "She will go back to her rabbits now, I'm sure. It's you I'm worried about." Bone Splinter put an arm under Sky Knife's shoulders and the other under his knees.

The world jerked and spun as Bone Splinter picked him up. Sky Knife screwed his eyes shut and rode the pain. It demanded so much of his attention, and he was so tired. So tired. He let himself slide down into the darkness.


As awareness seeped back into his mind, Sky Knife tensed against expected pain. But the pain had faded to a dull ache. He opened his eyes.

Bone Splinter sat beside him, eyes closed. Sky Knife lifted his head a bit and looked around the room. The room was large and brightly painted in orange, red, and blue. A scene of an assemblage of the gods dominated the walls. Sky Knife recognized Itzamna, Ah Mun, Ix Chel, and Ek Chueh right away though not all the deities depicted were equally as familiar. He pushed himself up on his elbow to get a better look. A red hot pain lanced down his arm and he gasped.

Bone Splinter's eyes snapped open. He put a hand under Sky Knife's neck and eased him back to the floor. "You've only slept a short time," said the warrior. "But you shouldn't get up yet."

Sky Knife closed his eyes against a sudden pounding in his skull. The *chic-chac* moved slightly, its tongue brushing lightly against Sky Knife's skin. For some reason, he felt better for that.

Sky Knife's stomach growled and tightened. "Can I have some food?" he asked. "Death Smoke said I should eat something after I left the acropolis. But then Nine Dog . . ."

"Food is being brought," said Bone Splinter. He paused and fidgeted. "What happened to you?" the warrior finally asked.

"I was attacked," said Sky Knife. "You were there. At least, I think I remember you being there."

"That's not what I meant," said Bone Splinter. "You were hurt yesterday by the jaguar, but you walked to the House of the Warriors. Today you were not injured as badly and you passed out immediately."

"I . . ." began Sky Knife. He stopped, wondering how much of what had transpired in the northern acropolis he could relate. "I had a lesson in sorcery," he said at last. "I was weak. Death Smoke and Stone Jaguar warned me I would be. But what about you—aren't you going to war?"

"The king has decided to cancel the war," said Bone Splinter, "and he ordered the release of the prisoners. Kan Flower wasn't happy about that." The warrior sighed. "I knew Nine Dog would be looking for you, so I sought you out. But he found you first."

Bone Splinter fell silent. Sky Knife relaxed and the pounding in his head receded a bit. He let his thoughts drift and his awareness of the world faded slightly.

"How is he doing?" asked a female voice. Sky Knife jerked to wakefulness and his eyes snapped open. Turtle Nest stepped up to the doorway, the hem of her purple dress swirling about her ankles.

"I am fine," said Sky Knife before Bone Splinter could reply. His heart pounded against his ribs and his headache returned full-force. Sky Knife winced.

"Perhaps we define 'fine' in different ways," said Turtle Nest. She came in and sat down next to Sky Knife opposite Bone Splinter. "You still seem to be in pain."

Sky Knife said nothing. Turtle Nest reached across his chest and pressed her fingers to his shoulder. Sky Knife gritted his teeth at the pain, but made no sound.

"You're lucky," said Turtle Nest, "and not only because of the serpent. There was a poison on the blade that struck you, slow-acting enough that it wouldn't have killed you for hours. I and my nuns, with the help of Ix Chel, managed to defeat the poison."

"Filthy merchant," said Bone Splinter softly.

"Then why did he follow me onto the patio?" asked Sky Knife. Itzamna! None of this made any sense.

"What?" asked Turtle Nest.

"If the blade were poisoned, why pursue me after stabbing me?" asked Sky Knife. "He already knew I'd die a slow death."

"The wise assassin never puts his trust in a bit of poison," said Bone Splinter. "He probably wanted to make sure of you."

"I suppose," said Sky Knife. He sighed.

Footsteps approached. "Here is the food I promised," said Turtle Nest. "Help him sit, Bone Splinter."

Sky Knife allowed Bone Splinter to pull him up. He pulled his legs up inside the skirt and sat cross-legged. He looked up. His heart froze in his chest a moment, then started beating wildly. Jade Flute stood in the doorway, a wooden tray piled with meat, cornbread, and fruit in her hands. She smiled at Sky Knife.

"Come, girl, the man needs to eat," said Turtle Nest. Jade Flute's gaze dropped demurely to the floor. She knelt and placed the tray in front of Sky Knife. He grabbed a hunk of cornbread and bit into it. The bread was still hot. Sky Knife ate it greedily.

Sky Knife was glad of Bone Splinter's presence. He was uncomfortable with the two women, who sat silently and watched him eat. All of the food tasted wonderful, especially the fruit. It was sweet and perfectly ripe.

Sky Knife ate until his stomach ached. He sighed.

"So," said Turtle Nest. "Have you discovered anything?"

Sky Knife shook his head. He wouldn't air his suspicions of the king again, especially not with Bone Splinter in the room. Bone Splinter was duty-bound to protect the king no matter what. Sky Knife did not want Bone Splinter to be his enemy.

Itzamna—he didn't want the king for an enemy either! Sky Knife's stomach rolled unpleasantly as doubt assailed him. He suspected, but he didn't *know*. How could he know for certain?

"The *chic-chac* has not been able to help you?" asked Turtle Nest in the ensuing silence. She frowned.

"I was told not to put my trust in a serpent, even a rainbow serpent," said Sky Knife.

"Told? By whom?" demanded Turtle Nest. "Stone Jaguar? Surely he's not as much a fool as that."

Sky Knife shook his head.

"It was the woman who lives in the jungle," said Bone Splinter. "She said serpents can see clearly, but won't see the same things a man sees."

"Or a woman," said Jade Flute. She tossed her head. Her silky black hair flew around her head and settled over her shoulders heavily. Sky Knife stared at her. She wore the same purple dress he had seen her in the other night. Sky Knife tried not to let his gaze fall below her collarbones.

Jade Flute smiled at him and shifted slightly so that her dress gapped open and showed even more of her than before. Sky Knife blushed and looked away.

"Girl, have you no shame?" asked Turtle Nest, though her voice was more tired than angry. "What shall I do with you?"

"Nothing," said Jade Flute. "I'll decide what's to be done with me."

"Entice the wrong young man and you'll be meeting an adulteress's death in the courtyard," said Turtle Nest.

Jade Flute pouted, but her gaze remained on Sky Knife. He stared at the tray in front of him studiously.

"That old woman was mindless before I was born," said Turtle Nest. "She knows nothing."

"She knew of the *chic-chac* before she saw me," said Sky Knife. "She said she knew Jaguar Paw."

"She probably did," said Turtle Nest. "No one remembers when she was born."

Bone Splinter touched Sky Knife on the knee. "Do you feel well enough to leave?"

Sky Knife nodded. Well or not, he wanted out of this place. Somehow, his thoughts always seemed muddled around Jade Flute. He wanted to think. About the king. About Red Spider. About Nine Dog.

And about how he was going to tell Bone Splinter his fears.

"Let's go," he said.

Bone Splinter nodded and grabbed Sky Knife by the elbow. Sky Knife let Bone Splinter pull him to his feet. His headache had faded and his shoulder only throbbed. He sighed in relief.

Turtle Nest and Jade Flute stood also. Sky Knife bowed slightly to Turtle Nest. "Thank you for the healing, and for the food," he said.

Turtle Nest smiled. "I and my nuns stand ready to serve you and the king," she said. "Only let us know how we can help."

Sky Knife nodded. Jade Flute stepped closer to him, but he stumbled toward the door.

With Bone Splinter's guidance, Sky Knife walked back to the entrance of the temple and shoved aside the drapery. Outside, the darkness of dusk colored the horizon, though the shadow of the temple was still long.

"Come again, Sky Knife," laughed Jade Flute. "It's not often I find a man sleeping in the temple. Next time, who knows what I'll do."

Sky Knife flushed red and walked across the patio without looking back.

# 17

›››››

Although the plaza was not as full of merchants and customers as usual, it was a lot more crowded than it had been earlier in the day. Bone Splinter gestured toward the crowd.

"No bad luck has happened since the rain," he said. "See how soon they forget?"

Sky Knife looked around the plaza. "Do you see Red Spider?" he asked Bone Splinter.

The warrior scanned the crowd. "No," he said. "Wait—there, on the very northeastern end."

"Fine," said Sky Knife. "It's time I asked him a few questions, I think."

Sky Knife wound his way through the crowd. Few vendors, it seemed, were doing much business. The love-gift vendor sat in her place by the temple, but no customers stood around her. The people in the plaza seemed more interested in looking around rather than doing serious bargaining.

Except at Red Spider's area. Red Spider was surrounded by gawkers. Most of them stared at his assistant. Red Spider crossed his arms over his chest and surveyed the scene approvingly. He smiled when he saw Sky Knife and Bone Splinter. He waved to them.

"Come," he called. "My assistant is just preparing a demonstration."

Sky Knife pushed through the small crowd to stand next to Red Spider. "What is he doing?"

Red Spider smiled. "We happened to bring some good luck trinkets with us, though I had thought to sell them in Palenque. Merchants coming from there say the king has suffered a rash of bad luck in the past couple of years and the people are worried it will spread. But if I can sell the charms now—why not?"

"And the demonstration?"

Red Spider gestured toward his assistant, who sat on the plaza stones and held a bead of jade between his teeth. "Very simple," said the tall man. "My assistant will invoke the spirit of the charm and it will drive away any bad luck that might be affecting him today."

"How do I know this is true?" asked Sky Knife.

"Just watch."

Sky Knife kept his eyes on the assistant. The man jerked and sweat rolled down his face. There was a slight popping sound and the bead dissolved into a puff of green smoke. The assistant sniffed the smoke and smiled.

"You see?" said Red Spider in a loud, dramatic voice. "Good luck is assured for the day. Since I didn't foresee that the people of Tikal would have much of a need for the beads, I didn't bring along very many. I do have a few. Speak to my assistant and he'll supply you with what you need until our stores are gone."

"Wouldn't you rather do the negotiating?" asked Sky Knife softly.

Red Spider shook his head. "I try not to bicker with my customers. Then if they feel they weren't treated well by my assistant, they'll come to me with their concerns."

"And trust you to set things right," said Bone Splinter.

"Even so."

Negotiations between the assistant and the crowd around him were quick. The few beads he had were purchased for exorbitant sums. Sky Knife's mind boggled that the people were willing to exchange so much of their wealth for a single jade bead. One woman traded twelve cotton blankets and a handful of salt. Sky Knife shook his head.

"You're doing a good business," said Bone Splinter, "but how will you manage to get all that home with you?"

Red Spider laughed and flicked a braid back over his shoulder. "I only need to get it to the next city," he said. "And if my luck holds there as well, I'll have made a fortune on just this one trip."

"Based on the misfortune of others," said Sky Knife.

"That's what being a merchant is all about," said Red Spider. "You have no salt, so I'll trade you some for corn. You have no corn, so I'll trade you some for obsidian. People never have everything they need. Or everything they want. You just have to be able to supply their needs. Or their wants."

The crowd dispersed as the assistant sold the last bead. The assistant packed away Red Spider's newly acquired wealth.

"What is it *you* want?" asked Sky Knife.

"Oh, wealth appeals to me," said Red Spider. "What about you, Sky Knife? I see your fortunes have improved as well. In two short days you've turned from lowly, poor, temple assistant, to a priest with the beginnings of a jewel hoard."

"I want some answers," said Sky Knife.

"That's right," said Red Spider. "You came by earlier with questions. And then the stinging rain came. What is it you'd like to know?"

"What are things like back in Teotihuacan?"

Red Spider cocked his head. "Why? Are you thinking of going there? I thought your people didn't leave their home cities much."

"I mean, how is the king?"

"Our king is just fine, and thank you for asking," said Red Spider. "With the Feathered Serpent's grace, he'll rule for many, many more years."

"And the king's brothers?"

Red Spider laughed. The sound was deep and bright, not menacing at all. Sky Knife hated Red Spider for his laugh. The man was tall, exotically beautiful, and graceful, and that should have been enough to hate him for. But that the man who was probably responsible—or was at least one of the men responsible—for Tikal's misfortune could laugh so gaily offended Sky Knife. The sound was as beautiful as Red Spider. How could the man be evil and be so graceful and fair?

"Oh, I see," said Red Spider, wiping a tear from the corner of his eye. "You want to know which of your king's elder brothers might want to replace Storm Cloud, seeing him perhaps as an easier target than the eldest who sits on the throne of Teotihuacan."

Sky Knife frowned. "Perhaps," he said.

"And that would make me one of the conspirators," said Red Spider. "Because I could come into the city and move about freely without inviting suspicion."

"Something like that."

Red Spider's assistant came up to him, bowed, and spoke a few words in his own tongue. Red Spider nodded. The man hurried off along with two other men, each loaded down with Red Spider's gains.

"Well, I'm afraid I don't have much reason to tell you the truth, do I?" asked Red Spider evenly. "If I am conspiring against Storm Cloud, I'd be a fool to say so. If I'm not, you're in no way obliged to believe me."

"That may be," said Bone Splinter. "But I, for one, would like to hear your answer."

Red Spider sat down on the steps to the northern acropolis and bent down to adjust his sandals. "Then my answer is this: I am innocent of any wrongdoing against Storm Cloud. I have not been sent by one of his brothers to prepare the way for an invasion. I have my own reasons to be here—acquiring wealth being the main one. Another is personal."

"Personal business with whom?" asked Sky Knife.

"With Storm Cloud," said Red Spider. "You can find out from the chief of his household that I requested an audience with him several days after first entering the city. That was two weeks ago. I am still awaiting a response to my request."

"I'll ask the chief of the household," said Sky Knife.

"Do that."

The sun dropped behind the tops of the trees in the west and the shadows in the plaza grew longer. A faint warm breeze stirred the air.

"Are you sure you will not trade for that serpent at your throat?" asked Red Spider.

"No," said Sky Knife quickly. His hands went to the serpent. "No one in the world has enough wealth to purchase this."

"Of course not," said Red Spider. He stood and bowed slightly to Sky Knife. "If you need to speak with me again, you can find me here in the plaza or to the west in the merchant's quarter."

The tall man walked away, his stride unhurried, his shadow stretched out impossibly long and thin behind him. Sky Knife watched him go and blinked against the bright orange of the setting sun.

"I don't trust him," said Bone Splinter. "We should search his possessions for charms or other items that could store bad luck."

"Perhaps," said Sky Knife. "But he's smart—I don't think he'd keep items like that with him. Not only because we might find them, but also, who'd like to be around that much bad luck all day and all night? If he's the one responsible, then he probably has the bad luck stored in various places around Tikal."

"We can't search the whole city, not even with the entire household guard to help us."

Sky Knife scanned the plaza. Except for a few stragglers, he and Bone Splinter were the only occupants. The plaza seemed unusually quiet and lifeless. "Maybe we don't need to search the entire city," said Sky Knife. "Most of the bad luck has taken place right here. Why don't we search the plaza?"

"Good idea, but let's get some help."

Sky Knife nodded and set off toward the House of the Warriors, Bone Splinter a tall and silent presence in his wake.

# 18

>>>>>

An hour later, Sky Knife stood in the plaza with Bone Splinter and Kan Flower. Other warriors stood on the perimeter of the plaza and held torches to light the area. The shells in Bone Splinter's ear spools reflected the torchlight.

"What do we look for?" asked Kan Flower.

"Anything in which a sorcerer could store bad luck," said Sky Knife. "Or anything that shouldn't be here."

Kan Flower laughed. "Sky Knife, this is the *plaza*. Everything in the city comes here at one time or another. Everything and everyone."

Sky Knife shrugged and grinned. "I know. But I don't know exactly what we're looking for. I have a feeling we'll know it if we find it."

"Right," said Kan Flower. "Well, anything to escape a poetry contest in which Bone Splinter doesn't compete." Kan Flower knelt on the pavement stones and held his torch in front of him.

Sky Knife walked to the Great Pyramid. None of the warriors could touch it, so it would be his to search. Sky Knife held his torch high and tilted his head back to stare at the summit of the pyramid. Normally, only the priests, attendants, and sacrifices would have been on the temple. But a sorcerer strong enough to bring a black jaguar full of butterflies or a stinging black rain probably wouldn't bother to obey that prohibition. If a sorcerer wanted to hide something, there would be no better place than the temple.

Sky Knife climbed the red step and walked along the step from end to end, bent over, torch held in front of him. When he was satisfied that nothing was out of the ordinary, he moved to the second step. Sky Knife thought briefly of calling a ball of fire to light his way, but it seemed too much like showing off. He had a torch and that was sufficient. Besides, if the power to fuel the blue flame came from Sky Knife's own soul, he shouldn't waste it. He might need the strength later.

By the time he had searched the first eighteen steps, Sky Knife's back and knees ached. He sat down and scanned the plaza. The torches held by the warriors below shone like the brilliant stars above. Sky Knife looked up into the sky toward the stars he had been named after. The Knife of Stars glittered in the humid air.

Sky Knife sighed. It was not wise to stare at the stars for too long. One might attract the attention of one of the monsters that lived in the dark shadows of the stars. It would come and devour the stargazer and digest his soul. Attracting such a monster would bring bad luck not only to the unlucky person but to an entire city.

Not that there wasn't already more than enough bad luck to go around Tikal just now.

Sky Knife's torch sputtered. "Itzamna!" he whispered through teeth gritted together. Now he'd have to go back down to the plaza and get another torch before this one left him entirely in the dark. Sky Knife stood up.

The *chic-chac* squeezed his throat slightly. Sky Knife hesitated. What did the serpent want him to do?

The torch sputtered a final time and died. Sky Knife tossed

it down the steps and prepared to follow it—albeit more slowly. But the serpent squeezed his throat again.

Sky Knife stroked the *chic-chac* and looked back up toward the stars. Everything was as it had been. He turned and looked back toward the summit of the pyramid.

A small object glittered on the end of the next to last step. Sky Knife climbed several steps until the one he wanted was at eye level. He leaned forward. The glow from the serpent was enough to illuminate the small object.

Sky Knife reached forward and grabbed it. It was a small point, like one would put on an arrow or a dart. An obsidian point. Its many glass facets gleamed brightly green in the serpent's light.

Sky Knife climbed the last few steps and looked around the flat top of the pyramid. Another shiny object sparkled on the altar itself. Sky Knife stepped forward and snatched the object. It was another small point.

Sky Knife looked around. Surely there were more. Leaving two of anything made no sense. Four was a number of power. Two wasn't anything at all.

But no more objects glittered in the serpent's glow. Sky Knife glanced back down to the plaza. The warriors had gathered around Kan Flower, who held something in his hands.

Sky Knife went down the steps of the pyramid as fast as he dared. The warriors moved aside as he approached.

"What did you find?" he asked.

Kan Flower held his hand out, palm up. In his hand glittered a third obsidian point. In the torchlight, the dark stone had a green cast to it.

"I found two more on the pyramid," said Sky Knife. He held out his finds.

"On the pyramid, even," snorted Kan Flower. "The evildoer has no shame."

"There is probably a fourth somewhere," said Sky Knife. "I

found the first of these on the second to last step. The other was on the altar itself."

"This one was in a crack in the pavement stones at the west end of the plaza," said Kan Flower.

"Which end of the step?" asked Bone Splinter.

"North," said Sky Knife.

"North, east, and west are accounted for, then," said Kan Flower. "Only south is left."

The warriors and Sky Knife walked carefully to the south end of the plaza and spread out. Sky Knife leaned down to examine the edges of the pavement stones carefully. Originally, they had been foot-square pieces of limestone. But years of weathering and constant traffic had cracked them along many fine lines. A few weeds poked out of the larger cracks, although the attendants to the temple usually kept plant growth away from the plaza itself. Apparently, in the midst of the bad luck, no one had thought to weed the plaza.

Sky Knife stuck his fingers into the crack, pulled out the weed, and tossed it aside. He ran his fingers along the edge of the crack, searching for anything unusual. Nothing.

Sky Knife moved along the south edge of the plaza, pulling weeds and searching cracks with his fingers. The warriors knelt on the pavement and did the same. Some of them stepped out of the plaza itself and pried up a few loose pavement stones to see what was underneath.

"Here," said one. Sky Knife jogged over to the western edge of the plaza. A warrior held up a pavement stone with two hands while another pulled something out from under it. As soon as his hand was free, the first warrior set the stone down gently.

The warrior held the object up to the light. A fourth obsidian point sparkled in the torchlight. Sky Knife's heart raced with anxiety. Green obsidian again. There was only one place to get it.

"Teotihuacan," spat Kan Flower. "It *is* that merchant with the pretty face."

"But why?" asked another warrior. "If he drives away his customers, what does he get?"

"I'll tell you what," said Bone Splinter. "Profit. He made a fortune this afternoon by selling jade beads as charms to protect against bad luck."

"Then let's find him," said Kan Flower. "I'd like to talk to him about these points."

"Wait," said Sky Knife.

"What is it?" asked Bone Splinter. "Now we have proof."

Sky Knife pulled Bone Splinter aside. "Wait," he said again softly. When they were out of earshot of the other men, Sky Knife whispered, "What if Red Spider is working with someone else?"

"What if he is?" asked Bone Splinter. "We'll get the truth out of him."

Bone Splinter turned away, but Sky Knife grabbed his arm. "What if he's working with the king?"

Bone Splinter froze. Very, very slowly, he turned back to Sky Knife. "What did you say?"

Sky Knife took a deep breath and stepped close to Bone Splinter. "What if Red Spider and Storm Cloud are working together?" he asked. "Two priests are dead, and Death Smoke has seen his own death. Stone Jaguar may be next. What if Storm Cloud wants to bring in foreign priests?"

"Why would a Teotihuacano priest come here?" asked Bone Splinter. "Their gods are different from ours."

"Maybe Storm Cloud wants to worship his father's gods," said Sky Knife.

"And what about us? Are we supposed to just stop worship of Itzamna?" asked Bone Splinter. "I won't worship the Feathered Serpent. Or their storm god, either."

"Who knows what they might have planned? It might not even be true," said Sky Knife. "But why should we go after Red Spider tonight? If he is behind all this, let him think we don't know."

"Sky Knife! Bone Splinter!" called Kan Flower. "Come on—let's go."

"No, wait," said Bone Splinter. He held up a hand to Kan Flower. "Sky Knife has an idea. Let's not go after Red Spider just now."

"What?" shouted another warrior. "No!"

"Shut up," said Kan Flower to the warrior. He turned to Bone Splinter. "This idea had better be good."

Sky Knife strode toward Kan Flower. He threw his shoulders back and held his head high, though he was still several inches shorter than Kan Flower. "Let Red Spider think we don't know about him," he said. "Have him watched at all times, but do not approach him. If he or any of his assistants come to claim the points, we have him."

"And if no one comes?"

"Someone will come," said Sky Knife. "So the plaza must be watched at all times, too."

Kan Flower hesitated. His gaze slid down toward the serpent at Sky Knife's throat. "All right," he said. "I would rather take Red Spider now, but I suppose a day or two won't matter as long as we watch him closely."

"Thank you," said Sky Knife. His heart pounded in his ears, and he realized he hadn't really expected Kan Flower to follow his orders. For the first time, Sky Knife was glad of the long skirt—it hid the trembling of his knees.

Kan Flower and the other warriors moved away. Kan Flower issued orders and they split up.

"Sky Knife!"

Sky Knife turned. Stone Jaguar strode across the plaza.

"Good," said Stone Jaguar. "I'm glad I found you. We have to prepare for a sacrifice."

"What?" asked Sky Knife. "When?"

"At dawn," said Stone Jaguar. "I convinced Storm Cloud that another sacrifice might turn the bad luck if we coincide the sacrifice with the birth of the sun."

Sky Knife nodded. "Perhaps it will work," he said, though the plan sounded desperate. The gods could reverse bad luck—but why should they bother? Sky Knife believed only the discovery of the men behind the bad luck would stop it. But perhaps a sacrifice would help in some way. Itzamna knew Tikal needed all the help it could get right now.

"It had better," said Stone Jaguar. "Anyway, come back to the acropolis. You and I must prepare."

"And Death Smoke?"

"Taken ill," spat Stone Jaguar. "It looks as though he was right. I don't expect him to last another day."

Stone Jaguar turned and walked toward the southern acropolis, Sky Knife at his heels, Bone Splinter a few strides behind.

"How did you find a sacrifice?" asked Sky Knife. Normally, it took days to collect the names of the volunteers and to choose from among them.

"Storm Cloud found one," said Stone Jaguar as he mounted the steps of the acropolis. "His wife's niece. She's in the temple of Ix Chel now. She's been told to prepare herself."

Sky Knife's heart dropped and he stopped. Stone Jaguar slipped behind the drapery and disappeared into the acropolis. Sky Knife remained on the patio, motionless.

"Itzamna," he whispered, a cold twisting in his gut making him feel suddenly ill.

At dawn, he would have to assist Stone Jaguar in the sacrifice. Stone Jaguar would reveal the Hand of God and slice into the sacrifice's stomach, rip out the heart, and offer it to the gods. And Sky Knife would hear the screams.

Sky Knife stumbled forward, but sobs caught in his throat. Jade Flute. Morning would come, and she would die.

# III

>>>>>>>>>>

# NORTH

## WHERE THE RAIN GIVES BIRTH TO IDEAS

9.0.0.0.2
10 IK 15 CEH

# 19

››››

Someone shook his shoulder. Sky Knife opened his eyes and yawned. Thoughts danced around his head in confusion. Vague memories of several hours spent reciting prayers to the gods before being sent to his bed squirmed in his mind.

"Stone Jaguar says it is time," said Bone Splinter. "Dawn will be here soon."

Suddenly, Sky Knife was awake. "Jade Flute," he said.

"Yes," said Bone Splinter.

Sky Knife got up and wrapped the skirt around his waist. Today, he didn't apply any paint to his skin—he was not Sky Knife, unmarried youth, this morning, but a representative of the gods.

Bone Splinter had reapplied grease to his hair and his ear spools were different. These had been carved of the light green jade that came from the mountains. Sky Knife stared at them in awe. Not even Stone Jaguar sported such exquisite ear spools.

"My father's," said Bone Splinter when he noticed Sky Knife's stare. "And his father's before him."

Sky Knife dropped his stare, embarrassed and envious at the same time. His father had never owned anything as fine to leave Sky Knife. The jade strand around Sky Knife's neck was the only jewelry he'd ever owned.

Sky Knife straightened the skirt and chided himself inwardly. He was only thinking of Bone Splinter to keep himself from thinking of Jade Flute.

His heart twisted as though a knife pierced it. How could he do it? She was the most beautiful woman in the city. She had a fiery spirit, too. Why her?

Why not her? She wasn't an asset to her uncle, considering the way she'd treated her suitors. If Storm Cloud couldn't marry her off to a foreign prince, perhaps he thought sacrifice was the best answer to the problem of what to do with Jade Flute.

"Stone Jaguar said to come quickly," said Bone Splinter. He ducked his head apologetically. For some reason, the gesture touched Sky Knife. Bone Splinter was everything he was not, and yet the other man treated him as a friend. Sky Knife felt warmed by that.

Sky Knife left his quarters and walked out of the acropolis. The night was still dark. The Knife of Stars sliced the darkness overhead.

Very few people stood in the plaza. No doubt word had not gotten out to the outlying areas about the sacrifice. Probably only the craftspeople and merchants who lived in the areas immediately adjacent to the ceremonial center would attend this morning's sacrifice.

Sky Knife walked to the Great Pyramid and mounted the first step. The skirt wrapped around his ankles and knees as if to trip him. Sky Knife jerked to straighten the skirt and lift the hem a few inches higher. Slowly, he climbed the remaining thirty-five steps.

Stone Jaguar stood on the pyramid with several young men Sky Knife didn't recognize. Stone Jaguar must have conscripted more help while Sky Knife had been busy elsewhere. Families of craft trades were always willing to donate younger sons to assist the priests of the temple.

The four attendants knelt at the four corners of the flat-topped pyramid. Stone Jaguar bowed slightly to Sky Knife. Sky Knife resisted the urge to kneel before Stone Jaguar as he would have two days before. But he was a priest now, and if not equal to Stone Jaguar in status, at least near enough in status to require no more than a bow in return. He bowed.

Stone Jaguar wore his jaguar-skin cloak and shell mask. Feathers stuck out from the mask around the edges, making Stone Jaguar's head seem larger than normal. Sky Knife walked to the small north altar, assuming he would be needed to light the cigars that drove away bad luck and the death gods.

Cigars that *usually* drove away the death gods, Sky Knife amended to himself. But surely Cizin wouldn't be strong enough to breach the good luck of a sacrifice twice in a row.

"Dawn comes," said Stone Jaguar. He gestured to the attendants, who stood and moved to the altar. They hesitated before kneeling at their respective places.

Sky Knife did not envy them. The first sacrifice he had attended had been hard on him. He had fled the pyramid as soon as he had been allowed and had run away on shaky legs to be sick in the fringes of the jungle. There had been so much blood. All over the altar. All over *him*.

Normally, only one new attendant was trained for sacrificial duty at a time, so that if he ran, the other three could still complete the sacrifice. With *four* new attendants, anything could happen. Sky Knife swallowed hard and prayed the young men would be brave enough to stay.

Guilt wracked him. At the same time he wanted the young men to be able to do their sacred duty, he wanted with all his heart for the sacrifice to be canceled. He didn't want to watch Jade Flute sacrificed. Even to save Tikal.

Not that Stone Jaguar was likely to stop a sacrifice he had

talked Storm Cloud into. Jade Flute would die. Sky Knife bit his lip and tried to push aside his bitterness and grief. The gods would not be pleased if he were not able to offer sacrifice with a pure heart.

The first gray tinges of dawn brightened in the east. Pink and gold followed quickly.

Stone Jaguar invoked the gods of the cardinal directions, but Sky Knife didn't listen. He let the booming voice of Stone Jaguar rush past him.

"It is time!" shouted Stone Jaguar when he had finished the invocation. He turned to Sky Knife. Sky Knife reached into a sack at the base of the altar and pulled out a cigar. He concentrated on it, recalling the feeling of calling fire to his hands. For a long moment, nothing happened. Sky Knife took a deep breath and tried again.

The tip of the cigar burst into flames. Sky Knife laid it on the altar quickly and stepped back. Stone Jaguar gestured toward another sack, this one crumpled at the base of the eastern stone bowl. Sky Knife walked over, reached in, and pulled out a handful of *copal.* He threw some of it in the eastern bowl, then walked to the southern and threw in the rest.

The sickly sweet aroma of the temple glow wafted by him, mixed with the scent of *copal* and tobacco. Sky Knife's stomach, knotted in grief as it was, gurgled and turned against the smell. Sky Knife prayed he wouldn't embarrass himself on the temple, and walked back to the northern altar.

"Let the sacrifice come forth!" said Stone Jaguar. Musicians struck up the beat. Sky Knife looked at the rapidly brightening sky. He didn't want to see Jade Flute stride across the plaza in time to the drums. He didn't want to see her naked before the world. He didn't want to see Stone Jaguar plunge the knife into her belly.

But he had to look. He'd never see her again. Sky Knife gazed down on the sacrifice. It helped a little to think of her only as the sacrifice and not as Jade Flute, but not much.

Flowers had been plaited into her hair, and she was swathed in blue cotton as befitted the sacrifice. She walked slowly and held her head high. Sky Knife's throat swelled with pride and sadness.

Jade Flute climbed the thirty-six steps without hesitation. She shed the lengths of cotton until she stood naked upon the temple platform. Sky Knife flushed with embarrassment but didn't look away. Jade Flute noticed his stare and frowned.

Stone Jaguar pointed toward the altar. Jade Flute tossed her head and glared at him but obeyed. She walked to the altar and lay down upon it. The four attendants pinned her there.

Stone Jaguar held the Hand of God over his head. It glowed frightfully, brilliantly blue. Sky Knife tensed, his knees threatening to give way beneath him at any moment.

"Hold!" shouted someone from the plaza.

Stone Jaguar hesitated. Sky Knife rushed forward in surprise. Who would make noise at such an unlucky time?

Red Spider stood in the center of the plaza. Around him, the rest of the people shrank away, unwilling to invite attention to themselves if the gods of ill luck noticed Red Spider's outrageous display of gall.

"You!" said Stone Jaguar. "I should have known you were behind all of this. Now it's over—this sacrifice shall return Tikal to glory and luck."

"Never!" said Red Spider. "I know why Storm Cloud—and you—decided upon her as a sacrifice. The gods do not appreciate such deviousness."

"You do not know what the gods want," said Stone Jaguar. "You are not a priest here."

"Yet I am a magician and a warrior," said Red Spider. "And I want this woman. I will stop you if I can. The Feathered Serpent will stand with me."

Once again, Stone Jaguar raised the blade above Jade Flute. She tensed and trembled, her eyes following the movement of the blade. A tear slid down her cheek and trickled into her ear.

Sky Knife's heart went out to her. Like all the other sacrifices, she was afraid. He wanted to rush forward, to offer himself in her place, to do anything to make her trial easier.

"No!" shouted Red Spider.

Something slammed into Sky Knife from the side and knocked him down. He lay on his back a long moment, staring at the brightening sky, while a great weight pressed him against the stones of the temple. He couldn't move. Panic crept into his thoughts.

Then it was gone. Sky Knife sat up quickly. The four attendants ran down the steps screaming and batting at something Sky Knife couldn't see.

Stone Jaguar stood in the center of the temple platform, arms upraised. His cloak fluttered about him, blown by a strong wind that rushed up the temple steps and swirled around the summit. The wind moaned like the dead in Xibalba. The sound cut through Sky Knife's nerves. He trembled uncontrollably at the shrieking of the gale.

A blue haze surrounded Stone Jaguar. He thrust the Hand of God out before him and sketched an outline in the air. Water slapped Sky Knife in the face.

Sky Knife wiped the water away and turned his back to Stone Jaguar. Water rained outwards from Stone Jaguar toward Red Spider, who stood in the center of a circle of green light. Sky Knife inched his way forward on hands and knees toward Jade Flute, who lay still on the altar.

Sky Knife got to the altar and reached a shaky hand up to touch Jade Flute's arm. She jerked and screamed.

"It's me!" Sky Knife shouted over the gale. "Sky Knife!"

Jade Flute must have heard him. She didn't hesitate, but rolled toward him and off the altar. Sky Knife caught her around the waist and held her tightly against the wind and the driving rain. Jade Flute shook and sobbed into Sky Knife's shoulder. He trembled, too, but held her close and prayed the battle would be over soon.

Sky Knife prayed, but didn't know what outcome to pray for. If Stone Jaguar won, Jade Flute died. If Red Spider won, Jade Flute would be lost to him. But at least then she would be alive.

Sky Knife hated to pray for victory for Red Spider, but he couldn't pray for Stone Jaguar.

The wind died down suddenly. Sky Knife raised his head above the altar. Red Spider knelt in the plaza, hands clutched to his abdomen. The green circle was gone.

"Die, bringer of bad luck," said Stone Jaguar. "And take your Feathered Serpent with you. He has no power here."

Red Spider crawled a few feet away from the pyramid. Sky Knife swallowed hard at the effort it cost the man. Blood ran from Red Spider's nose and ears and from under his fingernails. Each time he moved, his face contorted in agony.

Stone Jaguar laughed. His laugh, coming from behind the mask, roared forth in deep, thunderous peals that made Sky Knife shiver anew.

"Crawl away, *magician*," said Stone Jaguar. "Your evil days are finished."

One of Red Spider's attendants came forward and would have helped him, but Red Spider waved him away. The Teotihuacano merchant continued to inch his way off the plaza by dragging himself with hands and elbows.

Sky Knife turned to Stone Jaguar. Without attendants, he couldn't complete the sacrifice. At least, Sky Knife hoped he couldn't.

Stone Jaguar stared down at Sky Knife and Jade Flute. "It's too late for this morning," he said. "The sun has touched the horizon without being fed her heart."

Stone Jaguar stepped down off the temple and strode down the steps, across the plaza. The few people who remained scattered before him.

Sky Knife sank back on his haunches and held Jade Flute tightly. If he had any say in it, he knew he'd never let her go.

# 20

››››››

Sky Knife watched as the last few people in the plaza hurried away. Only Bone Splinter remained.

Sky Knife sighed and stood. Jade Flute stayed hunched down at his feet. Sky Knife untwisted the knot in his skirt and let it drop to his ankles, leaving him clad only in his blue loincloth. He stepped out of the skirt, bent down, and picked it up.

The skirt was wet from the rain and heavy. Sky Knife held it out to Jade Flute. "Here," he said. "You can wear this until you get back to the temple."

Jade Flute snatched the skirt and slipped it over her head. She gathered it under her arms and twisted it into a knot similar to the one Sky Knife had used. She stood. The skirt covered her from her chest almost to her knees. On impulse, Sky Knife removed his jade necklace and looped it over Jade Flute's head.

Jade Flute smiled, but tears flooded her eyes again. "Thank you," she said. "But I suppose I can only wear it until tomorrow."

Sky Knife put an arm around her shoulders and Jade Flute leaned against him. "Perhaps," he said. "But maybe I can talk Stone Jaguar out of another sacrifice. There is just too much going on—I don't believe a simple sacrifice is going to help Tikal."

"I don't want to die," said Jade Flute. "I thought I could do my duty to my family and my city, but . . ." Jade Flute's voice dropped to a whisper and she trembled. "But when I saw the blade, I didn't want it to happen. The gods won't find me acceptable—I'm afraid."

"They all are," said Sky Knife. He led her around the altar and down the steps. Bone Splinter stood, arms folded across his chest, at the base of the pyramid.

"I'll take her back to the temple," said Sky Knife.

Bone Splinter nodded.

Jade Flute pulled away. "No," she said. "I don't want to go back there."

"Why not?" asked Sky Knife.

Jade Flute spat. "They wanted me to be the sacrifice because they would rather see me dead than alive and unmarried."

"Then become a nun," said Bone Splinter, "and you will never have to marry."

"I don't want to be a nun," said Jade Flute. "I've lived with them. I know what their lives are like. Pray, pray, pray. That's all they do. They stay shut up in their temple and talk to Ix Chel."

"Then what do you want?" asked Sky Knife.

Jade Flute pulled away slightly and looked up at him. "I want a husband who wants me because I'm Jade Flute, and not because my aunt's husband is the king."

"It may be difficult to find a man like that," said Bone Splinter. "Many men will want to marry into the family of the king."

"I know," said Jade Flute.

Sky Knife hated himself for asking, but he did. "What about Red Spider?"

Jade Flute sneered. "He wanted me to be a prize to take back home to Teotihuacan. He petitioned Storm Cloud for me. But I don't want to marry a foreigner. I said so to Storm Cloud. I will marry a man of Tikal."

Bone Splinter laughed. "Then who will you marry?"

Jade Flute glanced at Sky Knife and dropped her gaze. "I don't know," she said. She sounded thoughtful.

"Well," said Sky Knife. His voice cracked with nervousness and his heart beat wildly against his ribs. Did Jade Flute consider him an eligible suitor? When dozens of others, more wise, more learned, more wealthy than he had failed? "If you won't go to the temple, where will you go?"

"Oh, I suppose I'll go back," said Jade Flute softly. She gazed west toward the temple in the distance. "I really have nowhere else to go. And it will only be until tomorrow anyway."

Sky Knife didn't know what to say to that. He couldn't promise Jade Flute she wouldn't die tomorrow as a sacrifice. He could only try to convince Stone Jaguar to choose another.

Jade Flute stepped away from Sky Knife and took several steps toward the temple. She hesitated slightly, and her shoulders shook. Sky Knife went to her and put an arm around her shoulders. Jade Flute buried her face in his shoulder and sobbed.

"Come," said Sky Knife softly. He led her away toward the temple of Ix Chel. Bone Splinter followed them.

Sky Knife didn't hurry to cross the city. He didn't want to leave Jade Flute, but he'd have to as soon as he'd delivered her back to Turtle Nest.

They reached the temple far too quickly. Jade Flute stepped away from Sky Knife as soon as they reached the patio of the temple. She walked ahead of him, back straight, without looking back.

Sky Knife followed her into the common room. Turtle Nest was there, along with several other nuns and Jade Flute's servant, Mouse-in-the-Corn.

Mouse-in-the-Corn rushed to Jade Flute but Jade Flute brushed her away. Turtle Nest stood.

"So, our sister did not please the gods?" she asked.

"She did," said Sky Knife, almost choking on the words.

"But Red Spider attacked Stone Jaguar with sorcery, and the duel was not finished until after dawn. Too late for the sacrifice."

"Stone Jaguar won, of course," said Turtle Nest. "So the sacrifice will happen tomorrow morning?"

"Perhaps," said Sky Knife. He did not add, *not if I can help it*, but Turtle Nest seemed to hear the words anyway.

She smiled. "I see. Well, many things can happen between now and tomorrow's dawn." She turned to her nuns. "Take Jade Flute to her room. She will spend the day praying and preparing herself for tomorrow." The nuns led Jade Flute away. Sky Knife watched her go, but she didn't look back.

Sky Knife turned to go. "Wait," said Turtle Nest. Sky Knife turned to her. "An aborted sacrifice is the worst news you could bring," she said. "Bad luck piles on bad luck."

"We could hardly have any more," said Sky Knife.

Turtle Nest sighed. "You must discover who is behind this soon," she said. "Or there will be no one left in Tikal for Storm Cloud to rule. Merchants and craftspeople are leaving—in small numbers for the moment—and even some of my nuns have left the temple."

That caught Sky Knife's attention. For a nun to leave the temple was the same as death. Her family would not take her back, nor would the temple. She might find a place in another city, but a faithless nun was not a person other people wanted around. A nun who left the temple asked for a short, brutal life among strangers. That several nuns had left the temple meant they preferred taking such a terrible chance rather than trust to Ix Chel to protect them.

"The city will survive," said Bone Splinter. "And the king. Sky Knife will perform his duty."

Sky Knife wished Bone Splinter hadn't said that—the warrior had more faith in Sky Knife than Sky Knife had in himself. Turtle Nest nodded and left the room.

Sky Knife turned back to the doorway. A feather-light touch

on his arm stopped him. He looked over. Mouse-in-the-Corn stood beside him, eyes downcast. She appeared nervous.

"Yes?" asked Sky Knife gently.

"You said . . . you said you wanted to know if I knew anything," said Mouse-in-the-Corn. Her accent was thick and it was difficult for Sky Knife to understand her.

"What do you know?" he asked.

"Nothing," she said. "But I heard from the cook that something is happening in the fields. Something strange. She said she hadn't been able to get the food she needs to feed the nuns."

Mouse-in-the-Corn fell silent and stepped back. Sky Knife nodded to her. "Thank you," he said.

Sky Knife and Bone Splinter left the temple.

"What do you think?" asked Sky Knife. "Shall we go to the fields?"

Bone Splinter frowned. "Priests and warriors do not go to the fields," he said. "The fields are for peasants."

"If that's where our answer lies, then we go," said Sky Knife.

"She's just a servant," said Bone Splinter. "She doesn't know anything about what's going on."

"That's what priests and warriors like to think," said Sky Knife. "But if the cook here has noticed something strange, perhaps the cooks at the acropolis have noticed as well. It won't hurt to ask."

Bone Splinter said nothing, but his frown spoke for him.

# 21

›››››

Sky Knife hurried back to his quarters at the acropolis. Now that he was no longer a representative of the gods, he could return to being just a man. He knelt down by the bench that served him as a bed and reached underneath it for his pot of blue paint.

The *chic-chac* squeezed his throat tightly. Sky Knife coughed and put his hands to his throat in alarm. Why would the serpent harm him now?

As soon as Sky Knife touched it, the serpent relaxed. Sky Knife waited a few tense seconds before he reached under the bench again. The *chic-chac* squeezed his throat.

Sky Knife stood and backed away from the bench. The serpent had to be warning him about some danger.

"Bone Splinter!" he called.

The tall man was behind him in a moment. "Yes?"

"For some reason, the *chic-chac* doesn't want me to put my hand under the bench for the paint pot," said Sky Knife, his voice high and nervous. "What do you think it means?"

"I don't know," said Bone Splinter. He knelt by the bench

and looked underneath. "Itzamna!" Bone Splinter stood and backed away from the bench quickly.

"What?" asked Sky Knife. He got no further. From under the bench came a long brown and black serpent with the diamond pattern on its back. Yellow Chin.

Sky Knife backed out of his quarters and Bone Splinter followed. Yellow Chin slithered toward them.

"The fire," said Bone Splinter. "Get behind the fire."

Sky Knife hurried around the firepit in the center of the room. Bone Splinter grabbed a half-consumed stick from the fire and jabbed it toward the approaching serpent.

Yellow Chin raised its head and dodged the flaming stick. Sky Knife expected it to retreat from the fire, but the serpent tried to approach again. Bone Splinter thrust the stick toward the serpent a second time. The serpent rolled away. Sky Knife blinked, unbelieving—serpents did not *roll!* But this one did. It stopped rolling once it was out of the way of Bone Splinter's stick.

Yellow Chin raised its head again and stared at Bone Splinter, then Sky Knife. It hesitated a moment, then slithered straight toward Sky Knife, completely disregarding Bone Splinter's attempts to ward it off.

Sky Knife yelped and jumped up onto a bench. Yellow Chin reached the floor beneath the bench more quickly than Sky Knife believed a snake could move. Yellow Chin's head peered up over the rim of the bench. It opened its mouth. Yellow fangs glistened wetly in the faint light in the room.

Bone Splinter leaped forward and grabbed the serpent by the base of the throat. Yellow Chin thrashed, tongue licking the air, but Bone Splinter did not let go. A dull snap, and Yellow Chin went limp except for a tremor in the tip of its tail. Bone Splinter stood holding the body of the serpent, but he did not let it go.

"What? How?" asked Sky Knife. He jumped down off the bench. "That's no true serpent!"

"Like the jaguar," said Bone Splinter. "Someone has called up an evil spirit in the form of a true animal."

"Who could do such a thing?" Sky Knife stepped off the bench carefully.

"Not Red Spider, unless he did this before the sacrifice this morning," said Bone Splinter. Bone Splinter threw the body into the fire. The fire popped and sizzled as it consumed the offering. Sky Knife stepped back from the foul odor of the fire's smoke. The fire burned brightly yellow, then abruptly went out.

"*Bolon ti ku,*" whispered Sky Knife through clenched teeth. He held out his hands and concentrated on fire. Energy buzzed through him, causing goose bumps to raise over his arms and shoulders.

Fire leapt from his hands to the firepit and the flames took hold in the wood once again. Bone Splinter's eyebrows shot up. "Impressive," he said.

"A waste," said Stone Jaguar from the doorway to the inner rooms. "Why did you do that?"

Sky Knife faltered at the harsh tone in Stone Jaguar's voice. "I . . . I don't know," he said.

"Be careful of your power," said Stone Jaguar a bit more calmly. "You're still new to it. You'll need to practice a great deal before the power becomes easy for you to control. Until then, you should never use your abilities without me to guide you."

"Of course," said Sky Knife. "I am sorry."

Stone Jaguar smiled. He walked over to Sky Knife and put a hand on the younger man's shoulder. "Well, perhaps I did something like that, too, when I was a new priest."

Sky Knife ducked his head in embarrassment.

"Perhaps you would like to know what caused the fire to go out," said Bone Splinter.

Stone Jaguar said, "Is it important?" though he didn't look at Bone Splinter.

"Yellow Chin," said Sky Knife. "He was in my room. He

followed me out here and tried to attack me. Bone Splinter killed him."

Stone Jaguar frowned. "Yellow Chin again? Where does Cizin get this kind of power?"

"I don't think it's Cizin," said Sky Knife. "We found green obsidian in the plaza—on the temple, even. I think Red Spider—and probably several others—have more planned. But I don't know what."

"Perhaps some of Red Spider's assistants are more than they seem," said Bone Splinter.

Stone Jaguar glanced at the warrior. He nodded. "Possible," he said. "But Red Spider will die before the sun sets. His assistants will have to manage whatever they have planned without him."

"If Red Spider is the man behind our bad luck," said Bone Splinter.

Stone Jaguar grunted and walked toward the doorway.

"Wait," said Sky Knife. Stone Jaguar turned to him but said nothing.

"Does . . . does there have to be a sacrifice tomorrow morning?" asked Sky Knife. The question was awkward, but Sky Knife didn't know if he'd have a chance to ask again.

"You haven't the rank to discuss sacrifices with me," said Stone Jaguar.

"But Jade Flute . . ."

Stone Jaguar spat toward the fire. "She is an insolent girl. Let the gods deal with her."

Anger flared up in Sky Knife's heart. Stone Jaguar didn't care about Jade Flute being a good sacrifice for Tikal—he wanted her dead. "She's not a volunteer," said Sky Knife. "You should have a volunteer for the sacrifice."

Stone Jaguar strode forward and slapped Sky Knife across the face. Sky Knife yelped at the unexpected force of Stone Jaguar's blow. His ears rang with the impact.

Sky Knife slipped to his knees. Someone moved in front of him and he flinched.

"Do not touch him again," said Bone Splinter. "Or I will kill you, priest or no. He has the king's grace."

"He is just a boy, and under my command," said Stone Jaguar. "And just as insolent as the girl he's mooning over."

"Even so," said Bone Splinter. "Do not touch him again."

Sky Knife shivered at the cold, flat tone in Bone Splinter's voice. There was no anger, no hate, no fear. Just a kind of calm finality. Sky Knife had no doubt that Bone Splinter would do his best to carry out his threat.

"Bah," said Stone Jaguar. "Out of my sight, both of you. Jade Flute is just a girl. There are hundreds more in the city, all just as pretty and just as suitable. Choose another. Jade Flute dies at dawn tomorrow. Storm Cloud has agreed."

Sky Knife said nothing as the older priest left the room, but his heart sank. He had tried, but it hadn't been enough.

Bone Splinter put a hand under Sky Knife's elbow and helped him stand. The tall man said nothing.

Sky Knife took a deep breath. "Time to talk to the cooks, I think," he said. He plunged into the darkness of the inner corridors of the acropolis, wound his way around to the entrance to the courtyard at the back, where the temple servants ground corn and cooked meals for the priests and attendants of the temple.

Several of the servant women were out in the courtyard, grinding corn on their granite *metates*. They glanced up nervously as Sky Knife approached. He knelt down by one woman, an older woman whose hair was streaked with gray, and whose corn-flour-covered hands were wrinkled with age.

"Good morning," he said. The woman ducked her head and mumbled something back.

"I'd like to ask you a question," said Sky Knife. "I'd like to know if you've heard of anything strange happening in the fields. Something that would prevent food from coming into the city."

"No, nothing," said the woman. "Please, sir, I haven't done anything."

Sky Knife was alarmed at the fear in the woman's voice. Was she merely afraid because he belonged to the temple? Priests were awesome—Sky Knife remembered being in abject terror the first time he'd been in the same room as Stone Jaguar—but surely this woman would be used to priests.

"What's wrong?" he asked. "I know you haven't done anything. I just want to know if you've heard any rumors about what's happening in the fields."

"Please, sir, I have to get back to the corn," the woman said.

Sky Knife stood and backed away from the woman. As soon as he got several feet away, the woman began grinding corn again. She did not look at him or acknowledge his presence in any way.

Sky Knife considered the rest of the servants in the courtyard. All of them seemed just as frightened as the first. In fact, they were acting just like Mouse-in-the-Corn.

Itzamna! If the servants couldn't trust him because he had rank and they didn't, how could he expect them to tell him anything?

Sky Knife retreated to the acropolis and sat down on the steps. Bone Splinter climbed the steps and stood at the top, staring down at those in the courtyard in a calm—but disconcerting—manner, judging by the renewed vigor in the women's grinding.

One of the women looked up from her work and screamed. Sky Knife tried to see what had frightened her. The source of the woman's alarm was not hard to discern.

Coming *over* the wall that surrounded the courtyard was another Yellow Chin. Two of them. No, three.

The serpents slid over the wall and dropped to the dirt of

the courtyard. Each raised its head and looked around. Three forked tongues tasted the air.

"Four of them in one morning," said Bone Splinter. "Let's hope four is all there is—I'd hate to think that someone has called nine."

Sky Knife shuddered. He didn't want to face three more of the deadly serpents, let alone eight more.

The serpents' gazes locked on Sky Knife, and the dingy-colored snakes slithered forward. Sky Knife backed up a step, but stopped. He would not run from Yellow Chin. Not again.

Something dropped to the dust at Sky Knife's feet and he jumped. A brightly colored serpent slithered toward the nearest Yellow Chin: the *chic-chac*.

Sky Knife retreated to the nearest *metate* and picked up the round *mano* used to grind on it. The *mano* was heavy and gritty with corn meal. Sky Knife approached the largest of the evil serpents.

The Yellow Chin hissed at him and lunged. Sky Knife dodged and threw the *mano* toward the serpent. The *mano* thunked to the ground on the other side of the snake. The snake paid no attention to the rock and slithered toward him again. Sky Knife ran to another *metate* and picked up the *mano* there. He turned to face the serpent.

Yellow Chin approached steadily and climbed up on the *metate*. Sky Knife slammed the *mano* down onto the serpent and jumped away.

The serpent thrashed about on the *metate*, its red blood leaking out into the corn meal. Its tail quivered, but the serpent went nowhere. Its spine had been crushed halfway down its back. The serpent opened its mouth and hissed toward Sky Knife.

Sky Knife picked up another *mano* and approached the Yellow Chin warily. The serpent kept its head toward him, mouth open, fangs bared.

Sky Knife crammed the *mano* into the serpent's mouth and crushed it against the granite *metate*. He pulled away the *mano*. The serpent lay limp across the stone, blood dripping from its disfigured head.

Sky Knife turned in time to see Bone Splinter smash a second serpent's head against the stone of the courtyard. He looked anxiously around for the third serpent. It was nowhere to be seen. Nor was the *chic-chac*.

Alarmed, and worried for the little rainbow serpent's safety, Sky Knife jogged forward, *mano* still in hand. "Where's the other one?" he asked Bone Splinter.

The warrior shrugged. "I wasn't paying attention," he said.

Sky Knife walked to the wall and followed it to a weed-infested corner. There, under a small flowering bush, lay the Yellow Chin, dead, and the *chic-chac*. Sky Knife dropped the *mano*, knelt down, and picked up the rainbow serpent carefully.

Two large puncture wounds marred the *chic-chac*'s back. It trembled and breathed heavily as if in great pain. Sky Knife stroked it and the *chic-chac* caressed his hand with its tongue.

"It is all right?" asked Bone Splinter.

"I don't think so," said Sky Knife. He choked back a sob. A rainbow serpent was not like an ordinary snake—perhaps it would be able to resist the poison of the Yellow Chin.

Sky Knife walked back to the acropolis steps and sat down. The *chic-chac* curled up in the palm of his hand. Sky Knife stroked it carefully.

Bone Splinter sat down beside him. In the courtyard, the women stood as far as possible from the place where the serpents had appeared and did not return to their corn.

"What's going on here?" demanded Stone Jaguar. "Why aren't you women working?"

The women stared at Stone Jaguar, fear in their faces, but remained where they were.

"We were attacked," said Sky Knife. "Three Yellow Chins came over the wall."

Stone Jaguar stepped down into the courtyard and examined the body of the Yellow Chin Sky Knife had killed. "Three, you say?" he asked.

"Yes," said Sky Knife. "I killed one, and Bone Splinter killed one. The *chic-chac* killed the other."

Stone Jaguar straightened and turned to Sky Knife. "A rainbow serpent is harmless," he said.

"Not, apparently, to a Yellow Chin," said Bone Splinter. "Though the *chic-chac* may die."

Stone Jaguar strode forward and peered down at the little snake. "I wouldn't think anything could kill the good luck of a rainbow serpent," he said. "If the *chic-chac* dies, we may as well give up."

"It won't die," said Sky Knife, more in hope than because he believed it.

"Let's pray that it doesn't," said Stone Jaguar. "I'll get one of the attendants we've got left to clear the serpents' bodies from the courtyard. And we'll have to throw out all the corn that was ground this morning. It will have too much bad luck clinging to it to be edible."

Stone Jaguar disappeared into the acropolis. The women fled the courtyard. Sky Knife stayed and petted the rainbow serpent. His tears ran down his face and wetted the serpent's skin, making it glisten like jewels in the late morning sun.

# 22

›››››

Sky Knife held the serpent for a few minutes while it trembled. He didn't know what to do. He couldn't leave it behind, but could he do his duty while carrying a serpent in the palm of his hand?

The *chic-chac* seemed to sense his discomfort. It slowly crawled out of his palm to his wrist. It rested and breathed rapidly for a time. Then it continued toward his elbow. The slow, pain-ridden way it moved broke Sky Knife's heart.

The serpent raised its head a fraction of an inch as if it intended to crawl up his arm to Sky Knife's neck. But the serpent dropped its head down after a moment and took a long, deep breath. To Sky Knife, the *chic-chac* seemed exhausted.

"Bone Splinter, help me," he said.

Sky Knife lifted the serpent's tail carefully. Bone Splinter reached around Sky Knife's shoulders and gently grasped the front half of its body. Together, they picked up the serpent and wrapped it around Sky Knife's neck.

"Now what?" asked Bone Splinter as he released the serpent.

Sky Knife stroked the serpent a moment. It relaxed against

his neck and stopped trembling. "The fields," he said. "If the servants don't know, or won't say, we have to go see for ourselves."

Bone Splinter said nothing.

Sky Knife stood and walked out of the side entrance to the courtyard. Outside, a small crowd had gathered. No doubt the women had told everyone they met about the evil spirits disguised as snakes that had attacked them and disturbed their work.

The people in the crowd were a mixed bunch—most were servants and wore the undyed cotton of the unranked. But several merchants and craftspeople also stood in the crowd. Sky Knife walked away from the acropolis and the people parted before him. One woman reached out to touch Sky Knife, but Bone Splinter batted her hand away.

The awe in the faces of the crowd spooked Sky Knife. He wanted to run away, but priests did not run like children. Sky Knife threw back his shoulders and walked steadily, though his spine crawled with the thought of dozens of eyes on him.

The crowd did not follow them very far. Sky Knife had walked hardly the length of the plaza before the people fell away and dispersed. He sighed with relief and stopped.

The midday sun was bright and hot. Sky Knife shaded his eyes with a hand and debated which way to go first. The *milpas* of the farmers of Tikal completely surrounded the city, but the greatest concentration of them were to the south.

Sky Knife turned his feet toward the south and walked among the smaller temples that clustered around the great plaza and the acropolis of the priests of Itzamna. Many gods besides Itzamna had temples in the city, some of them staffed with priests and attendants, but no other god had a pyramid as fine or priests as rich and learned as Itzamna. Some of the temples were cracked and weeds had obscured much of their original facework.

A tree grew from the steps of one small structure. Sky Knife had watched the tree grow for years, curious about what god had once been worshipped at the temple and how he felt about a tree taking root in his temple. But no one worshipped there now, and the tree grew taller each year without being disturbed. Apparently, the god did not mind.

Something moved ahead, just out of sight in a grove of trees. It was too small to be a person. Sky Knife froze, visions of dozens of Yellow Chin serpents coming for him creeping into his thoughts.

"What?" asked Bone Splinter.

"There, in the trees," said Sky Knife. "Something moved."

"Somebody must be there."

"No," said Sky Knife. "It wasn't a person."

"No animals are out at midday," said Bone Splinter. "It has to be a person. Perhaps one of Red Spider's people, watching you."

"No," Sky Knife insisted. He moved forward slowly, prepared to run if necessary, aware he couldn't outrun an animal in the open.

"Wait," said Bone Splinter. "Stay behind me."

Bone Splinter moved ahead of Sky Knife. He walked toward the trees slowly, Sky Knife just behind and to the right of him.

Something rustled in the undergrowth. Sky Knife froze. Bone Splinter walked forward another step.

The something limped out into the open. It was a small animal, not even as tall as Sky Knife's knee. Its reddish coat looked dull and wiry in the bright sunlight: a coati. Sky Knife relaxed for a moment; coati were harmless enough.

But coati came out only at night. Why would this one be abroad in the daylight? Especially out in the open, in the city of Tikal. The animal had to be possessed by an evil spirit.

Sky Knife tensed, not sure what to expect. With sorcery, normal rules did not apply. Serpents could roll and attack in groups. Jaguars could bleed butterflies out of their wounds.

There was no reason to assume this coati meant no harm. Not today.

Something about the animal appealed to Sky Knife, though. Its eyes seemed to seek out his. Behind its eyes was a spirit that spoke to Sky Knife in the depths of his soul, like the deep sound of water moving in the cave under the northern acropolis. This was no ordinary coati, but suddenly, Sky Knife did not doubt its intentions.

"Wait," he said to Bone Splinter. "It won't harm me."

"Don't be a fool, Sky Knife," said Bone Splinter. "Remember the Yellow Chin."

"I know this animal," Sky Knife insisted. "I'm sure I do." Sky Knife moved in closer. The coati blinked its amber eyes and stared at him down its long snout. It halted and lifted its right foreleg off the ground momentarily before putting the paw down and letting weight rest upon it.

"It's hurt," said Sky Knife.

"Then it will be dangerous," said the warrior.

"No," said Sky Knife in a whisper. He knelt beside Bone Splinter and watched the coati. It panted in the heat, but did not come any closer.

Sweat trickled down Sky Knife's face. The coati was in the meager shade of the trees, while he sat full in the noontime sun. For some reason he couldn't name, he knew the coati was important. But he didn't understand how.

"Go away," said Bone Splinter. He waved his arms toward the wounded animal. It jumped and backed away a few feet.

"No," said Sky Knife, climbing to his feet.

"It's got you in a spell," said Bone Splinter. "Let me handle it."

The coati circled around Bone Splinter and tried to approach Sky Knife again. Its tail was down between its legs and it panted heavily.

Bone Splinter ran for the coati, but it leaped aside and dashed for Sky Knife. Before he could react, the coati had run to his feet and leaned its weight against his legs. It looked up at him beseechingly.

"What?" he asked it.

"Careful," said Bone Splinter. He walked forward slowly. "It might bite."

"I don't think so," said Sky Knife. He knelt down and looked more closely at the coati. There was a wound in its shoulder. In fact, right about in the place where Sky Knife had been stabbed the day before by Nine Dog.

A cold feeling clutched Sky Knife's gut. Quickly, he grabbed the coati and examined its knees and elbows. Scabs coated fresh scrapes on them, just like Sky Knife's.

Oh, Itzamna. It was worse than he ever dreamed it could be.

"It's my *nagual*," said Sky Knife. His voice shook uncontrollably. His *nagual*, his spirit-animal, was a coati. How could he not have understood earlier?

Every person had a *nagual*, an individual animal that the Totilme'iletik kept safe in a special corral in the corners of the world. If a person were evil, the Totilme'iletik might release his *nagual* to suffer danger and death like any other animal of the forest. As long as a person obeyed the gods, though, his *nagual* remained safe in the corral.

Someone had loosed Sky Knife's own particular spirit animal from the safety it had known since Sky Knife had been born. Either Sky Knife had lost the protection of the Totilme'iletik for some reason, or the animal had been stolen from them.

"It's your *what?*" asked Bone Splinter. "That's not possible." The tall man seemed shaken.

The coati pressed against Sky Knife. He ran his fingers through its coarse fur. Bone Splinter knelt beside him.

"Now what?" asked the warrior. He stared at the wound in the coati's shoulder. "If this is your *nagual*, you cannot put it or yourself in further danger. You must go back to the acropolis. Take the coati with you. Stay there where you will be safe."

"I'm safe with you, aren't I?" asked Sky Knife. "Besides, I can't hide. That's probably just what the men who are behind this want. Whatever it is they're planning, they don't want me to interfere with it. They think this will stop me."

"It should."

"It won't."

Bone Splinter sighed. "So we take it with us? If you collect any more animals, we're going to look ridiculous."

"I can carry it," said Sky Knife. "But I think it will follow me anyway." He stood. The coati watched him expectantly. "Let's go," he said.

A scream rent the air. Sky Knife turned toward the sound. A woman in a gaily patterned red and yellow dress stared in horror at an animal that stood in front of her. Sky Knife ran to the woman.

"What is it?" he asked. The animal, a small monkey, jumped toward the woman making a chik-chik noise. The woman backed away from it.

"It can't be," said the woman. "It can't!"

"Your *nagual?*" asked Sky Knife, though he knew. Oh, Itzamna—the *nagual* animals of everyone in Tikal must have been set free.

"No!" screamed the woman. She turned and ran, the monkey right behind her.

"Sky Knife," said Bone Splinter in a low voice.

"Yes?" asked Sky Knife absently. He watched the monkey run after the woman. Now, more than ever, he knew he had to complete his duty to the king and the gods. Tikal could not withstand much more bad luck. The people were now unprotected from everything. Even their spirit animals were in danger.

"Sky Knife," insisted Bone Splinter in a whisper.

"What?" asked Sky Knife. He turned to the warrior.

Bone Splinter's face was pale. His hands trembled. Before the warrior stood a large, sad-looking hoofed beast with dark fur and a long, almost pig-like, snout: a tapir. It stood as high as Sky Knife's waist. It blinked black eyes framed by long lashes.

"Your *nagual*," said Sky Knife.

"What am I to do?" asked Bone Splinter. "What can I do?"

Sky Knife was alarmed at the helpless fear in the other man's voice. "Sit down," he said sharply. "And control yourself. It looks as though everyone in Tikal is in the same predicament."

Bone Splinter sat on the steps of a crumbling pyramid. The tapir ambled up to him and laid at his feet. Bone Splinter shrank from it. Sky Knife's coati approached the tapir and sniffed its ear, then settled down beside it.

Rage filled Sky Knife, slowly at first, and then with more force. Whoever had done this was willing to sacrifice everyone in the city for something. Without the protection of the Totilme'iletik, the people were exceedingly vulnerable.

Perhaps the plan was merely to frighten everyone in Tikal. After all, if one were powerful enough to take all of the *nagual* of the citizens of Tikal away from the Totilme'iletik, surely one would be powerful enough to return them. But the populace was already frightened. What more was behind this?

Sky Knife would find out. And the next step was to go to the fields and see what had happened there.

Sky Knife glanced at the coati and the tapir. They were going to look ridiculous after all.

# 23

## ⟩⟩⟩⟩⟩

Come on," said Sky Knife. Bone Splinter glanced at him but seemed unwilling to get up. Some of Sky Knife's anger settled on the warrior. "Your *nagual* is safe for now," he said sharply. "Now we must find out how to rectify the situation."

"*Everyone's nagual* is loose," said Bone Splinter slowly and distinctly, as if Sky Knife hadn't already figured that out. "The city is doomed. All the people are doomed."

"Not as long as their *nagual* are safe," said Sky Knife, "and so far, they are. It's bad luck, but no worse than what we've had. Wasn't it evil luck when Cizin stood on the very summit of the temple? Wasn't the jaguar bad luck—and the butterflies, too? And the black rain, and the Yellow Chin—bad luck is all around us. We have to go through it and go on."

Bone Splinter grunted, a hint of a smile crossing his worried frown. "You speak like a man born to lead other men."

Sky Knife, who had been about to speak, closed his mouth in surprise. After a moment, he said, "I'm just a priest. And not even a trained one at that. I'm no leader of men."

"You're wrong," said Bone Splinter. "But," he said with a

sigh, "you're right about one thing. We have to go through the bad luck to find the good on the other side."

"Then let's go."

Bone Splinter nodded and stood. The tapir watched him with adoring eyes and clambered to its feet. Sky Knife's coati yawned and stretched, then stood and bounded toward him.

"Oh, my," said a female voice.

Sky Knife whirled to see who watched them. Jade Flute crouched behind the pyramid. In front of her stood an ocelot. Its pink nose twitched as it sniffed the air near Jade Flute.

Jade Flute was dressed in a purple gown that covered her from neck to ankles. Sky Knife's jade necklace still hung around her neck, and a shell bead choker peeked over the dress's high neckline.

"Shouldn't you be in the temple with the nuns?" asked Bone Splinter.

Jade Flute reached out and stroked the ocelot. "I never thought I'd actually *meet* it," she said. "My *nagual*, I mean. I thought it would remain with the Totilme'iletik and I'd never see it."

Sky Knife shook his head. Trust Jade Flute to find a face-to-face meeting with her spirit animal a reason to rejoice rather than despair. He'd never understand her.

"Aren't you afraid?" asked Bone Splinter. "If it comes to harm, so will you."

Jade Flute brushed her hair back over her shoulders and stared up at Bone Splinter, her manner defiant. "I'm to die to-morrow at dawn, anyway, in case you've forgotten," she said. "I don't suppose I'll come to more harm than that today."

She had a point. Still, she hadn't answered Bone Splinter's question. "Why aren't you at the temple?" asked Sky Knife.

Jade Flute frowned. "What does it matter where I go or what I do anymore? I wasn't chosen to be a perfect sacrifice. You know that and I know that. My uncle just wants rid of me. Marriage or sacrifice—it's all the same to him."

"It's not good to say such things about the king," said Sky Knife. "Even if it's true."

Jade Flute stood and spread out her hands to either side. "So punish me," she said.

Sky Knife shook his head and looked away.

"Where were you going?" asked Jade Flute. "Before you met your *nagual*, that is."

"To the fields," said Sky Knife. "Something is wrong there, and I'm going to find out what it is."

"Then I'm coming, too."

"You're going back to the temple," said Bone Splinter. "Women of your rank don't go to the fields."

"You're going."

"I am with him, and he is on a mission from the king," said Bone Splinter. "That's different."

Jade Flute walked up to Bone Splinter. She barely stood as tall as his chest. "Well, I'm different, too," she said. "No one tells me what to do today. I'll die tomorrow because it's my duty, but today, no one but I say what I will do."

"You are disrespectful," said Bone Splinter.

"You're tall," she said.

That struck Sky Knife as funny and he barked out a laugh. Embarrassed, he tried to keep his amusement to himself, but he couldn't. The laughter rolled out of him until tears streamed down his face.

"Let her come," he said when he was able to talk again. Bone Splinter turned away, but Jade Flute smiled. Sky Knife walked toward the fields to the south. The tapir and the coati ambled along behind him and Bone Splinter, apparently content. At least the coati no longer limped and the tapir didn't look quite as dour—a good trick for a tapir. Jade Flute and her ocelot trotted along quite happily.

Jade Flute hummed a tune as they walked. Sky Knife didn't look back at her, but her voice was enough to make him flush hot and cold. His knees felt weak. What was it about this woman that made him feel this way? Sky Knife cursed the fact she'd be taken from him at dawn. He'd never have a chance to find out more about her.

The fields to the south of Tikal were dry, only the brown stubble of the corn stalks remaining this long after the harvest. Burned trunks of dead trees poked up out of the earth of the *milpa*. Bright green weeds and the hardy *achiote*, a small shrub, dotted the otherwise brown fields. All around the *milpa*, just outside the brush fence that surrounded it, the trees of the forest crowded as if waiting for a chance to capture the fields from the farmers.

Several houses sat in a cleared area, a low stone wall marking the boundary between civilization and jungle. Inside the wall, between the houses, were several hollow logs. The friendly *colecab* buzzed around them, intent on their honey. *Manos* and *metates* sat by the houses, unused.

The houses had been made in the traditional *chuyche* style: poles had been set in the ground and bound together with the sturdy *anicab* vine. Thatch formed a pointed, rainproof roof. Sky Knife had grown up in such a house. They were mustier and draftier than stone buildings, but they were more familiar. Sky Knife felt a pang of homesickness and realized how much he missed living with his family. A house like this was meant for families, for children and laughter.

Sky Knife stepped up to the nearest house and brushed away a curious *colecab*. "Hello?" he called out.

A breeze rustled the thatch of the house roof, but no other sound came from the area.

"Where is everyone?" asked Bone Splinter. "Have the peasants fled the bad luck like the merchants?"

Doubt gnawed at Sky Knife. "I don't think so," he said. "A merchant is free to walk away from a city, but a farmer would not leave his land. My father wouldn't have."

"Well, they're not here."

Sky Knife stepped up into one of the houses. The interior

was dark; no fire had been laid in the firepit in the center of the one-room structure. A drying rack leaned against a wall, one strip of meat still clinging to it. The meat strip was dry and old. Sky Knife looked up over the rim of the *peten*, the flat plate woven from the *anicab* vine. Fruit and spices were piled on the *peten* to keep it from rats. The fruit was wrinkled and overripe.

Sky Knife knelt by the firepit in the center of the room. A few half-consumed sticks lay at the bottom, along with a small pile of ash. Sky Knife touched the ashes. They were cold.

Nothing seemed out of order. The family's possessions were stacked along the walls neatly or hung from the rafters overhead on other *peten* or were strapped to the rafters by vines. The pungent smell of crushed chiles hung in the air.

Sky Knife got up and walked back outside.

Bone Splinter emerged from another house. A few of the friendly bees encircled him. The warrior ignored them. "No one lived here," he said. "And there's a pile of overturned dirt on the floor. Probably where they lived before the house you were in."

Sky Knife nodded. It was customary for peasants to bury their dead underneath their houses, but few families chose to live in a house where someone had been buried. Some thought it was unlucky, though not everyone believed that.

"Oh, look," said Jade Flute. She knelt down in a corner of the dirt yard. Sky Knife walked over to see what had caught her eye.

A simple cornhusk doll lay crumpled in the dirt. Jade Flute picked it up gingerly, but the dried husk was too fragile. It disintegrated in her hands and drifted back down to earth in tiny fragments.

"I used to play with one just like that," said Jade Flute. "I never thought that the peasant girls did the same things I did. I never thought about them at all."

"It looks like they've been gone a while," said Sky Knife, "which can't be, or we'd have heard rumors of it before now.

Besides, if this house had been deserted for any length of time, the jungle would have crept up around it."

Jade Flute continued to stare at the remains of the doll. "I wonder who she was," she said.

"What?" asked Bone Splinter.

"The girl who loved this doll," said Jade Flute. "I wonder where she is now."

"I wish I knew," said Sky Knife. He walked around the rest of the cleared lot. *Manos* and *metates* sat squarely in place, their surfaces worn smooth from extended use. A cracked pot lay discarded on the far side of the house.

"Well," said Sky Knife, "let's check some other places. Surely the peasants can't *all* be gone."

Sky Knife set off farther south. A larger group of houses sat at the far side of a wide *milpa*.

"Ugh," said Jade Flute. "Worms."

Sky Knife turned to her. Large, green grubs wiggled blindly in the *milpa*. Sky Knife shuddered in disgust.

"Perhaps the peasants are fleeing the worms," said Bone Splinter.

"Or maybe the worms are more bad luck," said Sky Knife. "Perhaps they were brought here by sorcery to destroy the fields of Tikal. Perhaps someone wishes to starve the city."

"My bet is Red Spider," said Bone Splinter. "He could have done this days ago, a week ago, and no one would have noticed. No one of consequence comes out here."

"What about Nine Dog?" asked Sky Knife. His shoulder tingled where Nine Dog's blade had struck and he shivered slightly. "He did try to kill me. He may be part of the conspiracy."

"Assuming there's a conspiracy at all," said Jade Flute. "Who is Nine Dog?"

"A merchant from Monte Alban," said Bone Splinter, "who has already left the city if he knows what's good for him."

"Why would someone from Monte Alban bring us bad

luck?" asked Jade Flute. She grimaced in disgust as one of the worms wriggled near her foot. She stomped on it. She picked up her foot and wiped the bottom of her sandal on a clod of sun-dried dirt. Only a blob of green and yellow liquid remained of the worm.

"I don't know," said Sky Knife. "They have different customs, different gods. And Monte Alban is so far away."

"Not nearly as far as Teotihuacan," said Bone Splinter. "And they are always looking for a chance to expand their control. Red Spider is a better bet."

Sky Knife set off again toward the next group of houses. "Hello!" he called as he approached. The angry squawking of some monkeys in the trees was his only answer.

Sky Knife wiped sweat from his face and stepped into the *caanche*, the small kitchen garden by the house. The plants in the garden were wilted and the soil cracked and hard.

"No one here, either?" asked Bone Splinter.

"It's so sad," said Jade Flute. "All the houses empty, without people, without children playing."

Sky Knife turned to go.

"Wait!" shouted someone from the house.

Sky Knife jumped. Bone Splinter pushed Sky Knife behind him.

"Who's there?" asked Bone Splinter.

"Where did everyone go?" A short, old woman with more skin than flesh hobbled to the doorway of the house. Her sparse white hair stuck out from her head at odd angles. She blinked in the sunlight.

"Tell me where they went, Lord," she said to Bone Splinter. "I want to go with them."

Bone Splinter glanced back at Sky Knife. Sky Knife took a deep breath.

"Let us come inside," he said, "and we'll talk about what happened."

The old woman seemed not to have heard. Tears rolled

down her face. "Maybe they'll forgive me," she said. "Do you think they'll forgive me?"

"Forgive you—for what transgression?" asked Sky Knife.

"I disobeyed the gods," said the woman. "I betrayed the people." She walked back into the house. "It's all my fault," she said. "Do you think they'll forgive me?"

"Of course they will," said Sky Knife. He walked around Bone Splinter and followed the old woman into the house.

# 24

›››››

It happened at least a *uinal* ago," said the old woman. She sat on a thatch mat on one side of the cold firepit in the center of the house. Bone Splinter, Sky Knife, and Jade Flute also sat by the firepit.

"Twenty days," mused Bone Splinter. "That's time enough to plan any sort of sorcery."

"But what was it that happened?" asked Sky Knife.

"A vision," sighed the old woman. "Ah Mun came to each of the men in the night and told them he needed their services in his own *milpas*. And so the men went to serve him. The next night, Ah Mun came in our dreams again and told us women we should go, too. And take our children with us. He said we were needed in the fields of the gods."

"Then why didn't you go?" asked Bone Splinter.

The old woman put her hands over her face. "I have failed him," she said. "Our beloved Ah Mun, the soul of the corn, the giver of bounty!"

Jade Flute reached out and gently took the woman's hands down. "How did you fail him?" she asked.

"I was too proud," sobbed the woman. "I said I was too old

to work in Ah Mun's fields, that he should not expect me to serve him when there were so many younger hands to help. I was wrong! If Ah Mun finds me worthy, who am I to refuse him?" The woman grasped Jade Flute's wrists. "Tell him I am ready! Tell him I'll come if he'll forgive me. I have fasted and offered blood every night since the rest of the women left, but I have received no vision. Tell him I'm ready!"

A strange look crossed Jade Flute's face. She sat up very straight. "I will tell him," she said. "When I see him tomorrow, I shall ask him to forgive you before I ask for anything else from the rest of the gods."

The cold tone in Jade Flute's voice sent shivers up Sky Knife's spine. Jade Flute sounded as if she had not only resigned herself, but accepted her place as a sacrifice. If she accepted her duty voluntarily, she would be more powerful in her death than any bad luck plaguing Tikal.

The old woman sighed and slumped down. "Thank you, child," she said.

"And so everyone left about twenty days ago?" asked Sky Knife. "All together and all at once?"

"No," said the woman. "I have seen others go by since. I think Ah Mun is calling the farmers to him one family at a time."

"So they have left the fields in small groups, first the men, then the women," said Bone Splinter. "And gone where?"

"East," said the woman. "In the vision, Ah Mun said to go east. A guide would meet us and take us to the fields of the gods."

"And when was the last time you noticed people walking by here?" asked Sky Knife.

"Just yesterday," said the woman. "But today I have seen no one but you."

Sky Knife looked at Bone Splinter and found agreement in the other man's eyes. "East," he said. "We'd better go take a look."

"Oh," said Jade Flute. She reached for the old woman, who had slumped over onto the floor.

Sky Knife jumped up and went to the old woman's side. Her breathing was fast and shallow.

"Tell him . . . tell him I'm ready," the old woman sighed. Then she let out her breath and didn't catch it again.

"No," said Jade Flute. "Don't die."

"She said she had fasted for twenty days, and had offered blood every night," said Sky Knife. "Perhaps Ah Mun has forgiven her and finally taken her himself, since she was too weak to walk."

"You don't believe that the corn god is actually calling the peasants away?" asked Bone Splinter. "I might believe it if he had called one or two especially worthy people, but *all* the farmers? And their entire families, too?"

"Whatever happened to the others, at least this woman was faithful to Ah Mun at the end," said Sky Knife. "The others may have been misled, but that doesn't mean this woman wasn't found worthy."

"Should we bury her?" asked Jade Flute.

"We don't have the time," said Bone Splinter.

"We have to have the time," said Sky Knife. "This woman deserves a burial at least. There ought to be some hoes around here, unless the farmers took all their tools with them."

Bone Splinter stood. "I'll look. We'll have to do this quickly. Midday is already here and we have work to do."

While Bone Splinter was gone, Sky Knife and Jade Flute wrapped the old woman in a cotton blanket.

"We should bury her with something," said Jade Flute. She untied her shell bead choker and placed it inside the blanket.

The light of the sun was temporarily blotted out as Bone Splinter entered the doorway. "Here," he said. He handed a hoe to Sky Knife.

Bone Splinter struck the ground with the hoe and turned up

a clod of dirt. Sky Knife did the same. Soon, they had dug a
shallow trench.

A third hoe struck the ground. Sky Knife glanced up in surprise. Jade Flute looked back at him. "Well, Bone Splinter
didn't bring me one," she said. "I had to go find my own."

"You're going to dig?" asked Bone Splinter.

"Why not?" asked Jade Flute. "The old woman died right
beside me. It only seems right to help bury her."

"Have you ever used a hoe before?"

"Have you?"

Bone Splinter closed his mouth and said nothing. He went
back to his digging. Between the three of them, the hole was
completed quickly. Bone Splinter and Sky Knife lifted each end
of the cotton blanket and lowered the woman into the ground.
Filling in the hole took very little time.

"Come on," said Bone Splinter when the last clod of dirt
had been thrown onto the mound that marked the grave.

"I'm thirsty," said Jade Flute.

Sky Knife nodded. "We need to find some water, especially
since we're not going back to Tikal just yet."

"There are water jugs in back of the house," said Bone
Splinter.

Bone Splinter led the other two to the water jugs. The jugs
had been made from gourds. They were tied to the poles that
formed the back wall of the house. Two of them contained
water. No doubt the old woman had consumed the rest during
the last *uinal*.

The *nagual* waited patiently inside the *caanche* for them to
finish. Sky Knife approached his coati and petted its wiry fur. A
dead brown lizard lay at the coati's feet. The coati nosed the
lizard, then stared into Sky Knife's eyes with a sadness Sky
Knife didn't understand.

"What is it?" asked Jade Flute. Her ocelot bounded over
to her.

"A dead lizard."

"It must be the old woman's *nagual*," said Jade Flute. "We should have buried it with her, but I didn't think about it."

Sky Knife thought he understood the coati's sadness now. Perhaps the two animals had known each other when they had lived under the protection of the Totilme'iletik. He petted the coati again.

"We need to go," Sky Knife said.

Jade Flute picked up the lizard and took it inside the house. She came back almost immediately.

Sky Knife set off toward the east. The *nagual* animals followed the people eastward.

Sky Knife led the others across *milpa* after *milpa*. They encountered more green worms in the fields, but no people.

By mid-afternoon, Sky Knife was tired and angry. In the weed-choked fields, it was impossible to tell whether anyone had even come this way. No weeds seemed bent or stomped down.

"Let's rest," said Jade Flute, "and start back. I haven't noticed anything unusual besides the worms—have you?"

"No," said Sky Knife, "but I'm not giving up yet." He looked around for a place to rest. Somewhere away from the fields and the squirming grubs.

"There," he said, pointing to a tall stand of trees just ahead. "Among the trees."

They pushed on. The trees were dense, but broken branches on the meager undergrowth showed someone had been here before. A path had been worn between the trees, and all the plants in the way had been trampled.

"Let me go first," said Bone Splinter. He shouldered on ahead. Sky Knife followed him. Jade Flute and the spirit animals came behind.

The path wound between the trees for nearly a hundred yards, as nearly as Sky Knife could figure. This deep in the jungle, the sounds of the birds and monkeys should have filled his ears, but only the crackling of the dying plants at their feet could be heard.

"Where are all the animals?" he asked no one in particular.

Suddenly, Bone Splinter stopped dead in his tracks.

"What?" asked Sky Knife.

"Take a look." Bone Splinter stepped aside. "But be careful."

Sky Knife took a small step forward. Through the branches of a shrub, he saw a deep hole in the ground—a *cenote!* Sky Knife parted the branches. Water glistened at the bottom of the circular hole. The steep limestone sides were bare of anything but the merest bushes. Sky Knife realized the bush he touched was actually rooted in the side of the *cenote* rather than the surface around it. He stepped back quickly, afraid the rim might give way beneath his feet.

"What is it?" asked Jade Flute. "Let me see." She pushed her way up to stand beside Sky Knife.

"An entrance to the underworld," said Sky Knife. "Perhaps the old woman was right. Maybe Ah Mun called the farmers here and took them from the *cenote* to his fields."

"And maybe there are just a lot of dead farmers at the bottom of the *cenote*," said Bone Splinter. "Only a proper sacrifice can die in a *cenote* and petition the rain gods. I doubt the farmers qualify."

"Do you suppose they just came here and jumped in?" asked Jade Flute. "Why?"

"The path ends here," said Bone Splinter. "Or, rather, here." He stood aside. Just to the right of the bush Sky Knife had held was a gap in the shrubbery that edged the rim of the *cenote*. Bone Splinter leaned over the edge and stared at the water.

"The water is very blue," he said. "I would think, with hundreds of dead farmers at the bottom, it would be fouled."

"Maybe they're not here at all," said Sky Knife. "Or maybe

this is where they met their guide, and they turned around and walked out of the jungle."

"And the guide came from where—the *cenote?*" asked Bone Splinter.

"I don't know," said Sky Knife. "But we're not finding any answers here. Let's go home."

The three of them and their *nagual* left the *cenote* behind and went back to the sunbaked fields. After the stuffiness of the air in the jungle, the open fields, though hotter, were a relief.

Sky Knife set his face to the sun and walked back to Tikal. The coati trotted along beside him.

# 25

›››››

The familiar sight of Tikal's temples eased Sky Knife's mind somewhat. The temples reminded him that, even though bad luck had come to Tikal, the gods remained, eternal and vigilant. Bad luck would fall away eventually. Only the gods were forever.

Sky Knife went straight to the Great Plaza. Today it was almost deserted. It seemed the merchants really were leaving the city. The love-gift vendor remained in her prime spot on the eastern edge of the plaza in front of the great pyramid. Several other merchants remained, but only a handful of people milled about their goods. The plaza, normally a busy, loud place, was eerily quiet.

"I don't like this," said Bone Splinter. "It's as if the city is dead already."

"The city won't die," said Jade Flute. "I'll ask the gods to save it."

"Why should you?" asked Sky Knife. He turned to the young woman. "You're being sacrificed for no good reason. Why should you ask the gods for anything?"

Jade Flute smiled. "That's my secret," she said. She winked

at him. Sky Knife blinked in surprise and his heart beat rapidly. A wink—normally, a young girl would only do that to encourage some young man she thought attractive. Jade Flute had to be teasing him. She couldn't be interested in a junior priest who should never have been more than a mere temple attendant.

"Girl—what are you doing here?"

Sky Knife whirled in surprise. Stone Jaguar strode across the patio of the southern acropolis, a solid blue skirt knotted about his waist and large blue-green jade ear spools in his ears. Jade necklaces of various colors dangled around his neck, and his wrists and ankles were heavy with shell ornaments. His hair had been freshly greased. A small green parrot with blue feathers on its forehead and shoulders sat on his shoulder.

"Go on, back to the nuns," said Stone Jaguar as he stepped down from the patio level. "You should be fasting and praying you will be found worthy tomorrow."

"It is you who should be praying, priest," said Jade Flute, "that I do not ask the gods to strike you down."

Stone Jaguar raised his hand to hit her, but Jade Flute darted out of the way. She and her ocelot ran off toward the temple of Ix Chel. The sound of laughter drifted back behind her.

"Foolish girl, she'll ruin everything," muttered Stone Jaguar. His *nagual* hissed. "With the *nagual* running loose, everyone should be more careful than ever. She's not worthy of the honor."

"Then find another sacrifice," said Sky Knife, "if her worthiness is truly an issue."

Stone Jaguar jabbed a finger toward Sky Knife. "Watch your mouth," he said. "You haven't the rank to question what I do."

"It doesn't take rank to question your actions," said Bone Splinter mildly.

Stone Jaguar refused to be drawn into an argument with the warrior. He didn't even glance toward Bone Splinter. "We have to continue your instruction," he said to Sky Knife. "Death Smoke grows weaker by the hour. How he lasted this long is a mystery in itself. By tomorrow, you and I will be the only priests of Itzamna in Tikal, and you do not yet know any of the important things you should know. Come."

Stone Jaguar set off across the plaza. Sky Knife glanced toward Bone Splinter, then followed. The love-gift vendor waved to Sky Knife as he passed. He nodded to her, relieved to see she was all right.

Stone Jaguar stopped short of the steps to the northern acropolis. He waved to Sky Knife to stand beside him. Bone Splinter stepped up as well, but Stone Jaguar turned to stare at him. After a few moments, Bone Splinter bowed slightly and stepped back. One step. Sky Knife fidgeted, sure Stone Jaguar would be angry at Bone Splinter's continued refusal to be awed by the priest. But Stone Jaguar accepted Bone Splinter's slight retreat and turned to Sky Knife.

"Since the temple has been violated, I was sure the acropolis would be next, so I have left it under the protection of Itzamna," the priest said.

Sky Knife was momentarily confused by the reference of the violation of the temple, until he remembered the obsidian point he had found there. Someone who wasn't afraid to dare the wrath of the gods by going onto the temple probably wouldn't let the legends about the acropolis stop them, either. Protecting it was a wise move.

Stone Jaguar held his hands out in front of him, palms out. In a calm tone, he chanted, "Hail, Itzamna, giver of life, giver of luck. Release this sacred area from your protection until I deliver it to you again. Hail, Itzamna, giver of life."

To Sky Knife, nothing seemed to change. He had expected Stone Jaguar's hands to glow blue as they did during a sacrifice, but the other priest's hands remained unchanged. Stone Jaguar dropped his hands and grunted. The parrot flew into a tree and stared down at them. "All right," said Stone Jaguar. "We can go in now."

The cracked stones of the patio and the twisted tree roots

that grew out of them seemed even more menacing today than before. Sky Knife watched his step and carefully avoided stepping on any roots.

Sky Knife turned back to the plaza before entering the acropolis. Bone Splinter stood at the bottom of the steps to the acropolis, watching Sky Knife. The tapir and the coati watched him also. The warrior nodded to him. Sky Knife waved and then plunged into the darkness of the acropolis.

It took a moment for the significance of the darkness to register with Sky Knife. It *was* dark—the glow of the *chic-chac* did not light his way. Sky Knife stopped and his hands flew to his neck. The serpent was still there, but it was cold now. So cold. Sky Knife thought it was dead, but he felt it move slightly. Its tongue touched his hand briefly.

"Sky Knife—where are you?" demanded Stone Jaguar.

Sky Knife walked forward into the room where he had saved the *chic-chac's* life. Bright blue fire blazed over his head in the highly vaulted ceiling.

Stone Jaguar spread his hands. "What is the perfect number?" he asked.

"Four."

Stone Jaguar nodded. "There are four directions, four Bacabs to hold up the sky, four great *chacs* to bring the rain, four great *chic-chacs* to guard the waters of the world. Four is the number of completeness."

Stone Jaguar dropped his hands and pointed toward the firepit in the center of the room. A blue tongue of flame flashed upward, then retreated and burned, bright and hot, in the bottom of the pit.

"Sit."

Sky Knife approached the pit and sat next to it. Stone Jaguar sat opposite him.

"There should be four priests to instruct you," said Stone Jaguar. "I am grieved I am the only one left to teach you what you should know." Stone Jaguar smoothed his skirt down over

his knees. "I am *Ah nacom*, He Who Sacrifices. I am not quali-
fied to teach you everything Death Smoke could about being
*Ah kin*, He Who Divines the Will of the Gods. But I will try."

Stone Jaguar reached into a bag and pulled out a handful of
*copal*. "Death Smoke can divine the will of the gods through the
spirit of *copal*," he said. He threw the *copal* into the sorcerous
flames. Thick white smoke billowed out of the firepit all around
Sky Knife.

"Breathe in the smoke," said Stone Jaguar, "and let your
mind rest."

Sky Knife closed his eyes and breathed in deeply. The
musky odor of the *copal* filled his nostrils. His fingers tingled
and thought suddenly seemed unimportant. Sky Knife let his
mind drift and his awareness of his surroundings fade.

"Beware!"

Sky Knife jerked, heart pounding, and opened his eyes. He
looked around for the source of the voice, but saw nothing but
white smoke tinted blue by the sorcerous fires above.

"Who's there?" he asked.

"You should be relaxing, not talking," said Stone Jaguar.

"But the voice . . ."

"Voice?" shouted Stone Jaguar. "What was that about a
voice?"

"I . . . I heard someone say 'beware,' " said Sky Knife. "It
sounded as though the person were right beside me." His heartbeat slowed slightly but Sky Knife could still feel its pounding
in his ears.

"A deep voice? A shrill voice? What?"

Sky Knife thought for a moment. "Neither," he said. "I can't
put any quality to it. It just *was.*"

Silence.

"Stone Jaguar?" asked Sky Knife, afraid the other man had
deserted him in the smoke.

"Amazing," said Stone Jaguar.

Sky Knife waited to see if Stone Jaguar would say anything

else. The serpent at his throat stirred briefly and he stroked it.

"I have never heard the voice," said Stone Jaguar. "Sometimes, I thought Death Smoke only imagined it or I'd hear it too. But you heard it—the first time you listened. I thought your ease at learning to call fire was a fluke. Now I see I was wrong."

"But what does it mean?" asked Sky Knife. "Beware of what?"

"The gods don't explain themselves to men," said Stone Jaguar. "The warning might not even have been for you personally, but for the priesthood, or perhaps Tikal in general. Death Smoke would smoke and fast after he listened to the voice, so that he could determine what the voice meant by its messages."

"It seemed very personal," said Sky Knife softly.

"I imagine it did," said Stone Jaguar. "Try again."

"Again?" Sky Knife hovered between excitement and terror. A god had spoken to *him*—Sky Knife could barely imagine what that meant. He had never thought to be so honored. But catching the attention of the gods was not necessarily something Sky Knife had ever desired. Even Itzamna, Lord of All, could spread chaos and destruction in turn with giving life and security to men. Ix Chel his wife was a healer, but she also caused plague. The gods had many duties and wore many faces, not all of them beneficial to men.

"Yes, again," commanded Stone Jaguar. "Relax and open yourself to the gods."

Sky Knife closed his eyes, let out the air in his lungs, and then took a deep breath. He held his breath a moment and let it out slowly. His skin tingled as if the smoke caressed him with its feather-light touch. The touch of the smoke brushed up from his fingers to the backs of his hands. Up his arm to his elbows and then to his shoulders. The *chic-chac* tensed and squeezed Sky Knife's neck weakly.

Sky Knife opened his eyes and squeaked in surprise. He sat

in a large room—larger than the one he had been in—lit by blazing globes of yellow light that drifted across the vaulted ceiling. Brightly painted murals displaying scenes of torture and sacrifice crowded the walls. The scene on the wall before him showed a priest offering the heart of a sacrifice. Tears of blood were shed by the people in the crowd below while Itzamna himself looked down from above.

A slight rustling sound came from behind him. Sky Knife leaped to his feet and turned around.

"Oh, Itzamna," he whispered.

In front of him stood an iguana the size of a tapir. Its tail stretched out behind it into the darkness of the corridor beyond. Its bright green scales sparkled in the light and its sides were marked by dark brown stripes that stopped just short of the ridge of spines that ran down the center of its back.

The one eye the iguana had turned toward him was dark brown. The iguana blinked the eye slowly, the lid sliding from the bottom up.

Sky Knife fell to his knees and banged his forehead against the floor. "Itzamna, Lord of All," he whispered. "I am honored to be in your presence."

Sky Knife waited, but heard nothing. He raised his head slowly. The iguana lowered the dewlap at its throat and opened its mouth. Inside its mouth, its pink, slightly forked tongue wriggled from side to side. Slowly, the iguana shut its mouth.

As Sky Knife watched, the brilliant greens and browns of the iguana's scales faded to yellow. Even the brown of its eyes lightened until they were bright, bright gold.

The iguana sneezed.

Horrified, Sky Knife stood up and backed against the wall. This couldn't be Itzamna. It was a trick, a evil spirit in disguise.

"Itzamna curse you!" he cried.

The iguana writhed and shrank until nothing remained of it but a small green worm like the ones in the fields. Sky Knife hesitated, but walked to the worm and stomped on it.

Instead of a satisfying splat, cackling laughter rose from the floor. Sky Knife jerked his foot back, but it was too late. A yellow ooze surrounded his foot and quickly worked its way up to his knee.

Sky Knife tried to shake the goo off, but it spread so quickly it was to his waist before he could shake his foot a second time.

"No!" he screamed. But the ooze climbed higher, past his chest, to his neck.

To his neck. It stopped. Sky Knife felt the *chic-chac* go rigid.

All the feeling in Sky Knife's body and limbs faded away. He sank to the floor. Terror burst from his gut and rushed up his throat. He screamed.

Then a terrible pain in his throat blazed through his terror and shoved him down into a flaming world where only the sound of laughter could be heard.

That, and a small, thin scream, almost too high to hear. Sky Knife screamed, too, knowing the sound for what it was in his soul. It was the dying scream of a rainbow serpent.

# 26

>>>>>

"Sky Knife! Sky Knife!"

Someone was calling him, but the sound was so far away and he hurt all over. Sky Knife resisted the pull of the voice, but it insisted.

"Sky Knife! Come on, boy, snap out of it! What happened?"

A stinging pain in his face. Someone had slapped him. Sky Knife opened his eyes in anger. Then he remembered.

"The *chic-chac!*" he shouted. "Where is it?"

Sky Knife sat up but the pounding in his head told him he'd made a mistake. He held his head in his hands like a man who had had too much *pulque*. Every movement sent more spikes of pain jarring into his skull.

"Sky Knife?"

Sky Knife took a deep breath before turning toward the voice. Stone Jaguar sat next to him, sweat glistening on his face and chest. The older man's hair was wild despite the grease on it and his eyes were wide. Sky Knife blinked in surprise. Stone Jaguar looked terrified.

"What happened?" asked Stone Jaguar. *"What happened?"*

Higher ranked priest or no, Sky Knife had other priorities

besides Stone Jaguar's questions. "The *chic-chac*," he said again. "Where is it? I thought I heard it die." He felt his neck, but his fingers touched only smooth skin.

Stone Jaguar pointed toward Sky Knife's neck. "It . . . I . . . I don't know how to explain. Wait." Stone Jaguar got up and brought back a bowl of water. "Look."

Sky Knife leaned over the bowl. The serpent was still around his neck.

"It's a tattoo," said Stone Jaguar. "I don't understand what happened."

"I was attacked," said Sky Knife. He couldn't keep his hands away from the tattoo of the serpent. It looked so real.

"By what?"

"I don't know. It looked like an iguana, then a worm. Then it laughed and became a yellow ooze that tried to consume me. Somehow, the *chic-chac* stopped it."

"Cizin," growled Stone Jaguar. "He is still here."

Sky Knife paid no attention. Grief wracked him at the thought of the *chic-chac* dead. It had given his life for him. It had taken the poison of Yellow Chin and fought off the yellow ooze. And it had left its mark on his neck. Sky Knife didn't know what the tattoo meant, but he knew in his heart it could not be bad. The *chic-chac* may have perished, but it had left something of itself behind. At least its love. Maybe more.

Tears rolled down Sky Knife's face and he choked back sobs. His chest felt tight. "Why?" he asked.

"Why what?" asked Stone Jaguar.

Sky Knife shook his head. He didn't expect an answer. He could only be grateful that the rainbow serpent, an immortal being, had chosen to put his life before its own.

Stone Jaguar smoothed his hair down. He spat into the blue fire in the firepit. "Cizin here, and the rainbow serpent dead." Stone Jaguar's gaze slid to Sky Knife's neck. "Apparently dead," he amended. Stone Jaguar sighed. In the flickering light of the blue flame, he suddenly seemed older and very worried. "Come back to the fire," Stone Jaguar said. "You still have much to learn."

Sky Knife slid back to his place. The *copal* smoke had dissipated, but the thick musky smell remained in the room.

"Normally, we work for days to get new priests to be able to sense the voice of the *copal*. Sometimes, we work for weeks and they never do hear anything. Apparently, the gods have already deigned to speak with you through the *copal*," said Stone Jaguar. "So I won't repeat that lesson." He reached into the bag and brought out a cigar. He held the cigar to the blue flame until it caught and handed it to Sky Knife.

Sky Knife took the cigar and put it to his lips. A tingle in his neck stopped him. He put the cigar down quickly.

"What's wrong?" asked Stone Jaguar.

"I don't know. I think there's trouble."

"Trouble? Where? How?"

Sky Knife shook his head and looked around the room. Shadows slid in and out of the blue balls of flame in the vaulted ceiling. The shadows merged at the western end of the room and fell to the floor.

"Itzamna!" whispered Stone Jaguar. "What sorcery is this?"

The cigar Sky Knife had put down smoked and then went out. Sky Knife stood, feeling naked without Bone Splinter to help him. The shadow in front of him whirled as if stirred by an invisible ladle. Slowly, it coalesced into a dense fog that took on the shape of a man.

A man with a fleshless face and chest. A man whose skin was covered with black and yellow blotches.

"Cizin," muttered Stone Jaguar. "I curse you and all you've done to this city."

"Death to you!" screeched the terrible figure. Its fleshless jaws flapped loosely and its teeth rattled against each other. Maggots crawled in the hole where its nose should have been.

"Death death death!" whispered other voices. Sky Knife whirled, but the room behind him was empty.

"Watch!" said Cizin.

Sky Knife turned back to the god of death, but the voices around him did not stop. "Watch watch watch!" they cried, over and over. Sky Knife shivered. The temperature in the room had dropped since Cizin had appeared. Already, Sky Knife was colder than he could remember being in his life.

Cizin hopped on his swollen, bruised feet. His lidless eyes rolled loosely in their sockets.

"Come, Sky Knife, we must dispel this hideous creature," said Stone Jaguar. The older man spread his hands and chanted in a language Sky Knife did not recognize. But the chant flowed into his soul like rain onto the dry *milpas* in spring. Sky Knife concentrated on the chant and put his hands, palms out, toward Cizin. He shivered again, anxious to clasp his arms to his chest to conserve warmth. But he had to help Stone Jaguar now.

Cizin laughed. The high, screechy sound grated on Sky Knife's ears. It sent shivers up and down his spine. Cizin hopped closer.

"Bad luck!" shouted the god of death.

The voices snickered. Sky Knife dropped his hands and clasped his arms together across his chest to control his shivering. Fear pushed his heartbeat faster and he panted in terror.

A strange fog appeared before Sky Knife. He stared at it and realized it was formed by the breath coming out of his mouth. What magic was this? Sky Knife backed away from the fog, but couldn't escape it.

"Cold!" said Cizin.

"Cold cold cold!" echoed the voices.

Stone Jaguar stopped his chant. "Foul monster!" he shouted at the prancing figure.

"Eat your bones!" screeched Cizin.

"Bones bones bones!" said the voices.

Cizin took a step toward Stone Jaguar and pointed a finger at the priest. Then, slowly, Cizin turned to Sky Knife and swung the blotched finger toward the younger man.

Voices chittered and gibbered in Sky Knife's ear. "Death death death!" they sang.

Anger rushed over Sky Knife in a searing wave, forcing the cold from his bones and the fear from his mind. "No!" he shouted. He stepped forward and picked up the cigar. He reached outward with his mind and called fire to the cigar. The end of the cigar burst into flames. Sky Knife took the flaming cigar and shoved it into the maggoty dark hole in the center of Cizin's face.

Cizin screamed. The high, piercing sound hurt Sky Knife's ears. He stepped back away from Cizin and clamped his hands over his ears.

The god of death writhed in agony. He reached for the cigar but his hands smoked where he touched it. Cizin fell to his knees. Yellow fluid oozed out of his blotched skin and puddled around him. Cold winds swirled around the room and battered at Sky Knife, but he stood firm against them.

Cizin melted away until only a puddle of yellow ooze and a cigar remained. The puddle drained toward the firepit. As the ooze touched the fire, the blue flame sprang up to consume it.

Sky Knife watched until the last bit of slime had disappeared into the firepit. At that moment, the cold wind ceased and the room returned to its normal temperature. The shock of the much warmer air against his skin nauseated Sky Knife. He fell on his knees and heaved, but had nothing in his stomach to bring up.

When Sky Knife's guts stopped twisting and fighting to come up his throat, he sat back, trembling and exhausted.

Stone Jaguar sat on the other side of the firepit, his hands in his face. Sobs wracked the other man.

"Oh, Itzamna," said Stone Jaguar. "Are we truly doomed?"

"Doomed?" asked Sky Knife weakly. "How? Cizin is gone."

Stone Jaguar dropped his hands and looked up at Sky Knife. A terrible anger blazed on the older man's face. "You understand nothing," he said. "Nothing!"

"Nothing nothing nothing!" echoed the voices. Sky Knife jerked and looked around the room.

Stone Jaguar stood. "I will defeat you, Cizin!" he cried.

Sky Knife stared at the sacrificial scene on the wall. The painted figures moved! He was sure of it. Sky Knife stood and walked toward the wall.

"What are you doing?" barked Stone Jaguar.

Sky Knife didn't answer. He stared at the image on the wall.

There! They *did* move! The priest in the scene plunged his knife into the chest of the sacrifice. Bright red blood ran down the wall.

"What?" shouted Stone Jaguar. "What is this?"

Sky Knife backed away toward the door. He didn't want to be here any longer. He wanted back out in the sunshine. Back out in the fresh air under the blue sky.

"Watch out!" shouted Stone Jaguar. Sky Knife ducked and whirled. A knife swung over his head. Sky Knife backed up and looked at his attacker.

The man looked odd. Flat. Sky Knife stared, at first not understanding. But the blank spot on the wall behind the man made it obvious. The painting had not only come to life, it had leaped off the wall.

The man approached in a strange, stilted gait. He raised his knife again.

Sky Knife ducked under the knife and pushed the man from behind. His hands encountered a surface that gave readily but sprung back as soon as he pulled his hands back.

The flat man advanced on Stone Jaguar next. Stone Jaguar circled the fire, keeping it between himself and the painting. Sky Knife glanced around. Other figures climbed down from the walls.

"Run!" shouted Sky Knife. He hesitated a moment to see if Stone Jaguar had heard him. The older man nodded. Sky Knife dashed for the black hole of the doorway and darted through just as another flat man stabbed at him with a spear.

Sky Knife ran outside, across the patio, and leaped down the steps. Bone Splinter reached out and grabbed him. "What happened?" he asked.

Sky Knife turned to see if Stone Jaguar had escaped. The older priest emerged and stumbled across the patio. Blood flowed from a wound in his leg.

Stone Jaguar sat down on the steps of the acropolis and tore his skirt to make a bandage for his leg.

"This is no longer any of your concern," he said to Sky Knife. "Whatever the king may say. This is sorcery, and no untrained priest wandering around asking questions is going to help us now. Go back to your quarters and stay there until morning. By then, perhaps, I will have been able to deal with Cizin and his ilk."

Sky Knife couldn't believe his ears. "I was the one who fought Cizin," he said. "Why send me away? I can help."

"You are braver than you are wise," said Stone Jaguar without looking in Sky Knife's direction. "Which is only to say you are young. Go. Without the *chic-chac*, you can't help anymore. Take your bad luck name out of my sight."

Sky Knife backed away from Stone Jaguar slowly, then turned and walked toward the southern acropolis. He was confused. He could help—he knew he could! Why would Stone Jaguar turn him away?

Bone Splinter put a hand on his shoulder when they reached the patio. "What are you going to do?" asked the warrior.

Sky Knife sat on the steps. "I'm not going to my quarters tonight," he said. "That much I know."

"Good."

Sky Knife glanced at the warrior. Bone Splinter smiled.

"I'm going to disobey a direct order from Stone Jaguar and you say that's good?"

Bone Splinter laughed. "You don't answer to him first. Or even to the king. You're different from the rest of us, Sky Knife, even if you can't see it yet. I believe you'll know what to do."

Sky Knife sat on the steps, rubbed his hands over his snake tattoo absently, and thought. The coati curled up at his feet, laid the tip of its tail over its nose, and went to sleep.

# 27

›››››

The sun just touched the tops of the trees in the west before Sky Knife got up. The coati yawned and stretched. Bone Splinter's tapir had wandered over to some weeds growing on the far side of the plaza. It looked up as Sky Knife joined his coati in a stretch.

"Where are we going?" asked Bone Splinter.

"Stone Jaguar said Red Spider would be dead before sunset. If we want to ask Red Spider anything, we're going to have to do it now."

Bone Splinter hesitated. "We should take some warriors with us, then," he said. "Red Spider may be dying, but his attendants aren't. Some of them may want revenge for Red Spider's death."

Sky Knife watched as the sun began to dip behind the treetops. "If Stone Jaguar was right, we don't have much time."

"Time enough to die if things go wrong."

Sky Knife weighed his decision. "All right," he said. "I'll go on ahead to the merchant's quarter. But I won't go in. You come as soon as you can with some others."

Bone Splinter nodded and jogged off in the direction of the

House of the Warriors, the tapir ambling along after him. Sky Knife watched them until they disappeared around the ball courts. Then he turned his face toward the sun and walked to the merchant's quarter.

The quarter was a meandering system of permanent buildings and tents that sat outside the city proper. The tall trees of the jungle crowded close to the buildings. The colorful woven tents were often strung up between two trees. Many people slept in the open, in hammocks strung between trees.

Several people noticed Sky Knife standing there, but no one approached him. Sky Knife leaned against a tree and waited impatiently. The sun dropped lower, and shadows covered the quarter. By the light of the fires in the quarter, Sky Knife saw merchants and their attendants moving around, but outside the firelight, the evening was dark under the trees.

Eventually, Sky Knife saw Bone Splinter, carrying a torch, approaching. Several people followed him. Sky Knife was glad to see Kan Flower was one of them.

"Do you know where Red Spider is?" asked Bone Splinter.

"No," said Sky Knife. "But a merchant from Teotihuacan shouldn't be difficult to find."

Sky Knife straightened his shoulders, took a deep breath, and walked into the quarter. The warriors followed him.

Red Spider's camp was centered around one of the low stone buildings that dotted the quarter. Campfires and tents surrounded the structure and the jungle growth that plagued the other camps was completely absent. No doubt Red Spider made his people keep the area clear.

Sky Knife approved. A clean, weedless area around the building made it look more liveable, more civilized, than the other buildings in the area.

"What . . . you want?" asked a heavily accented voice. An attendant, short, dumpy, and clothed only in a white loincloth, stepped out of the tent to Sky Knife's left.

"I want to speak with Red Spider," said Sky Knife.

The man stared at him, apparently uncomprehending. "Me. Speak Red Spider," said Sky Knife, hoping the man knew a few important words, even if he couldn't understand entire sentences.

"No speak," said the man. He followed that with several sentences in his own harsh tongue and spat on the ground at Sky Knife's feet.

Bone Splinter stirred, but Sky Knife waved for him to be silent. "I am going to speak to Red Spider, like it or not," he said.

Another attendant, this one clad in a fine cotton skirt and shell bead jewelry, stepped out of the building.

"You are Sky Knife?" he asked. His accent was thick, but not nearly as distracting as the first man's.

"Yes. I want to . . ."

"I know, speak with my master. He wishes to speak with you, too." The second man shouted something at the first. The short man disappeared back into the tent.

Sky Knife walked up to the building. The other man bowed slightly. "Please enter our dwelling," he said. Then he said something in his own language.

Sky Knife hesitated.

The other man stood up. "It is only a blessing we give to strangers entering our home," he said without meeting Sky Knife's eyes. "I know you do not have a similar custom."

Sky Knife walked into the building. Its single room, though decorated in a Teotihuacan fashion, was a familiar, comfortable Mayan shape. Red Spider lay on a bench against the southern wall, covered in blankets. A third attendant sat beside him and wiped sweat from his face.

"Sky Knife."

Sky Knife was alarmed by how weak Red Spider sounded. He'd known Red Spider was dying, but somehow, hearing the pain and exhaustion in Red Spider's voice was troubling.

Red Spider waved his attendant away. The man bowed and

left the building. Sky Knife walked over to Red Spider's bed and sat down on the edge.

Sky Knife hardly recognized the other man. Red Spider had been exotically beautiful before. Now his face was deeply lined and his skin damp and pale, almost yellowish, in the firelight.

Red Spider moved his hand out from under a blanket and clutched Sky Knife's wrist. "You must stop him," he whispered.

"Stop who—Cizin?"

"No." Red Spider closed his eyes and his breath hissed out of his throat. He squeezed Sky Knife's arm and drew in another breath.

Sky Knife cringed at the pain in the other man's face. He waited without speaking.

After two shallow breaths, Red Spider opened his eyes again. "Stop the priest," he said.

"Stone Jaguar? Why?"

Red Spider licked his lips slowly. "She'll die."

Sky Knife's guts trembled. "I know," he said. "But the king and Stone Jaguar have agreed on it. I can't stop it." Sky Knife clamped his mouth shut, embarrassed by the anguish in his voice.

Red Spider smiled. "You want her," he whispered.

Sky Knife said nothing.

"So did I," said the merchant. "I asked Storm Cloud for her."

"What did he say?"

"He said he wouldn't give any Mayan woman to a Teotihuacano."

"But his mother . . ."

"I know," the other man interrupted. Red Spider fell silent and closed his eyes. "But he felt his mother should have been married to a Mayan lord." The last word faded away as Red Spider let out his breath.

Sky Knife leaned forward, afraid the merchant had died. But after a moment, Red Spider caught his breath.

"You mean the king doesn't want to extend ties to his kin in your city?" asked Sky Knife.

Red Spider nodded once, slowly. "His brothers made him leave," he said. "He barely tolerates our merchants here—a marriage was out of the question."

"Yet you asked."

A hint of a smile crossed the other man's features. "Wouldn't you?"

Sky Knife said nothing. He took Red Spider's hand and held it.

"Sky Knife . . ."

"Yes." Sky Knife leaned forward to catch the merchant's words.

"Stop him. You can do it."

"Why do you say that?"

Red Spider smiled. "The owl told me." The merchant's breath hissed out of his throat again, but this time, he did not take in another. The lines in Red Spider's face eased and his face grew slack.

Sky Knife trembled. He hadn't liked Red Spider, but he felt guilt at the other man's death. Red Spider had died at Stone Jaguar's hand, and Stone Jaguar and Sky Knife were priests to the same god, in the same temple. Sky Knife felt almost as if he were the one who had killed the other man.

Sky Knife said a silent prayer to Itzamna for the soul of Red Spider. Slowly, he stood and walked to the entrance of the building. Red Spider's attendants stood there, waiting.

"He's dead," said Sky Knife. "I can perform death rites for him if you wish."

The attendant shook his head. "No, we will perform whatever rites are necessary. But I thank you for your offer."

Sky Knife nodded and went over to Bone Splinter.

"What did he say?" asked the warrior.

Sky Knife sighed. "He said Storm Cloud wouldn't form an alliance with his kin in Teotihuacan because his brothers forced him to leave. And he said I could stop Jade Flute's sacrifice. An owl told him that."

"An owl?" asked Kan Flower. He stepped forward, his manner intent and serious. "He said an owl spoke to him?"

"Owl has spoken to Red Spider," said the heavily accented voice of the attendant in the fine skirt and jewelry. Sky Knife turned to face the man.

"The owl is the sacred guardian of their royal family," said Kan Flower softly.

"Owl has spoken," repeated the attendant. "He told Red Spider that this man," the attendant pointed toward Sky Knife, "was marked by the gods to strive against the evil that is here."

Sky Knife's hands went to the rainbow serpent tattoo at his neck.

"May the Feathered Serpent guide your hand, priest," said the attendant. He stretched out both his hands toward Sky Knife and said something in his own language. Then he went back into the building.

Sky Knife walked back toward Tikal. The others followed him, but he ignored them. If Storm Cloud and Red Spider hadn't planned to bring bad luck to the city, he'd been running around the fields and the city for no purpose.

Sky Knife's steps came more quickly. Something was going to happen tonight, or Stone Jaguar would not have sent him away. But he wasn't going to stay away. Whatever happened, Sky Knife was going to be there.

By the time he reached the city, he was running, the coati bounding easily beside him. Overhead, the Knife of Stars pointed toward the last place Sky Knife wanted to go, but where he knew he needed to be.

The northern acropolis.

# IV

››››››››››

# SOUTH

## WHERE WISDOM RISES ON THE WINGS
## OF THE WIND

9.0.0.0.3
11 AKBAL 16 CEH

# 28

›››››

Sky Knife slowed as he reached the Great Plaza. He turned to the warriors behind him.

"Kan Flower, you and your warriors return to your house. I thank you for your service."

Kan Flower and the others bowed. Bone Splinter stared at him.

"You know what you have to do?" asked the tall man. His tapir scratched an itchy ear against the steps to the northern acropolis and grunted in pleasure.

"No," said Sky Knife. "But I know where I have to go. Wait!" he shouted to Kan Flower as he and the other warriors prepared to leave.

"Yes, Lord?"

Sky Knife flushed. "Uh, I just thought of something. Go to the Temple of Ix Chel instead. Under no circumstances is the sacrifice to happen tomorrow. You will guard Jade Flute—even if Stone Jaguar himself comes for her."

Kan Flower bowed again. "It will be our pleasure." It was too dark to make out Kan Flower's expression, but the warrior sounded smug. Kan Flower and the other warriors walked off toward the temple of Ix Chel.

Sky Knife turned to the northern acropolis. Bone Splinter took a step forward.

"No," said Sky Knife. "We're not going to just rush in. Go to the House of the Warriors and bring your weapons. I'll go back to Stone Jaguar's quarters and get what I need."

Bone Splinter bowed slightly and jogged off. Sky Knife walked back to the acropolis. As he crossed the patio, an attendant stepped outside. He saw Sky Knife and screamed.

Sky Knife stopped, confused. The other man darted back into the acropolis. Sky Knife looked down at himself. He saw nothing unusual.

Sky Knife raised his hands and looked at them in the light. Nothing.

Only then did Sky Knife realize there *was* light. He'd become so used to the *chic-chac* at his throat lighting his way, he hadn't thought about the glow now that it was dead. He put his hands to his throat and the light dimmed a little.

Sky Knife assumed the serpent tattoo glowed as the little snake once had. No wonder the attendant had been alarmed— a man with a glowing necklace was approaching the acropolis.

The drapery at the entrance tweaked aside. Sky Knife couldn't see who was peering out at him. He walked toward the building and the person released the drape.

Sky Knife swept aside the drapery and walked into the room. The coals in the firepit glowed slightly, but no flames lit the room. Sky Knife gestured toward the firepit and reached out with his mind. Flames leaped up from the coals, but Sky Knife could see they wouldn't last long unless someone fed the fire.

Usually, the attendants took turns caring for all the fires within the acropolis. Without priests to watch over them, though, it seemed the remaining attendants were letting their duties go.

"Who's here?" called Sky Knife. "Someone take care of the fires!" Sky Knife walked down the corridor. A frightened attendant ducked by him, eyes downcast.

Sky Knife went into Stone Jaguar's quarters. No fire had been laid in the firepit. Sky Knife reached his hands over his head and called the flames. Blue light danced in the vaulted ceiling, illuminating the entire room.

Sky Knife went to the jars in the corner. Somewhere here he'd find what he needed.

The first jar contained fat for Stone Jaguar to put in his hair. The second held cigars. Sky Knife took several and wrapped them in a small cotton towel he found on the bed.

A small gourd lay behind the jars. Sky Knife took it and unstoppered it. The heavy, sweet odor of tobacco juice wafted out of the gourd. Sky Knife restoppered the gourd and looped the strap over his shoulder.

What else would he need? Sky Knife glanced around the room quickly. A carved wooden box stood open in the corner. Jade and shell beads reflected the blue light and shone like stars. But wealth was not what he needed.

The jaguar-skin cloak lay across a wooden frame in another corner. Sky Knife walked to it slowly. He'd never dared touch it, for only *Ah nacom*, He Who Sacrifices, could do so without bringing bad luck upon himself.

The black spots on the yellow fur reminded Sky Knife of Cizin. But the jaguar was not death. The jaguar was power. Stone Jaguar should have it with him.

Sky Knife reached out to touch the cloak when a glittering object caught his eye. In farthest recesses of the corner, something shimmered brightly green. Sky Knife walked around the wooden frame and the cloak and knelt by the object.

It was a small point, like one intended for an arrow or a dart. And its glassy facets were as green as the leaves of the *ceiba* tree.

Oh, Itzamna. It hadn't been Red Spider, or even the king.

*Stone Jaguar.* But why? He was High Priest of Itzamna in Tikal. Why should he bring bad luck to the city?

Anger rose in Sky Knife's throat, but he choked it back down. Whatever he wanted to know, he would have to ask Stone Jaguar himself when he got to the acropolis. He would save his anger for Stone Jaguar. Still, a deep sense of betrayal burned in his heart.

Sky Knife picked up the point and put it with the cigars. He looked again at the jaguar skin cloak and anger twisted in his chest. The cloak was for the High Priest to wear, for only he was sacred enough, pure enough, for such an honor. But Stone Jaguar had thrown all that away. Sky Knife took the cloak and put it around his own shoulders. The rough fur felt strange under his fingers.

Sky Knife took the cotton tie, knotted it at his throat, and shook his shoulders to settle the cloak in place. The forepaws of the cloak fell down his arms while the back paws and tail trailed down his back and legs. The neck wrapped around the back of his neck and ruffled his hair. Sky Knife smoothed his hair back down, gathered his things, and left the room.

Sky Knife passed no one on the way out, and he sighed in relief. It felt right to wear the cloak, but he was uncomfortable—now he not only glowed, he wore the most holy garment in the entire acropolis.

Sky Knife stepped out into the night air. The Knife of Stars continued to point toward the northern acropolis. Sky Knife walked forward, angry and afraid. He bit his lip and tried not to think about the kind of power Stone Jaguar must have to bring about all the bad luck. To call Cizin, to free all the *nagual*, to bring a stinging rain and to call Yellow Chin and the black jaguar—all these things had taken a great deal of strength to do. How could Stone Jaguar have done it all and still had time to perform his duties, to train Sky Knife?

The power needed to call fire must come from within the priest himself. But the power to bring bad luck would take so much more effort, Sky Knife was sure one man could not do it alone. It would take a group of men, at least. And where could Stone Jaguar find a group of men to aid him in destroying his own city? The Maya belonged to their cities as much as the cities belonged to them. So why one man—let alone a group—should act against the interests of Tikal was mystifying.

No doubt he would learn more when he confronted Stone Jaguar. Who knew—perhaps Sky Knife was wrong. Perhaps Stone Jaguar had another reason to have the Teotihuacan obsidian in his quarters. Some other reason than to plant it in the plaza and make Sky Knife run to Red Spider. Or the king.

Sky Knife walked across the plaza and breathed deeply of the humid night air. The cloak made his skin itch and was hot. Sky Knife sweated freely under it.

Bone Splinter stood in the plaza next to the steps to the patio of the northern acropolis. He glanced over at Sky Knife as the younger man approached. Sky Knife waited for Bone Splinter's reaction to the cloak, but the warrior merely nodded.

"I felt there wouldn't be enough room for a sword or a sling, so I brought a knife," said Bone Splinter. He hefted a heavy flint blade before Sky Knife. The flint had been hafted onto a wooden handle. "It would please me if you would bless it before we begin."

Sky Knife felt heat rising in his cheeks, and was glad the darkness hid it. He reached out and touched the cool stone surface of the knife. "Itzamna grant that this blade strike true and remain as strong and faithful as the hand that holds it. May knife and wielder gain favor in your sight, Lord of All."

Bone Splinter bowed slightly. "Thank you."

Sky Knife ducked his head, a bit embarrassed by the warrior's deference.

"Did you get what you needed?" asked Bone Splinter.

"Yes." Sky Knife reached around for the juice-filled gourd. "I've got tobacco juice here. Put it behind your knees, elbows, and ears."

Sky Knife unstoppered the gourd and poured a small amount onto Bone Splinter's outstretched hand. When the warrior had anointed himself, Sky Knife put the sticky, smelly liquid on himself as well. He restoppered the gourd.

"You think the dead will bother us, then?" asked the warrior.

"I don't know," said Sky Knife. "But this place is supposed to be haunted. And Cizin himself was here this afternoon. Where Death is, can the dead be far behind?"

Bone Splinter grunted. "You are probably right," he said. "Here, pour some of the juice on my knife. Flint is no weapon to use against the dead."

Sky Knife took out the stopper and dribbled some of the liquid onto the knife.

"Good," said Bone Splinter. "At least they won't like the smell, if nothing else."

The cloyingly sweet smell of the tobacco juice hung around them both. Sky Knife fought the urge to sneeze. "I'm not sure *I* like the smell right now," he said.

Bone Splinter laughed. "Are you ready now?"

Sky Knife looked toward the dark gaping hole that marked the entrance to the acropolis. "One thing more," he said. "I found a green obsidian point in Stone Jaguar's room. Just like the ones we found last night in the plaza."

Bone Splinter stiffened. "What?"

Sky Knife didn't answer. He let the silence stretch out between them and answer the question for him.

"Stone Jaguar," Bone Splinter said at last. "But why? Destroy Tikal and he destroys himself."

"I don't know," said Sky Knife. "Maybe I'm wrong."

"No," said Bone Splinter. "I don't think you are."

"No," said Sky Knife. "I don't think I am, either."

Bone Splinter hefted his knife and waited. Sky Knife sighed. "All right," he said. "Let's go."

Sky Knife walked up the steps. Bone Splinter moved around to a place slightly behind and to the right of him.

Something was missing. Sky Knife turned around. The tapir and the coati stared at him, ears up and expectant. But they came no farther than the first step.

"Wait here for us," Sky Knife said, feeling a little silly to be speaking to animals. The coati flicked an ear at him and sat down. The tapir looked forlorn.

Sky Knife turned back around and set his feet down carefully onto the broken surface of the patio. The tree roots seemed to come to life in the rainbow glow. They seemed to reach out for his feet as if to trip him.

Heart in his throat, Sky Knife paused and stared at the roots. When he looked at them squarely, they remained in place. Slowly, he moved forward again.

They crossed the patio without incident. Sky Knife paused before the doorway. He glanced up. The Knife of Stars seemed to be pointing right toward him.

Sky Knife took a deep breath and clenched his fists. He stepped forward and was swallowed up by the darkness.

# 29

››››

Sky Knife stepped forward confidently into the room where he had saved the *chic-chac*. The glow at his throat lit it only dimly. Sky Knife glanced around for the living paintings, but only colored dust marred the floor. Blank spots stood out in the colorful murals on the walls.

Bone Splinter came in and stood beside him. "Where would he be?"

Sky Knife shook his head. "I'm not sure. This is the only room I've been shown up here. Perhaps we should search around, though, before we go down to the cave, to make sure no one will be behind us."

"Cave?" Bone Splinter sounded excited.

Sky Knife bit his lip. The cave was a secret that only the highest-ranked priests were supposed to know, and he had just revealed the secret to a warrior.

Not just a warrior. His friend. And the only man in Tikal he knew he could trust tonight.

"Yes," whispered Sky Knife. He understood Bone Splinter's excitement. A cave—especially one containing a pool of water—was a holy place. In all of Tikal, there was nothing holier.

"Then I doubt we need to search up here," said Bone Splinter. "Whatever's going to happen will happen in the cave. And if there is anyone behind us—well, Itzamna knows our names."

Fear clutched at Sky Knife's heart and his knees shook. Bone Splinter spoke like a warrior. He planned to carry out his duty to the king without thought of surrender or retreat. Though it seemed strange to Sky Knife, he knew the warrior was right. Whether or not anyone followed them was immaterial. They had a job to do and could not waste time worrying about a safe passage out. They only needed to get in to carry out the king's command.

Sky Knife turned briefly and glanced toward the black hole of the entrance to the room. Through it, he could see nothing of the outside. Not a fire, not a star. He wondered if he'd ever see the outside again.

"Sky Knife, I know what you're thinking," said Bone Splinter. "It does no good to think like that."

"I can't help it," said Sky Knife. "I've never walked in to meet my death before."

Bone Splinter clapped him on the shoulder. "Don't think of it that way," he said. "Think only this—Itzamna holds us in his hands. Whether we live or die, it is for his glory and the glory of Storm Cloud our king."

Sky Knife took a deep breath. "For Itzamna," he whispered. He walked toward the steps. Only a blank wall stared at him.

"Where are you going?" asked Bone Splinter.

Sky Knife pointed at the wall. "Here," he said. "Yesterday, there were stairs here. Leading down to the cave."

Bone Splinter tapped the wall with his knife. A deep thunk echoed back. "Solid," he said. "Surely Stone Jaguar didn't build it this afternoon."

Sky Knife pressed his hands against the wall. It was cool

and rough. The gritty, slightly uneven surface felt like any other wall. "Well, it wasn't here yesterday."

Bone Splinter grunted. "We don't have the tools to break it down," he said. "What do you want to do?"

Sky Knife stepped back. "I don't think Stone Jaguar could have done this. Built a wall with stone, I mean. But if he can call up Cizin and free everyone's *nagual*—how hard could it be to create a wall with sorcery?"

Bone Splinter rubbed his chin with one hand. "An interesting idea. How do you think we could get through a wall of sorcery?"

Sky Knife reached into the cotton towel and touched the obsidian point. The tattoo at his throat tingled. Sky Knife pulled out the point.

"Remember Red Spider's assistant, the one Red Spider said could get good luck from the jade beads?" asked Sky Knife.

"Yes."

Sky Knife looked down at the green stone in his hand. "Maybe, if there's bad luck, we can get it out of this point," he said.

"Why?" asked Bone Splinter. "We don't need any more bad luck."

"No, but Stone Jaguar could use a little."

Sky Knife held the green stone up to his face. The rainbow glow of his tattoo reflected blue off the stone. Sky Knife knelt and placed the stone at the foot of the new wall, then stepped back.

"Now what?" asked Bone Splinter. "You're not going to bite it, I assume."

Sky Knife walked back to the opposite side of the room and motioned for Bone Splinter to do the same. When the warrior stood against the wall next to him, Sky Knife held out a finger and pointed toward the stone. He called fire with his mind.

A brilliant blue ball of light no bigger than a corn kernel appeared at the tip of Sky Knife's finger. It hovered for a moment, then leaped across the room to the obsidian.

A terrible yellow flash blinded Sky Knife and a loud crack pierced his ears. He screamed and raised his hands to his face.

After a few moments, sight returned. The rumbling echoes of the blast still rang in his ears.

"Bone Splinter—are you all right?"

The warrior wiped tears from his face. "Yes," he said. "Did it work?"

Sky Knife blinked tears from his own eyes. He stepped forward toward the wall. Only a black hole of a doorway faced him now.

"It's gone," he said.

Bone Splinter walked over. "Then let's go."

Sky Knife started forward, but a hand on his shoulder stopped him.

"I'll go first," said Bone Splinter.

"You can't see the steps in the dark," protested Sky Knife.

"So make light," said Bone Splinter. "Whoever is at the bottom of the steps has already heard us. But I should go first."

Sky Knife frowned, but called up a ball of light. It danced over his head brightly. Sky Knife pushed the light with his mind until it hovered over Bone Splinter.

The warrior held his knife out in front of him and descended the stairs slowly. Sky Knife followed. The stairs seemed to go down endlessly. A slight breeze brushed by him. It was cold and smelled of rotted fruit. It smelled like the temple glow before the sacrifice touched the temple.

"Sorcery," whispered Sky Knife. "Someone is working sorcery."

"We knew that," Bone Splinter whispered back over his shoulder.

"I mean right now."

Bone Splinter nodded his understanding and continued. The smell grew stronger the lower they went. It filled Sky Knife's nose and throat and made him want to sneeze.

At the bottom of the steps, Bone Splinter stopped. "Get rid of the light."

Sky Knife hesitated. Stone Jaguar had never shown him how to dismiss the light he called up. It shouldn't be too hard, but Sky Knife didn't want to take the time to experiment now. He pushed the ball of light up the steps. It zoomed away.

Sky Knife stepped around Bone Splinter. The cave was lit by a ball of green light that hovered beneath the surface of the water. Above the light, the water churned and splashed angrily.

Beneath the water, something moved. Sky Knife inched closer to the edge of the pool, but he couldn't make out what the something was. It just seemed to be a flickering shadow against the brilliant green light.

It came closer to the surface. Closer. Bone Splinter pulled Sky Knife back.

A human head broke the surface of the pool. A head connected to neck and shoulders. The person paddled toward the side of the pool and hooked his elbows over the side. The man tried to pull himself out of the pool, but he was too weak. He slid back into the water.

Sky Knife ran over and knelt by the side of the pool. He reached out his hand to the man.

"No," said Bone Splinter. The warrior knelt beside him. "It could be a trick, or an evil spirit in the form of a man."

Sky Knife grabbed the man's shirt and pulled, but the man was too heavy for Sky Knife to pull out alone.

"Help me," he said. "He's no spirit. This is *zuhuy ha*, the Navel of the World. No evil could be in the water."

Bone Splinter reached out and grabbed the man by the elbow and helped Sky Knife drag the man out onto the rock shore of the pool. "If Cizin could be on the temple, there's no reason evil could not desecrate the Navel of the World," he said. "But I agree that this does not seem to be an evil spirit. For one thing, I assume that an evil spirit that knew it would be in a pool of water would also know how to swim."

Sky Knife rolled the man over on his back. The man coughed and sat up. His deeply lined face, worn clothing, and gnarled hands spoke of the hard life of a farmer.

"Hello," said Sky Knife.

The man did not react. Sky Knife waved his hand in front of the farmer's face, but the man did not blink.

"Look," said Bone Splinter. He pointed back toward the pool.

Another head broke the surface. And another.

Sky Knife glanced back at the first farmer. "I would guess that this is where they end up," he said. "They answer Ah Mun's call, go to the *cenote*, and are brought here somehow through the water."

"If that is so," said Bone Splinter, "where are all the others? Hundreds of farmers must have answered that call by now." Bone Splinter got up and moved out of the way of the farmers as they pulled themselves out of the water.

The first farmer stood shakily and joined the others. All ignored Sky Knife and Bone Splinter. Soon, several dozen farmers stood in the room, their faces blank, their movements shaky and stilted.

As the last farmer dragged himself out of the pool, the green light died and the surface of the water calmed. Another green light, this one coming from a passage to the left, shone brilliantly in the cave's gloom.

One by one, the farmers walked toward the light and entered the passageway. Even though they moved slowly, it did not take long for them to all file out of the room. The green light died, leaving the cavern lit only by the glow at Sky Knife's throat.

"Should we follow?" asked Bone Splinter.

"Yes," said Sky Knife. "But we'll keep back a ways."

"Perhaps I should go ahead alone," said Bone Splinter. "You can't hide. Whoever's at the other end of the passage will know you're coming."

"I think we announced ourselves upstairs," said Sky Knife. "When we destroyed the sorcerous door."

"Yes, but they don't know exactly where we are or when we're coming," said Bone Splinter. "I think I should go on alone."

"No."

Sky Knife walked to the passage and glanced down. Shiny flakes of obsidian dotted the floor.

Sky Knife eased down the passage. The rock here was gray and smooth. Someone had carved out this passage by hand. Sky Knife ran his hands along the walls, awed at the effort it had taken.

Ahead, he heard a low rumble. It bounced off the craggy walls of the passage and echoed strangely, so that several seconds after he first heard it, it no longer seemed to be coming from ahead of him. The strange rumble was behind him, then over. Sky Knife shook his head.

Bone Splinter touched him on the shoulder. "Pay no attention," he said. "Go on."

Sky Knife continued forward. The passageway curved around toward the left and opened up until it was wide enough for several people to walk abreast. Then it stopped. Sky Knife ran forward and put his hands on the wall.

"No," he said. "There's got to be a way to go on."

"Look around for an opening," said Bone Splinter. The warrior dropped to his knees and felt around the wall near the floor. Sky Knife glanced up. A dark hole in the wall gaped several feet over his head.

"Here," he said. "But how do we get to it? How do the farmers get to it, for that matter."

Sky Knife felt the wall beneath the hole. Several small, deep horizontal grooves marred the wall.

"Hand holds," he said. Bone Splinter came over and joined him.

Bone Splinter boosted Sky Knife up. Sky Knife hooked his

elbows over the rim of the hole and pulled himself up. Bone Splinter followed. This passage was rough, though the bottom was smooth as if ground down by hand.

There was only enough room to crawl. Sky Knife pulled himself to his hands and knees and crept forward. The air grew hot and sultry and the smell changed from one of sorcery to the thick, bitter smell of blood.

Light came from ahead, from around a corner. Sky Knife poked his head cautiously around the stone of the corner. Just past the corner was a drop-off, as the passageway met a huge, cavernous room. Several of the great pyramids could fit inside, with a few palaces tossed in for good measure. Sky Knife gaped in awe.

The entire room was lit by brilliant balls of blue and green light that danced around the highly vaulted ceiling. On the floor of the cavern, among piles of stones and in the shadows of boulders, sat hundreds of men.

"What is it?" asked Bone Splinter.

"I think we just found the farmers," whispered Sky Knife.

A movement caught his eye. Across the room, a man moved sprightly. He gestured for one of the farmers to come to him. The farmer did. The man led him away down another passageway.

The man turned back once and looked straight at Sky Knife. Sky Knife's heart jumped and he fought the urge to duck back down the passageway. Surely the man couldn't actually see him—but no doubt he'd see movement if Sky Knife pulled his head back.

Sky Knife bit his lip and stared back at the man. The man wasn't particularly tall, and his graying hair was swept back from his face with grease. Something about him was familiar.

Sky Knife's blood ran cold. He did know the man. He looked twenty years younger than he had yesterday, but it was he.

Death Smoke.

# 30

›››››

The strangely youthful Death Smoke turned away and the farmer followed him down a passageway. Both of the men were swallowed up in the darkness.

Sky Knife pulled his head back and sat down against the cold wall of the passage.

"Well?" asked Bone Splinter.

"A big room," said Sky Knife. "Hundreds of men, just sitting around. And Death Smoke . . ." Sky Knife's voice failed him and he couldn't go on.

"What about him?"

"He's . . . he's younger somehow," said Sky Knife. "He stands straight and his hair is only slightly gray."

Bone Splinter frowned. "More sorcery," he said. "Power had to be used for that, too. But where is he getting all this energy?"

Sky Knife shook his head. "I don't know. But the farmers are obviously part of it."

Bone Splinter eased forward and peeked around the corner. "Itzamna," he whispered. "It shouldn't be too hard to get across the room unseen, what with the rubble all over and the farmers. But getting down to the floor could be a problem."

"The farmers had to manage it somehow," said Sky Knife. "There are probably handholds carved into the wall."

"I would think so," said Bone Splinter. "What I meant was that we're sure to be seen."

"Oh." Sky Knife thought a moment. "But the farmers didn't react to us in the other room," he said. "Perhaps they won't react to us here, either."

"Could be. Only one way to find out."

Sky Knife took a deep breath. "Right." He got back on hands and knees and crawled around the corner. Cautiously, he crawled to the edge and glanced down.

The floor of the cavern was at least twenty feet below him, but near the wall, a pile of rock debris cut the distance in half. Sky Knife backed up to the corner and turned around. When he reached the edge, he lay on his stomach. The gritty floor of the passage scraped against his belly and chest as Sky Knife lowered his legs and then his hips down over the edge of the drop-off.

Bone Splinter caught his wrists. "I'll lower you," he said. Sky Knife nodded and let Bone Splinter support his weight. Bone Splinter lowered him down over the edge and then dropped him. He didn't drop more than a few feet, but the impact jarred him and he fell backward down the slope.

Sky Knife tumbled down the slope, scraping hands and knees on rough stone. The jaguar-skin cloak protected his back. He slid to a stop at the bottom, skinned but otherwise uninjured. A few rocks tumbled down after him and struck him in the legs. Sky Knife glanced around quickly. Surely someone had seen him, heard him.

But the farmers stared blankly in front of them, each appearing to be lost in his own thoughts. Sky Knife looked back up to the entrance to the passage. Bone Splinter peered down at him. Sky Knife waved and stood on shaky legs. Blood dripped from shallow scraped on his knees and forearms. Old scabs had been torn away. Some hung loosely along with small strips of skin. Sky Knife pulled them off. The wounds stung, but not badly.

Bone Splinter's descent was a little more graceful than Sky Knife's. The warrior lowered himself until only his fingertips supported him. He let go and dropped onto the debris. Bone Splinter half slid, half ran down the slope without ever losing his feet.

"Are you all right?" asked Bone Splinter.

Sky Knife nodded. "A little cut up, but nothing serious," he said. He pointed toward the passage where Death Smoke and the farmer had disappeared. "There's where Death Smoke went. We'd better see what he's doing."

Bone Splinter grunted. "Right," he said. He glanced around. "But what about all these peasants? Will they give us away?"

Sky Knife walked to the nearest man and waved his hand in front of the man's face. The man did not react. Sky Knife pinched the man's forearm hard. Still nothing. The man breathed deeply and easily as if asleep.

"I think they're drugged or there's a spell on them," said Sky Knife. "We can't help them now."

Sky Knife stood and looked around the room. In the shade of the next boulder sat a small girl. Sky Knife walked by a peasant woman to get to the girl and knelt by her.

"What's your name?" he asked. He touched the girl's hair. She stared ahead of her blankly as the others had done.

Bone Splinter knelt on the other side of the girl. Sky Knife held the girl's hand briefly. It was cold, but Sky Knife felt a pulse in her wrist.

Bone Splinter put a massive hand over Sky Knife's and the girl's. "Whatever Death Smoke is doing, it means the death of these people," he said. "You can smell it."

Sky Knife nodded. The smell of blood he had noticed in the passage was nearly overwhelming down next to the floor. Mixed with it was the pungent smell of decay. Over everything was the rotten fruit smell of the temple glow.

"Death," said Sky Knife, "would seem to have taken residence here. Perhaps that's why Cizin was in the acropolis—this place is his home."

"At least for now it is," said Bone Splinter. "Such a foul stench could only be pleasant to a foul creature like Cizin."

Sky Knife stood and reluctantly left the girl in the shade of the boulder. He wanted to take her away, but in looking around the room, he saw many such little girls, and small boys as well. Each of them stared blankly. If Sky Knife was going to rescue them, he would have to rescue them all. That meant facing Stone Jaguar. And Death Smoke.

Sky Knife walked carefully to the opposite side of the room. The rubble made footing tricky. Occasionally, Sky Knife had to climb over a large rock. He left blood behind on each of them, though the bleeding was very slow. He sat down on a dog-sized rock and looked at his knees and elbows. Blood continued to seep out of his wounds.

"What's the matter?" asked Bone Splinter.

Sky Knife shook his head. "I don't know. These scrapes should have stopped bleeding by now."

Bone Splinter knelt, grabbed Sky Knife's wrist, and examined the elbow. "What do you think it means."

Sky Knife looked toward the passageway where Death Smoke had gone. "Perhaps it's because of all the sorcery."

Bone Splinter released Sky Knife's wrist and stood up. Sky Knife stood up as well and continued toward the passageway.

Sky Knife stopped at the beginning of the passage. This passage was narrow and high, the top shrouded in darkness. No balls of blue and green lit the corridor; what light there was was provided by cavern behind them. Sky Knife's shadow stretched out ahead of him.

He stepped into the passageway, Bone Splinter just behind him. The glow from his serpent tattoo lit his way.

The corridor curved away slightly to the left. Although it looked flat, Sky Knife could feel the rise of a gentle slope as he walked.

Sky Knife had no idea how far he'd walked—one hundred yards? two hundred?—before the corridor widened out into a round room about twenty feet across. To his right, the narrow corridor continued.

Sky Knife stepped into the room and headed for the other opening in the walls.

"Wait," said Bone Splinter.

Sky Knife turned to him. "What is it?"

Before Bone Splinter could answer, Sky Knife felt it, too. Although Sky Knife thought he could hear something, he felt the vibration more in his gut than heard it. The vibration spread through Sky Knife's body. The pain of his wounds receded, and his fear bled away.

Death Smoke entered the room from the opening on Sky Knife's right. He walked up to Sky Knife, peered into his face, and grunted. The older man's fetid breath swept by Sky Knife, but it didn't disgust him as it usually did. He felt terribly, unshakably calm. He couldn't remember ever feeling this way before.

It was wrong, though. Sky Knife fought to struggle, fought to remember at least a little fear, a little pain. But it was beyond him. Only the heavy burden of stillness lay on him.

"I knew you'd come," said Death Smoke. The sound of the older man's voice slid into Sky Knife's mind like water. It dripped pleasantness and tranquility into his soul.

"Stone Jaguar said you wouldn't, but then, he's underestimated you from the start, hasn't he?" asked Death Smoke. "Saving the *chic-chac*—that was brilliant. Even now, after its death, it aids you."

Sky Knife fought to open his mouth, but the muscles of his face remained stubbornly outside his control. Sky Knife knew he should ask Death Smoke all the questions he had. But as soon as he thought of anything, it slid away beyond his reach.

"It doesn't matter now, anyway," said Death Smoke. He moved away, toward Bone Splinter. Sky Knife wanted to turn his head, to keep the older man in sight, but he couldn't move. "My spell holds you as it holds the farmers. Ignorant peasants that they are, they were easier to snare. But you are untrained and were unable to resist my spell for very long."

Death Smoke walked back to the opening from which he'd come. "Come along," he said.

Death Smoke walked away. Sky Knife's foot jerked forward and he took a step. Then another. And another. Awkwardly, but steadily, he made his way down the corridor.

At the end of the corridor, Death Smoke paused and glanced over his shoulder. "Once you see, you'll understand, Sky Knife," he said. "Your death will aid the greater glory of Tikal."

Death Smoke walked into another monstrously huge cavern lit by globes of blue and green fire high overhead. In the center of the room stood Stone Jaguar. He held a heart in his hands; before him, on an altar, lay the body of a man.

Light streaked from the heart around the cavern, but instead of rising to the heavens as usual, the light entered Stone Jaguar. Even through the terrible calm, Sky Knife felt a tinge of horror—Stone Jaguar did not offer the sacrifice to the gods. He kept it to himself.

Sky Knife stepped forward into the room unwillingly with a jerky step, right behind Death Smoke. The stench of blood and decay hit him all over again. Sky Knife wished he had control of his body so he could turn and run. Even under the spell, his gut twisted and Sky Knife felt like he might vomit.

When the light had faded, Stone Jaguar threw the heart behind him, where it joined others in a pile. Sky Knife stared at the quivering mass behind Stone Jaguar, his brain barely able to comprehend the meaning of it. The mass must represent hundreds of people, slaughtered on the altar to give power to Stone Jaguar and Death Smoke.

A single heart rolled off the pile and Sky Knife suddenly understood. The hearts were not dead—they lived. The heart at Stone Jaguar's feet continued to beat. Stone Jaguar picked it up and pitched it back onto the pile.

In the back of his mind, Sky Knife screamed.

# 31

›››››

Death Smoke descended the steps that led from the corridor to the floor of the cavern. Sky Knife followed helplessly. His skin crawled with the tingle of sorcery, but the feeling was vile, like the smell of fouled water.

At the bottom of the steps, Death Smoke strode easily forward around heaps of bodies, ignoring the way they jerked spasmodically. Death Smoke stepped on an arm of a young woman and her fist clenched as if in pain. Another arm, this one without a body, dug its nails into the rubble-strewn floor and crawled slowly out of Death Smoke's way. Sky Knife was suddenly glad he couldn't look around him. He could see more than enough without turning his head.

Stone Jaguar stood on the small pyramid in the center of the cavern. The man's face was ravaged with anger; his lips curled back into a snarl. He wore only a blue loincloth and a necklace of jade. Stone Jaguar stared at Sky Knife with such hatred, Sky Knife cringed despite Death Smoke's spell. The tingle of sorcery grew stronger until it thrummed along Sky Knife's skin from neck to ankles and made him want to scream.

Stone Jaguar motioned to two naked men who stood behind

him. The men, blood-coated and bent over with weariness, came forward, picked up the corpse on the altar, and threw it off the side of the pyramid. The two men returned to their places without blinking or reacting to the sights in the cavern in any way.

A small ray of warmth lit Sky Knife's heart from the tattoo at his neck. The dreadful calm in his mind shifted just a little. Sky Knife tried to move his hands, but they were still beyond his control. At least now, he had a little hope that he would be able to free himself from Death Smoke's spell. But what about Bone Splinter? Sky Knife could not turn around to see the warrior, but he heard the big man walking behind him. Perhaps if Sky Knife could free himself, he would be able to help the other man.

Death Smoke continued walking toward the pyramid at the center of the cavern while Stone Jaguar's gaze never left Sky Knife. Finally, they arrived at the base of the structure.

"Come here," commanded Stone Jaguar.

Sky Knife's legs took him up the nine steps to the top of the structure. His feet squelched in the layers of dried and almost-dried blood on the steps. Some of the blood slid between his toes. It was warm and slick.

Sky Knife's feet brought him halfway across the top of the pyramid, close enough to Stone Jaguar to touch him if his hands had been under his control.

"Pretentious boy," growled Stone Jaguar. "First you wear four stripes of paint as if you were royal, and now you wear the cloak of the High Priest! I will be well rid of you."

Another sliver of warmth crept into Sky Knife's heart. A healthy, warm feeling flowered in his chest and spread slowly to his shoulders. The sorcerous burden of calm relaxed a bit more.

Stone Jaguar reached out to grab the jaguar skin cloak, but it billowed up and back, out of his reach, as if a sudden wind had caught it. Sky Knife felt no breeze, only the awful tingle of sorcery against his skin.

Death Smoke laughed. The sound surprised Sky Knife, as it came from just behind him. He had not heard the other man come up the steps.

"I told you the cloak was no longer yours," said Death Smoke. "If Sky Knife is allowed to touch it, it is the will of the gods."

"What gods?" asked Stone Jaguar. "The gods of Tikal should be protecting me, not him. I am the one acting in their behalf. I am *Ah men* of Tikal."

"Perhaps the gods see it differently," said Death Smoke. "Or perhaps they have become too confused by the foreign influences in our city."

Stone Jaguar stepped back. "I will have my cloak back," he said. "Sky Knife will not wear it to his grave, confused gods or no."

Sky Knife wanted to ask Stone Jaguar so many questions, but his lips and jaw remained fastened shut.

"You will never wear it again," said Death Smoke. "I have seen it."

"You were the one who saw your own death, yet here you are, younger and healthier than I've ever known you," said Stone Jaguar. "Perhaps your sight is what is confused."

As the other men bickered, Sky Knife concentrated on his hands. Slowly, so slowly, he found he could twitch his fingers. He took a deep breath and a tendril of fear swept back into his mind. Sky Knife could have cried with relief.

"The time draws near," said Death Smoke.

"Oh, shut up, old man," said Stone Jaguar.

"Be careful what you say to me," whispered Death Smoke. "You could not have done all this without me. It was I who drew the farmers here for you to sacrifice. You have made nothing but mistakes. You called Cizin—and cannot now drive him away. You thought Sky Knife was no threat, yet here he is."

"He is under your power," said Stone Jaguar. "So he is no threat."

"But he got here," insisted Death Smoke. "He should not have been able to come so far without training. And you could not even kill him when you had the chance."

"It is just as well. He can die on my altar tonight. And don't forget your clumsy attempt to poison him. Drinking the water of the pool, a test of a priest—bah."

"What about you?" shouted Death Smoke. "You threw a rock! You, *Ah men* and *Ah nacom* of Tikal, threw a rock at a boy."

Sky Knife made a fist carefully and flexed his toes. The warmth from his tattoo had spread over his entire body and into his mind. Sky Knife fought to keep his revulsion at the sights in the cavern from showing on his face.

"Come, boy," said Stone Jaguar. Sky Knife took an unwilling step forward, but the overwhelming compulsion he had felt earlier had faded. He could not disobey. Not yet. But soon.

"Lie down on the altar," commanded Stone Jaguar. "Your Mayan blood will aid me in eliminating the foreign influences in our city. The merchants leave already. And tonight, when I have consolidated my power, the king will feel my wrath."

"A Teotihuacano as king," said Death Smoke. "It is an outrage we have borne these fifteen long years. Until the *katun* changed and our opportunity came."

Sky Knife stepped toward the blood-covered altar. The two naked men came around to stand on each side of the altar, prepared, no doubt, to pin him down. A touch of outrage colored Sky Knife's thoughts. There should be four attendants. The way Stone Jaguar had this set up, there were six people on the pyramid—assuming Bone Splinter had climbed the stairs with Death Smoke. Six people made no sense. There should be nine.

More and more, the warmth in his body spread into his mind, pushing against Death Smoke's spell. Suddenly, the love and comfort of the *chic-chac* burst into his mind in one swift stroke that nearly sent Sky Knife to his knees. Even his disgust of the stench in the cavern dissipated. In place of the smell of blood, flowers and the fresh smell of the jungle after a brief rain crowded in his nose. The tingle of Stone Jaguar's sorcery abruptly vanished. Sky Knife moaned in relief.

"What?" shouted Death Smoke. "What's happening?"

Sky Knife whirled. Death Smoke had aged. He looked now as he always had—stooped, wrinkled, white-haired. Blood ran from his nose and ears.

"He broke your spell," said Stone Jaguar. "Fool!"

Stone Jaguar began chanting, hands spread wide. The two naked men collapsed where they stood and lay, unmoving, on the stones.

Death Smoke straightened himself slowly and pointed a bony finger at Sky Knife. "You think to fight me, boy?" he said. "I was a sorcerer when your grandfather was an infant. You are nothing."

Death Smoke closed his eyes and clapped his hands together. A ball of yellow flame appeared over his head with a loud boom. Sky Knife raised his own hands and called fire. An intense white flame appeared.

The yellow and white flames shot toward each other and combined in a dazzling conflagration. Sky Knife covered his eyes with his hands, momentarily blinded. Death Smoke's laughter rose above the crackling and blazing of the flames.

"I will crush you!" shouted the older man.

Slowly, the whirling ball of flame approached Sky Knife. He pushed against it with his mind, in much the same way he'd sent the ball of flame away up the steps earlier. He could look at the flame now without it hurting his eyes. White and yellow tongues of fire danced around each other. Sky Knife stared at the white of the flames and pushed them away. In the back of his mind, he felt the returning tingle of Stone Jaguar's sorcery, but he couldn't take his attention from the flames. They pressed against him and he had to push with all the power of his concentration against them to keep them at bay.

Then the whirling slowed slightly and the flames edged toward Death Smoke. Heartened, Sky Knife pushed against them harder.

"No!" shouted Death Smoke as the flames touched him. Death Smoke dropped to his knees. Abruptly, the flames vanished. The air was clear for a moment. Then smoke rose from the pyramid. It swirled around slowly and coalesced into the form of a giant butterfly.

Sky Knife felt in himself a strand of sorcery that bound him to the smoke. It was his creature, to do his bidding. He pointed toward Death Smoke.

The butterfly wrapped its six smoke-legs around the old man and beat its blue-tinted wings. It rose over the pyramid, carrying Death Smoke with it. The old man screamed.

The butterfly rose to the ceiling and dissipated against the rocks. Death Smoke, released from the creature, fell, still screaming, to the stones below, just before the steps of the pyramid.

Sky Knife turned away, sickened at the thought he'd caused the old man's death. His knees trembled in weariness and he panted heavily. Calling the flames and the butterfly creature had weakened him. But he still had another opponent. Sky Knife looked over to Stone Jaguar.

"So he saw his own death, after all," said the priest. "Now it is your turn to die." Stone Jaguar clapped his hands together.

Sky Knife didn't wait to see what Stone Jaguar would do. He turned to Bone Splinter and rushed toward the warrior. Bone Splinter blinked, freshly released from Death Smoke's spell and apparently confused. Sky Knife had no time to explain. He felt the cold claws of Stone Jaguar's spell in his back.

Sky Knife ran headlong into Bone Splinter. He and the warrior tumbled off of the pyramid into the heap of quivering bodies below.

# 32

›››››

Sky Knife bit back a scream as he rolled down the pile. Intestines, blue-hued and rubbery, caught at his ankles and wrists. Sky Knife pulled away frantically, but his elbow slammed into another person's empty chest. Black goo coated Sky Knife's arm.

Sky Knife tried to push himself away from the bloody mess, but everywhere he turned, there were more lifeless limbs and gaping chest cavities. Stomachs, unaccountably limp and flat, hung out underneath gleaming white ribs. Sky Knife closed his eyes and pushed away with his feet, trying to stand.

Strong hands grabbed his shoulders and pulled him up. Sky Knife screamed, afraid Stone Jaguar had called up a smoke butterfly that would carry him to the roof and drop him.

"Shut up," said Bone Splinter. Sky Knife opened his eyes. Bone Splinter plopped Sky Knife down on the stones of the cavern floor.

Sky Knife turned to the warrior. Bone Splinter's eyes were wide and he looked as though he might scream himself.

"We have to get out of here," said Bone Splinter, his voice high with fright. "Itzamna! What a place."

Sky Knife glanced up. Stone Jaguar stood on the summit of the pyramid, chanting another spell.

"Let's go," said Sky Knife. "Anywhere away from the pyramid."

Sky Knife looked around, but here, against the pyramid's side, was the only spot clear of bodies he could see. "We'll have to climb over," he said, biting back his disgust. Resolutely, he stepped on a pale, blood-streaked back and started climbing the pile. His hand slipped on waxy skin and rubbery, slimy organs. Sky Knife kept his eyes on the top of the pile and tried to ignore what his hands and feet touched.

The hair on Sky Knife's neck tingled and the rotten fruit smell rolled over him, overpowering, for a moment, the stench of old blood and entrails. Sky Knife redoubled his efforts to put distance between himself and Stone Jaguar's sorcery.

At the top of the pile, Sky Knife threw his legs over and slid down the other side. Several bodiless limbs and heads rolled down with him. One head stopped just in front of him, the windpipe stiff and white amidst the red ruins of the throat and skin. Nausea rose in Sky Knife's gut, and this time, no spell held it back. He rolled onto his knees and heaved.

Behind him, he heard Bone Splinter doing the same thing. No doubt the warrior had seen death before, but never, ever anything like this. Sky Knife wished he'd never seen any of it.

Stone Jaguar screamed, "Kill them! Kill them!"

Sky Knife stood up and turned. Stone Jaguar stood in a globe of glowing green haze. Tendrils of green reached out toward the bodies in the cavern. As it touched them, they moved. One of them sat up and glanced toward Sky Knife. The dead man's eyes had rolled back; only white showed to Sky Knife. The man rose to his feet.

"Itzamna," whispered Sky Knife. "Come on, let's go!"

Bone Splinter wiped his mouth with the back of his hand and nodded. Sky Knife turned toward the corridor that lead back to the room where the farmers had sat.

More and more bodies rolled themselves into sitting positions and stood. All focused their white stares on Sky Knife. Sky Knife's gut cramped again, but he didn't stop running. The dead, with their abdomens gaping open, trailing intestines behind them, came after them. Sky Knife tried to ignore them and concentrate on where he put his feet. He feared if he slipped now, he'd go down under a mass of bodies that would grab him and not let go.

A young woman directly in his path reached out for him. Sky Knife bit his lip and pushed her out of the way as he ran past. The young woman grabbed his wrist, but let go immediately.

Sky Knife stopped. Between him and his goal stood an army of the dead now. Bone Splinter drew up beside him. Sky Knife glanced behind them. Thirty or forty more of the dead shambled blindly along, cutting off any route back toward the pyramid.

A terrible weariness crept over Sky Knife. The smoke creature and the ball of flame had taken a lot of energy from him. He thought about calling more fire, but knew he didn't have the power.

"We can't fight them all," said Bone Splinter.

Sky Knife kept his eyes on the dead behind them—they were closer. The young woman who had grabbed him before slowly climbed back to her feet and approached.

Bone Splinter raised his knife, then lowered it slowly. "She's already *dead*," he shouted. "What can we do?"

Sky Knife and Bone Splinter backed away from the woman. Sky Knife stopped. They would only end up backing into the rest of the dead guarding the entrance to the cavern.

The young woman paused and Sky Knife took a good look at her. Her hair was matted with dried blood and her skin slack all over her body, especially her face, making it look too large for her. Her hands were callused, her knuckles gnarled from hard work. Yet her nose was perfectly straight, her chin pointed delicately, her breasts full and round. She had been pretty in life, and young. Anger flooded Sky Knife's mind. Who was Stone Jaguar that he could take the gift of life from such people? Not just one, not just for the gods. But hundreds, and all for his own glory.

Sky Knife stepped forward and pushed the woman again, but she was too quick for him. She grabbed his wrists. Her grip was strong. Sky Knife groaned as her hold became painful. She might even be strong enough to break his wrists.

The woman let go and stumbled back. Sky Knife jumped back toward Bone Splinter, holding his bruised wrists close to his chest.

"What happened?" asked Bone Splinter.

"I don't know."

The woman stumbled backwards a few feet and sank to her knees. Softly, she tumbled over onto the floor of the cavern and lay still and dead once more.

Understanding crept into Sky Knife's thoughts. He reached for the gourd of tobacco juice. "It's the juice," he said. "The dead can't stay near it."

He unstoppered the gourd. Bone Splinter held out his hands. Sky Knife poured a few drops into the warrior's hands, then reapplied the juice to his knees and elbows. He let a drop fall to the floor. It struck the pale gray hand of an old man. The juice hissed where it touched the dead flesh and smoked. The hand jerked rapidly several times before being still again.

"Let's get out of here," he said. He walked forward, sprinkling a few drops on the corpses as they passed. The dead drew back from their path.

There were still the dead by the entrance. Sky Knife walked toward them and poured some juice into his hand. When he got close, he threw it onto the nearest corpse. The man withered and plopped to the ground immediately.

Sky Knife ran for the entrance, Bone Splinter on his heels. He sprinkled more juice as he ran, and the dead got out of his way. Finally, Sky Knife and Bone Splinter stood in the relative shelter of the narrow corridor. Sky Knife didn't stop until he reached the round room where they had encountered Death Smoke.

Sky Knife's knees would no longer hold him. He slumped to the floor. Bone Splinter did the same.

"Itzamna," the warrior whispered over and over.

Sky Knife clasped his hands to his shoulders. He shook so badly, he felt he'd shake his bones right out of his body. The bloody sights of the cavern seemed to hover in front of him whenever he closed his eyes.

Slowly, the trembling faded. Sky Knife glanced back down the corridor. Only a faint tingle of sorcery came to him and he heard nothing but the beating of his own heart.

"Stone Jaguar must be planning something new," said Sky Knife. His teeth chattered together in shock and fear. "We'd better get out while we can."

"We have to stop him," Bone Splinter said. "We have to defeat this evil."

"How?" asked Sky Knife. He looked the warrior in the eyes. The warrior was determined, but panic lurked in his eyes, too. "He has the power from hundreds of sacrifices to aid him."

"What do you mean?"

Sky Knife took a deep breath to calm himself. "There's always a great release of power after a sacrifice. Usually, the priest offers it to the gods. You've seen that."

"The dancing lights?"

"Yes. But Stone Jaguar is taking all of that inside himself. He's adding to his own power by killing others."

"Whatever for?"

"I'm not sure exactly how he plans to do it," said Sky Knife, "but he intends to depose the king."

Bone Splinter's face curled in a snarl and all trace of fear left it. "Then we must stop him before he harms the king. We have to go back to the cavern."

Sky Knife tried to push himself to his feet, but weariness overtook him and he dropped back to the floor. "I don't think I can walk," he said. "Defeating Death Smoke exhausted me."

"Then I'll carry you."

Sky Knife closed his eyes, humiliated. A familiar giggle startled him. Sky Knife opened his eyes and looked around.

Cizin stood in the corridor leading to the cavern.

"Eat your bones!" the specter cried.

"Bones bones bones!" gibbered voices from the walls.

Sky Knife forced himself to his feet and leaned against the wall behind him. He reached into the pouch where he had put Stone Jaguar's cigars.

Bone Splinter edged over to Sky Knife. "What shall we do?" he asked, his voice low and confident.

Sky Knife's trembling hand wrapped around several cigars. "I'm not sure," he said. "But I do know he doesn't like tobacco."

Sky Knife stared at the end of one of the cigars, willing it to burst into flames. Sweat trickled down his face even though the room was rapidly growing colder.

Sky Knife concentrated while the awful figure approached him. Finally, a small flame burst from the end of the cigar. He handed the cigar to Bone Splinter. "Attack him with it," he ordered.

Bone Splinter didn't hesitate. He grabbed the cigar and charged Cizin. The specter dodged. Bone Splinter missed his intended target of Cizin's chest and got instead the figure's right hand.

Hand and cigar slammed into the wall and Cizin screamed. Bone Splinter ducked as Cizin swung at him with his left hand. But the right was fixed to the wall just as surely as if Bone Splinter had run a spike through it. Cizin tugged, but his hand remained trapped between wall and glowing cigar.

Sky Knife focused on another cigar. For a long moment, nothing happened. Then, finally, the cigar lit. He handed it to Bone Splinter. The warrior approached Cizin warily, then jabbed the cigar into the specter's left hand. Cizin screamed again and yellow smoke came from his hands where the cigars touched them.

Sky Knife lit one more cigar, but it was so, so hard. He knew he would not be able to light another, so he lit the rest he had from that one.

"Pin his feet," Sky Knife whispered as he slumped to the floor. Bone Splinter nodded and took the three remaining cigars. With two, he pinned the figure's feet to the floor.

"What about this one?" Bone Splinter asked.

Sky Knife stared at the blotched figure quivering in agony on the wall. "Right into his heart," he said.

Bone Splinter shoved the last cigar into Cizin's chest. It sank into Cizin's flesh. Cizin screamed again. Bone Splinter backed up and covered his ears. Sky Knife did the same. The screams echoed through his brain and grated against his skull like gravel.

Cizin's entire body smoked. The yellow tendrils of smoke drifted down to the floor and disappeared into fine cracks.

"Death to you!" shouted Cizin, but the gibbering voices did not echo him this time. The terrible figure melted away little by little. His blotched skin separated from his body and slid down to the floor, becoming insubstantial as mist as it did so. Flesh dropped off Cizin in chunks, and his organs fell to the floor. Finally, only a skeleton remained.

With a final scream, Cizin's skeleton splintered into uncountable yellow pieces and dissipated into the air. One of his eyeballs fell to the floor intact and rolled toward Sky Knife.

It faded, too, but while it did so, its gaze remained firmly fixed on Sky Knife.

It may have been Sky Knife's imagination, but the eyeball of the death god seemed vengeful. Sky Knife swallowed heavily, convinced Cizin would remember his name in the future. It was not a comforting thought.

# 33

›››››

"Itzamna," whispered Bone Splinter. "Is he gone? From Tikal, I mean."

"I don't know. I'm sure we can't kill a god," said Sky Knife. His voice cracked with weariness and his breath came shallow and shaky. "Stone Jaguar called him, but couldn't make him go away."

"Of course not," said Bone Splinter as he retrieved the still-glowing cigars. He ground them out as he did so. "How could someone evil dispel evil? Even a child could see that wouldn't work."

"Stone Jaguar is no child," said Sky Knife. "And he doesn't see it. And we still have to face him."

"Then we face him."

Bone Splinter returned the remains of the cigars to Sky Knife. Sky Knife tried to return them to the bag, but his hands trembled violently. Bone Splinter held the bag open and put the cigars inside.

"Thank you," said Sky Knife. "It seems I'm not much use right now."

Bone Splinter grasped Sky Knife's shoulder. "Don't say

that," he said. "You got us through the cavern and killed Death Smoke. And you had the means to get rid of Cizin. You've been more use to us tonight than I have been."

Sky Knife would have protested, but the earnest look in Bone Splinter's face stopped him. He nodded.

Bone Splinter bent over to pick up Sky Knife.

"I can walk," protested Sky Knife.

"Perhaps," said Bone Splinter, "but for how long? You still have to fight Stone Jaguar. Conserve your strength."

Sky Knife clenched his fists in embarrassment, but nodded. Bone Splinter was right. But how could Sky Knife face Stone Jaguar when he was so weak?

Bone Splinter walked down the corridor, but stopped after only a few steps. Sky Knife looked down the corridor.

The narrow passage was crammed with the dead, piled upon each other. The first ones must have lain down on the floor while the other had lain down in layers on top of them. They had layered themselves all the way to the ceiling high overhead.

The dead had formed a wall of flesh Sky Knife had no idea how to get through.

"Whatever he's planning, it's obvious he doesn't want to be interrupted," said Bone Splinter. "I'm all for interrupting him."

"The tobacco juice won't get us through that mess," said Sky Knife. "They're jammed in so tight, they couldn't retreat from it if they wanted to."

"What next?"

Sky Knife closed his eyes and thought for a moment. "Whatever Stone Jaguar is going to do, he can't afford to expend more energy on us because his supply of power has run out. He has to use what he's got stored because no more farmers are going to be coming his way."

"Unless there's another way into the cavern."

"Could be," said Sky Knife, "but the farmers were snared by Death Smoke's spell. No Death Smoke, no spell."

"So we have time to plan something without being attacked," said Bone Splinter, "but at the same time, we have no idea how much time before Stone Jaguar strikes at the king."

Sky Knife sighed. "That's about it."

"Then I say we look for another way back into the cavern. There might be hundreds of passages around here. Let's go back to the cavern where the farmers were and start looking from there."

"All right."

Bone Splinter carried Sky Knife quickly back to the room and through the other narrow passage to the cavern. The balls of light that had lit it previously had disappeared. Against the immensity of the room, the glow from Sky Knife's tattoo was pitifully small.

Bone Splinter stopped. "I don't remember there being any steps," he said.

Sky Knife thought back. "I don't remember any, either."

"Good." Bone Splinter stepped forward again into the room. He moved slowly and put his feet down with care.

"What's that?" someone shouted.

A woman screamed. The sound of sobbing reached Sky Knife's ears.

"The farmers," he said. "They're still here."

"Well, they can't see to get out," said Bone Splinter. "Any more than we can see another way back to the other cavern."

Footsteps. Bone Splinter stopped while the other person approached them. When the other person was about six feet away, he came within the glow of the tattoo. A short, skinny farmer stood there. Grime stained his face and arms.

"Who are you?" he demanded. "And where is Ah Mun? We were told we were needed in his fields."

"You were told incorrectly," said Bone Splinter. "It was a trick to lure you away from your own fields."

"I am Sky Knife." Sky Knife tried to sound calm and confident. "I am a priest of Itzamna. I was sent by the king to find the source of our city's bad luck."

The farmer looked confused. Slowly, hope crowded out the fear and confusion. He knelt in front of them. "I should have recognized you by the cloak, Lord," he said. "I apologize for my stupidity."

Sky Knife was embarrassed by the display. "There is a way to get out of here, but it is high on a wall on the other side of the room. I can't stop to help you look for it right now."

"Look above a pile of rocks," said Bone Splinter. "It is a small crawlspace."

The farmer bowed and backed away without looking again at Sky Knife. "Thank you, Lord," he said.

Sky Knife waited until the farmer was well away. "He thinks I'm Stone Jaguar," he whispered.

"To a farmer, a priest is a priest," said Bone Splinter. "Why bother to tell one from another when they are all sorcerers?"

"Do you think they'll get out?"

Bone Splinter hesitated. "Probably not. Not without light. You're too weak to do that for them. Let them struggle on their own for now. If we fail in our task, Stone Jaguar will have them again anyway. If we succeed, we can worry about getting out then."

Sky Knife nodded. Bone Splinter was right. The farmers would be on their own until the struggle with Stone Jaguar was over.

"Put me down," said Sky Knife. "I've got to see if I can stand on my own."

Bone Splinter lowered Sky Knife slowly. Sky Knife planted his feet wide and stood. He kept a hand on Bone Splinter's shoulder, but his legs held him up.

"Good," said Bone Splinter. "You should face him on your feet and make him grovel before you and beg for his life."

Sky Knife flushed. "First I have to beat him."

"You will."

A deep rumble filled the air. It echoed in the cavern, and throbbed in Sky Knife's gut. A small stone struck him in the shoulder.

"The ceiling's coming down," he gasped. Bone Splinter grabbed him and pushed him down to the floor, covering Sky Knife with his own body.

Screams came from all around Sky Knife. The high, thin shrieks of children mixed with the deeper screams of their parents.

"Looks like we don't have a choice," said Bone Splinter as the rumble continued and rocks rained down around them. Sky Knife felt one of them strike Bone Splinter and the warrior grunted.

"Time to get out," said Sky Knife. "Which way?"

"I don't know."

Sky Knife closed his eyes and concentrated. He couldn't remember exactly where they were in relation to the entrances to the cavern. But a small tingle on his left shoulder grabbed his attention.

"To our left," he said.

"Are you sure?"

"Yes!"

Bone Splinter grabbed Sky Knife and picked him up. He clutched Sky Knife close to his chest and stepped as quickly and carefully as he could.

The tingle in Sky Knife's shoulder changed until it was in the center of his chest. "You're going the right way!" he shouted.

Bone Splinter stopped. "The wall," he said. He put Sky Knife down.

Sky Knife pressed himself against the wall. Fewer stones rained down from the ceiling here. His right shoulder tingled.

"To the right," he said. He made his way along the wall. Soon he came to the pile of rocks and climbed up. The slope was steep and he sent several rocks spinning down the slope behind him. "Careful," he shouted to Bone Splinter above the rumble.

The handholds were obvious in the tattoo's glow. Sky Knife tried to climb, but his arms would not pull him up. He slumped against the wall.

Bone Splinter came up behind him. "Here," said the warrior. "Hold onto the wall." He picked Sky Knife up by the hips and pushed him up the wall. Sky Knife hooked his elbows over the crawlspace's entrance, but he couldn't pull himself up. Bone Splinter shifted his grasp until he had Sky Knife by the knees and he pushed him up with a mighty heave. Sky Knife slid into the crawlspace.

Bone Splinter followed him quickly.

"The farmers," said Sky Knife. "We have to get them out." Sky Knife tried to ignore the screams, but they cut through him like a priest's obsidian blade.

"We have to defeat Stone Jaguar first," insisted Bone Splinter.

"How? We can't get to him from here."

"Back to the pool," said Bone Splinter. "We'll look for another way from there."

Sky Knife raised himself to hands and knees. Behind him, the rumble rose to a sudden shriek of rock against rock.

"What's that?" screamed Sky Knife, but his words were drowned out by the horrible crash in the cavern. Dust billowed into his face and he choked.

Bone Splinter gagged. "The ceiling," he said. "Itzamna. All those people . . ."

Sky Knife's heart twisted in despair and tears rolled down his face, warm and salty. "We have to stop him," he said. "We have to."

"Go, then," urged Bone Splinter. "Hurry. Whatever he's going to do is almost upon us. Can't you feel it?"

Sky Knife paused, unsure what Bone Splinter meant. A painful throbbing hit his ears as he did so and he winced. Stone

Jaguar must be doing some terrible sorcery right now. Sky Knife crawled back toward the room of the *zuhuy ha*.

Sky Knife was tired and couldn't move quickly. Bone Splinter half-pushed, half-prodded him through the last bit of the crawlspace. Sky Knife let himself fall down to the smooth floor of the corridor. Bone Splinter jumped down beside him, picked him up, and jogged back to the room of the water. Bone Splinter deposited Sky Knife by the water. Sky Knife let his hands and forehead sink to the floor, his energy spent. A deep exhaustion flowed into each joint, every muscle. Sky Knife felt as though he'd never move again.

"The stairs are gone," said Bone Splinter from the other side of the pool. "May the beasts of Xibalba burn his soul slowly and roast his heart for their dinner. We will have to find another way."

Sky Knife grunted in agreement, but the effort it cost him seemed to be too much. He closed his eyes.

Up the passage they had just come came the sound of laughter. "You are trapped," laughed the mocking voice of Stone Jaguar. "And powerless. When I finish with the king, I will see to you."

"No!" screamed Bone Splinter. "We will stop you."

"Too late," said Stone Jaguar. His voice faded away.

Bone Splinter ran to Sky Knife and grabbed his shoulders, propping the younger man up into a sitting position. "Sky Knife, we must do something—now!"

Sky Knife raised his eyes to the warrior's. "We could get to the king. . . ."

"There's no steps—and no time," said Bone Splinter. "There is only one way for you to get the strength you need to defeat him."

Suddenly, Sky Knife knew what Bone Splinter was going to say. He prayed he was wrong. But he knew he wasn't.

# 34

›››››

You have to do it," said Bone Splinter. "If Stone Jaguar can take unwilling peasants and use their energy for his own use, you could take a willing sacrifice and use the energy to beat him."

Sky Knife shook his head. "I've . . . I've never . . . I can't!" he screamed. "I can't."

It would work. Sky Knife damned the simplicity of it. A volunteer—a true volunteer—was more powerful as a sacrifice than someone who came unwilling. No doubt Stone Jaguar had had to use hundreds of peasants because of that. But Sky Knife had always been taught that the perfect sacrifice would be powerful enough to move the earth, powerful enough to breach the walls of the underworlds and bring the heavens crashing down into the seas. Powerful enough, certainly, to best Stone Jaguar.

But it meant Bone Splinter's death at Sky Knife's hands. He couldn't do it. Storm Cloud was his king, but he'd only met the man twice. Bone Splinter was his friend. Sky Knife didn't have enough friends to lose one.

Bone Splinter grabbed him by the shoulders and squeezed.

Sky Knife winced in pain and met Bone Splinter's eyes. The warrior's face reflected fear, but it wasn't fear for himself.

"We must do something, and this is the only way," said Bone Splinter. He frowned and shook Sky Knife. "Do it—or I will curse you with every evil I can name."

"I . . . I don't know how," said Sky Knife.

Bone Splinter released him. "There is nothing to know. You are a priest, you bear the Hand of God. You will do it."

Sky Knife glanced around the cavern helplessly, anywhere but Bone Splinter's eyes. "But there are no attendants, no other priests. . . ."

"It only takes one priest for a sacrifice," said Bone Splinter. "And as for attendants, well, you won't need anyone to hold me down."

Sky Knife shivered at the coldness in Bone Splinter's voice. It was the same tone with which he'd threatened Stone Jaguar in the southern acropolis after Yellow Chin's attack. There was no doubt in the warrior's voice, no fear. Only the sure knowledge that he would do his duty.

Sky Knife met Bone Splinter's eyes reluctantly. He felt as if a great hand squeezed his chest and he had to bite back sobs.

Bone Splinter nodded. "There is no other way," he said. "Come, do it quickly, before Stone Jaguar harms the king." The warrior grasped Sky Knife's shoulder and smiled. "I will miss you," he said. "But we will meet again in the seventh heaven. Believe it."

Sky Knife looked away and gestured toward the still pool of water. He couldn't bear to think about saying goodbye. "Bathe yourself," he said. "This is *zuhuy ha*, the pure water at the Navel of the World."

Bone Splinter dropped his arm and lowered his forehead to the floor at Sky Knife's knees. "As you will, Lord," he said.

Sky Knife struggled to his feet while Bone Splinter removed his sandals, skirt, and loincloth and stepped into the pool.

Where should he do this? Sky Knife still couldn't believe he was contemplating sacrificing Bone Splinter. He glanced around. Behind him, next to where the pool met the western wall of the cavern, was a boulder whose top surface was flat. Sky Knife went to it and bent over to examine it more closely. He leaned his weight on it as he did so, glad of the support.

The surface looked as though it had been ground down. No doubt it had been used as an altar before, but there was no way to know to which gods it had been sanctified. Sky Knife got out the cigars and placed them on the boulder. Then he removed the obsidian blade from its pouch and placed it next to the cigars.

"Itzamna," he whispered. "Bless this altar and accept the sacrifice I am about to give you." Sky Knife nearly choked on his prayer and the pressure in his chest grew. No wonder his mother had been told to give him a bad luck name—what worse luck could a man have than to sacrifice a friend?

Sky Knife picked up the blade and scratched his wrist. A thin trickle of blood ran down his wrist and dripped onto the stone. Sky Knife waved the blade over the blood. "With blood I change this from stone to altar, from earthly to divine purpose. Take my blood and hold it in trust, that I may always be true to you, Lord of Ali."

Smoke rose from the blood, deep blue in color. It glowed slightly, then dissipated. The cigars burst into flames and burned brightly blue for a moment. The flames died, leaving a small pile of glowing ash.

The gods approved. Sky Knife trembled and couldn't keep the tears from flowing. He closed his eyes and took a deep breath.

"Where is the sacrifice?" he asked as firmly as he could. Before the actual sacrifice, it was imperative to find a volunteer. Bone Splinter had already said he was willing, but Sky Knife wanted to conform to all the rituals he remembered. This had to go just right. Everything had to be perfect.

"I am here," said Bone Splinter. "I come freely to be the sacrifice for my god, my king, and my city."

"Then come forward." Sky Knife turned and held the Hand of God out in front of him.

Bone Splinter stepped into the circle of the tattoo's glow. He was naked—even his ear spools were gone. Water dripped off his skin and his wet hair fell over his ears and into his face. The warrior knelt in front of Sky Knife.

Sky Knife passed the Hand of God over Bone Splinter's head four times. "The time of sacrifice is set."

"When is the time?" asked Bone Splinter as ritual demanded.

"The time . . . the time is now," whispered Sky Knife, his voice deserting him. He fought the tears, but they ran down his face again.

Bone Splinter looked up and grabbed Sky Knife's wrist and that was definitely *not* part of the ritual. Sky Knife gasped in surprise and glanced into Bone Splinter's calm eyes.

"Be easy, my friend," said Bone Splinter. "I am the sacrifice come freely."

Sky Knife bit his lip and nodded. "Then stand."

Bone Splinter obeyed. Sky Knife stepped aside and Bone Splinter walked to the altar and laid himself upon it.

Sky Knife knelt before the altar. "Red Jaguar of the East, hear my prayer. Black Jaguar of the West, hear my prayer. White Jaguar of the North, hear my prayer. Yellow Jaguar of the South, hear my prayer."

A slight breeze caressed his face carrying the sweet smell of flowers. Sky Knife frowned. The temple glow odor had never smelled of flowers before. Perhaps it was a good sign. Sky Knife prayed it was.

"Lord of All, I beg you for help," prayed Sky Knife. "I must have the strength to defeat Stone Jaguar. Please, give me the power I need to protect Storm Cloud and Tikal. Stone Jaguar must die and the *nagual* must be returned to the Totilme'iletik.

All bad luck must be driven away so that Tikal will prosper in the new *katun*. Be my guide and my strength, Itzamna Kauil, friend of man and provider in times of need."

Sky Knife stood on shaky legs. Bone Splinter lay quiet and calm on the altar, eyes closed. He breathed evenly and slowly.

Sky Knife bit his lip. This was it. There were no more prayers to make, no more incantations, no more invocations— just the *p'a chi* itself. The time of sacrifice. Sky Knife held the Hand of God above Bone Splinter. It glowed, dimly at first, but then more and more brightly until it lit the entire cavern.

Sky Knife trembled. He couldn't do it. He lowered the knife a few inches. Bone Splinter opened his eyes.

"Do not fail me, Sky Knife," he said. "You must do this." Bone Splinter reached out and grabbed Sky Knife's wrist, stopped its descent. Sky Knife met the other man's eyes. This was the time when every sacrifice showed fear—when the knife was held above their hearts. If even a glint of fear showed in Bone Splinter's face, Sky Knife knew he wouldn't be able to go any further.

But there was none. Bone Splinter's face was calm, even under the knife. He released Sky Knife's wrist and settled himself back down on the altar. Awe colored Sky Knife's thoughts and soothed his heart. Bone Splinter was *not* afraid. He was a true sacrifice. Perfect.

Sky Knife raised the knife again, said a silent prayer to Itzamna for courage, and brought the blade down into Bone Splinter's stomach. The warrior's flesh parted easily before the glowing blade.

The warrior grunted but did not scream. His bright, bright blood splattered over him, over Sky Knife, over the cavern wall. It flowed down his sides and down the altar. It ran onto Sky Knife's feet, warm and slick.

Sky Knife withdrew the knife and shoved it into his left hand. With his right, he put his fingers into the gash in Bone Splinter's gut.

Bone Splinter's body was warm, his blood slippery. Sky Knife pushed his hand completely in, not sure exactly where in the chest he would find Bone Splinter's heart. His hand encountered a smooth, muscular barrier. Sky Knife gritted his teeth and shoved his hand through.

Bone Splinter grunted again, but still he did not scream. Sky Knife glanced at the warrior's face. It was contorted in pain, but it remained without fear.

Past the barrier, Sky Knife felt the warrior's strong heartbeat near his hand. He reached in farther and grabbed the slippery, pulsing organ, wondering how strongly it was rooted in the chest.

Sky Knife's hand was not large enough to encircle the heart, but it didn't seem to matter. The heart stuck to his hand as if bound to it. Sky Knife drew the heart toward him.

Bone Splinter screamed "Itzamna!" as the heart came loose from his chest. Sky Knife yanked the heart the rest of the way out and the other man went limp on the altar. His face went slack, losing all trace of his suffering.

Sky Knife held the beating heart in front of him over Bone Splinter's body. It glowed and dazzling flakes of light rained down from the ceiling. Others leapt from the floor and walls. They swirled around Sky Knife, tickling and teasing, before converging on the heart and pouring into it.

The heart swelled with the light and burst into a million small blue sparkling motes. Some of the blue sparkles fell onto Sky Knife, bathing him with warmth and a deep, soul-satisfying comfort. And with love, too. Sky Knife laughed with joy.

More of the sparkles fell on him. Sky Knife closed his eyes at the strength that flowed into him. Power flowed through his muscles, his veins, into his heart and mind.

In his mind, he saw himself flowing upwards, through the stone of the cave, to float in the air above the northern acropolis. He looked down at himself. To his own eyes, he looked solid. He reached down to touch his leg and his hand passed through it as though he were a cloud, or a streak of mist. Sky Knife knew he should be afraid, but he felt only the joy that Bone Splinter had bequeathed him.

Sky Knife glanced around for Stone Jaguar. The night was almost gone. The first gray streaks of pre-dawn light lay littered on the eastern horizon. Below, in the plaza, the love-gift vendor had just settled into her coveted spot.

Something else was to the east besides false dawn. A black cloud in jaguar shape hovered over the palace. In its forepaw it clutched something small and human-shaped.

Storm Cloud.

# 35

››››› 

"Stop!" shouted Sky Knife.

The black jaguar whirled. It hissed at Sky Knife. "You think to stop me? You are nothing."

The words hit Sky Knife and his gut quivered in fear. But Bone Splinter's love held him up. Sky Knife wrapped it around him like a cloak. "No," he said. "I have the strength of a perfect sacrifice. There is no power on earth or in any of the heavens or in any of the underworlds as great as that."

The cloud jaguar shrugged, dismissing him. "No power can equal me. I am *Ah nacom* of Tikal—I alone have the right to perform the *p'a chi* and wear the cloak you have stolen." The jaguar bared its fangs to Sky Knife.

"Leave the king alone," commanded Sky Knife. "I will not let you harm him."

"You can't do anything about the king now," said Stone Jaguar. The struggling figure in the jaguar's grip disappeared. Sky Knife leaped forward, thinking Stone Jaguar had dropped the king, but no sign of Storm Cloud remained.

"Where is he?" demanded Sky Knife. "Where is the king?"

The jaguar cloud shimmered slightly, the blackness bleeding out of it. In the span of only a few heartbeats, it had become merely a low-lying cloud, white and fluffy. It faded in the early morning air.

"Stone Jaguar!"

Monkeys began their ear-splitting daily ritual to greet the dawn. Their screeching set off the birds of the jungle. The noise normally meant stability and normality to Sky Knife, but today, the sounds seemed desperate, panicked.

Sky Knife floated to the palace. Courtiers, hair loose around their shoulders, skirts askew, ran around shouting. Sky Knife rose higher above the city. Around Tikal, the jungle stretched green and thick, broken only by the small cleared areas of the farmers' *milpas*. The city itself, its temples and plazas, the palace and the House of the Warriors, seemed tiny and insignificant. Sky Knife felt ashamed. He had always thought of the buildings of his city as impressive. But next to the jungle, they were nothing. Sky Knife wondered why the gods would ever smile upon a city that was so small when viewed from the skies.

The sky was cloudless. "Stone Jaguar!" shouted Sky Knife. "Where is the king?"

The squawking of the jungle animals was his only answer. Sky Knife descended until he was just above the roofs of the city's buildings. He flew over the plaza, past the Temple of Ix Chel. Kan Flower and several other warriors stood outside.

Where would Stone Jaguar take the king? Sky Knife skimmed over the jungle canopy, searching for any sign. In the east, the grayness grew brighter.

Sky Knife stopped his flight. Stone Jaguar believed himself to be the true priest of Itzamna. He believed he acted for the gods. He would want to make a sacrifice of the king. Not a *p'a chi*, not a willing sacrifice, but the sacrifice of an enemy. Stone Jaguar would want everything to be just right.

An enemy could be sacrificed in any number of ways, usually with a knife in the chest or a slit throat. But Stone Jaguar had used his blade most recently on farmers. He would need to resanctify it for more holy use if he wanted to use it to kill the king. Sky Knife doubted Stone Jaguar wanted to take the time that would require.

The cardinal directions were important, too, of course. Stone Jaguar would want to do this somewhere to the east, the most prestigious direction; or north, where the rain gods lived.

Water—water was another way to make sacrifice. It could symbolize the rain gods no matter in which direction it lay.

The *cenote!* Sky Knife flew over the treetops toward the east. The hidden *cenote* would be perfect. Not only did it have water to honor the rain gods, it was in the east to honor Itzamna.

Sky Knife broke through the canopy and hovered over the *cenote.* The black cloud jaguar hovered there, too, Storm Cloud still in its grip.

"It didn't take you long to find me." To Sky Knife, Stone Jaguar sounded disappointed. "Well, now that you're here, save the king, *priest,*" hissed the jaguar. It stretched out its paw and dropped Storm Cloud. The small figure of the king plummeted toward the water.

"No!" screamed Sky Knife. He dove for the king and reached him just before Storm Cloud hit the water. But the king passed through Sky Knife's insubstantial body and struck the blue water of the *cenote.*

Sky Knife followed the king into the water and wrapped his arms around the other man. But his arms continued to pass through Storm Cloud's flesh.

Panic nibbled at Sky Knife's thoughts. If he could not drag the king out of the water, Storm Cloud would drown, and Sky Knife would have failed Bone Splinter's trust.

Storm Cloud struggled, but bonds of blue light held his wrists behind his back and strapped his ankles together. Sky Knife grabbed at the sorcerous bonds. They stung his hands, but he could hold onto them. He flew upwards toward the air, toward life, dragging the king behind him.

He was not strong enough to pull the king into the air with

him, but he pressed down with his hands and felt the bonds weaken. Sky Knife reached out with the power of Bone Splinter's love and snapped the sorcery that bound the king.

Storm Cloud's head broke the surface and he took a deep breath of air. Sky Knife hovered over him, tremendously relieved.

A boulder struck the water near Storm Cloud's head. The splash sent the man under again, but he bobbed up after a moment. Sky Knife glanced up. The cloud jaguar was gone. In its place hovered Stone Jaguar himself, his arms spread wide.

"I will crush you both!" Stone Jaguar shook a fist toward Sky Knife. Suddenly, Sky Knife felt his body returning to him. He fell several feet into the cool water and came up, choking. The feeling of weight and a solid body seemed cumbersome to him now.

Another rock smashed into the water. Sky Knife tread water and closed his mouth against the spray. The king was not so lucky. Sky Knife heard the other man choking on a mouthful of water.

Stone Jaguar's plan was clear—he would pull down the walls of the *cenote* and crush Sky Knife and the king under them. Anger warmed Sky Knife's blood and power throbbed in his bones. He reached out with the power, down to the bottom of the *cenote*, and pulled it toward him.

The water became choppy and a deep rumble filled the air. Stone Jaguar threw more stones, but Sky Knife pushed them away with the strength that flowed through him. He concentrated on the rocks beneath them, pulling them closer and closer. . . .

The bottom came up to meet Sky Knife and the king, pushing them out of the water, granting them a small island in the midst of the pool. Storm Cloud lay on the wet stones, panting and coughing, but otherwise all right.

Sky Knife threw back his head and screamed out to the man he had held so high in respect and awe. "Itzamna sees the evil you do!" he cried. "He has given me the power to defeat you."

"Never!" shouted Stone Jaguar, though his voice held a note of doubt it had not before.

"You broke all your vows," said Sky Knife. "You are no longer a priest."

"Who are you to say that?" said Stone Jaguar. "You are just an ignorant boy."

Sky Knife reached into the calm, deep quiet in the center of his soul where Bone Splinter's power waited. Sky Knife tapped the power and let more flow through his veins. He rose from the water, leaving the king behind on the island. He floated in the air just before Stone Jaguar.

"Am I?" asked Sky Knife. "You showed me the way, and Bone Splinter gave me the power of a perfect sacrifice."

"That idiot? He was never the perfect anything," said Stone Jaguar. "Just a strong hand for the king to use."

Anger threatened to flood over Sky Knife, but he held it in check. "He is my friend," he said. "He died for Itzamna, and for the king. And for me."

Sky Knife gathered power in his mind and shoved the floating figure of Stone Jaguar into the wall of the *cenote*. Stone Jaguar screamed and clapped his hands together. A jaguar of fire burst into life in front of Sky Knife and leaped at him, fiery claws extended.

Sky Knife pushed against the jaguar but it was too strong for him. The flames of its paws came closer to his throat. Sky Knife reached down and pulled the water of the *cenote* to him and encircled the jaguar with it.

The jaguar dissolved in a puff of smoke and ash. The water, released from Sky Knife's control, rained back down to the *cenote*.

Stone Jaguar rushed toward Sky Knife and locked his hands around the younger man's throat. Pain lanced through Sky Knife's mind. Stone Jaguar's strong fingers dug into his flesh, closing off his throat.

Fear bubbled through Sky Knife, fear that threatened to become panic. But deep inside his heart was a wellspring of calm. Not the soul-crushing calm of Death Smoke's spell, but a gentle tranquility full of love and trust. Sky Knife drove his mind into the calm and made it a part of himself. The legacy of Bone Splinter eased into every nerve, every pore.

Sky Knife pushed his awareness of his pain aside and opened his mind to the other man, encircling Stone Jaguar with the power Bone Splinter had provided him. Stone Jaguar screamed and dropped his hold on Sky Knife. Frantically, Stone Jaguar jerked his limbs, trying to escape, but Sky Knife's power was everywhere the other man turned.

The power continued to pour through him, so that Sky Knife couldn't tell if he held it or it held him. But it didn't matter. They were part of each other.

Now that he had accepted the power into himself, Sky Knife saw that Stone Jaguar sat in the center of a sorcerous net like some obscene spider. One strand of the net branched outwards toward Tikal, toward the *nagual*. Sky Knife reached out and pulled the strand free.

Stone Jaguar screamed. Sky Knife felt Stone Jaguar's spell dissolve in his hands. The *nagual* faded with the spell, returned to their proper place in the corral of the Totilme'iletik.

Sky Knife yanked another strand from Stone Jaguar. On the other end, he sensed the smell of rot and putrefaction. Cizin. So he had not managed to banish the death god entirely. With a flick of his mind, Sky Knife sent Cizin spinning through the nebulous wall that surrounded the underworlds. The death god screamed as the spell was broken and he was banished from the waking world of men once again.

Other strands came loose from Stone Jaguar now of their own volition. Golden, ropy cords dangled briefly in midair, then dissolved into nothing. Stone Jaguar stopped screaming. He hung limp and unresisting in the center of Sky Knife's power.

"Your power is broken," said Sky Knife. "You are rejected by the gods."

"Think again," said the other man. He reached out to Sky Knife, obsidian blade in his hands. He moved so quickly, Sky Knife reacted without thinking. With his own blade still in his left hand, he stabbed the other man in the neck.

Bright blood, as red as the jungle flowers in the garden at the House of the Warriors, sprayed the trees, coated Sky Knife, gushed out of the gaping slit in Stone Jaguar's throat to the ground below.

Instead of collapsing, Stone Jaguar grew in size as if still bloated with power. "You'll never defeat me!" he screamed. Flames burst into the air around Sky Knife's head. He screamed and shielded his eyes from their glare. Rocks whizzed by his head. Sky Knife curled up in a ball to protect himself.

A rock hit him solidly in his wounded shoulder. Sky Knife cried out. Above him, Stone Jaguar laughed. "You're dead!"

Sky Knife uncurled himself. He had come too far and lost too much to give in now. He pushed himself through the air toward the other sorcerer. "No!" he shouted. "You're the one who's dead!" Sky Knife shoved his hand into the gaping hole in Stone Jaguar's neck, reached back until he found the hard solid bones of Stone Jaguar's spine. Stone Jaguar's eyes widened in fear.

Sky Knife let the power of Bone Splinter's sacrifice flow through him, down his arm, into his hand. He squeezed the other man's spine until it snapped with a loud crack.

Sky Knife let Stone Jaguar drop. Stone Jaguar reached out at the last moment and grabbed Sky Knife's ankle, sending him plummeting after Stone Jaguar into the blue waters of the *cenote*.

Sky Knife screamed at the pain that lanced through him when he hit the water. Then all screams were taken from him as cold water rushed down his throat.

# 36

›››››

Sky Knife used the last trickle of energy in him to push himself to the surface. He came up, spluttering and coughing. A strong hand grabbed him by the shoulder and hauled him halfway out of the water onto a rock.

Sky Knife gasped for air. "Stone Jaguar," he said. "Where . . ."

"He is gone," said a heavily accented voice. The king. "He fell into the water and has not come up."

Sky Knife relaxed a moment. The power that had coursed through him before had left him, but a trace of the love that had touched him remained. Bone Splinter—and the *chic-chac*—had not left him. He hoped they never would. "Thank you," he whispered to them both.

"It is I who should thank you," said Storm Cloud. "But don't you think we should leave now?"

Sky Knife raised his head. "The *cenote* . . ."

"Is no more," said the king. He slapped Sky Knife on the shoulder. Sky Knife's heart leaped in surprise at the familiarity. He blinked and scanned the area. He saw what the king meant. Instead of a *cenote*, there was now a pile of rubble. Small deep pockets of water remained, but the vertical walls no longer existed.

Sky Knife laid his head back down on the rock as the morning sun broke over the trees. Blackness threatened to overwhelm him, but it was a comforting sort of blackness that promised rest.

The king shook Sky Knife back to wakefulness. "I owe you my life," he said. "My kingdom. Anything that is mine you may have. You have only to name it. Wealth, status, power—they are all yours to take."

Sky Knife could no longer hold the darkness back, but he smiled. The king had promised he could have anything he wished. Well, there was something he wished very badly indeed—provided Jade Flute agreed.

He would go to the love-gift vendor and buy that rabbit. And if Jade Flute spit on his gift, he'd try something else. But Sky Knife had a strange feeling she'd accept.

The comforting tingle at his throat seemed to chime in agreement and an echo of Bone Splinter's laughter rang in his ears. Sky Knife sighed as darkness overtook him. He let himself slide into well-earned and much-needed pleasant dreams.